Max and the Gatekeeper
Book V
The Reign of Hudich
Part I

James Todd Cochrane

Special thanks to all my family and friends for their help and support. Thanks to all the kids who motivated me to keep writing.

Copyright © 2016 James Todd Cochrane

Published April 18, 2016

www.darkmoonpublishing.com

Library of Congress Control Number: 2016906151
ISBN 978-0-9915234-6-7

Cover by Kalen O'Donnell
Edited by Janet Michelson

CONTENTS

1

Camps

Boom! Boom! Boom! A loud bass drum vibrated through the air.

"Do you think they have a chance?" asked Sundance, a tall average built man, his reddish hair pulled back with a leather tie. He was dressed in black clothing.

"Not without our help," responded Sam, a twenty-something male. Thin, of medium-height, and freckled-faced with straight brown hair, he stared through his binoculars. Sam spied a make-shift fort, roughly the size of two football fields, surrounded by a wall of piled debris consisting of trees, bricks, old cars, and barbed wire piled approximately twenty feet high. The two men lay nestled among a cluster of tall weeds at the top of a small hill.

"I sometimes think there aren't enough of us to win this war," Sundance lamented. "Look at the sheer numbers we're up against. It's like a million to one. Granted, we have the technological advantage but, magically, we are behind the curve. They are destroying camps, towns, and cities left and right, or assimilating them."

"Don't worry. We are bringing in more every day. We have some powerful allies on our side fighting the same fight all over the universe. We will take Hudich's empire one piece at a time," Sam replied.

"I hope you're right. I, for one, would like to know more. Don't get me wrong. I love the weapons, but I would like my magical skills to be up to snuff," Sundance said. "And those drums mean we aren't in for a good night. The enemy is coming."

"Your talents will improve, just give it time.   You can't run a marathon without proper training," Sam continued. "It was only two years ago, I could only do a few things and they kept me and my friend, Linda, alive until help arrived." He handed the binoculars to Sundance.

"Let's hope we can keep these people alive a little longer too," Sundance muttered.

"We need to get them word to keep all the lights on. Trying to hide in the dark only puts them at greater risk," Sam noted.

"You and I know that, but you know how fond these groups are of strangers. It's hard to trust anyone now-a-days, but you can't blame them. Not only are there evil things roaming the lands, but clans fighting over food, land, and other supplies." Sundance focused on a section of the wall. "I think I found the front gate."

"Where?" Sam tried to spot the area with his naked eyes.

"The center of the left wall. There are an awful lot of guards at that location. Most of the other sections only have a handful of watchmen," Sundance indicated. "So, how do you want to do this?"

Boom! Boom! Boom! The drums pounded out again.

"Have we tried to establish radio contact?" Sam questioned, studying the section of wall his friend had pointed out.

"I put Jim on it." Sundance passed the binoculars back to Sam.

"Let's move back and see if he's had any luck." Sam slid down the small hill, with Sundance right behind him.

They wove their way back into a small stand of trees at the bottom of a gully and out of sight of the camp. A man named Jim sat in the shade with an old radio, trying to make contact on each frequency. Another dozen men occupied positions to watch the perimeter of the small base, each carrying a small arsenal of advanced Olik-type weapons.

"What's the word?" Sam asked Jim as he continued to fiddle with the radio.

"Well, I've had a couple of nice conversations with a few folks who are either in hiding or trying to lure victims out into the open. As far as the complex, nada." Jim frowned. "I've been warning them about the coming attack. If they are listening, they should know."

"Keep trying." Sam patted him on the shoulder.

"So, what do you want to do?" Sundance asked.

"I guess I'm going to have to go knock on their front door." Sam started handing his weapons to Sundance. "I'll keep my radio, although they will probably confiscate it. Take my communicator. If you think this is going to get ugly, call for backup."

"Will backup be able to respond in time?" Sundance questioned, accepting all of Sam's equipment.

"I hope so." Sam shrugged his shoulders. "Because there is no guarantee these people will believe me or let me go after I get in. You will have a hard time reaching me in that situation."

"Are you sure you want to go in?" Sundance questioned with raised eyebrows.

"Yeah." Sam checked his watch. "We only have about five hours until sunset. We better hurry. I want to give them as much time as possible, so at least they can release me before dark."

"Five hours isn't a lot of time to convince them to head west," Sundance observed.

"First things first, I'm just going to try to convince them to let us help them *and* keep the lights on. I'll worry about getting them to head to the Rocky Mountains later."

"Good thinking."

Boom! Boom! Boom!

"You better follow me up to a safe distance. I don't want to be caught out there by something we haven't seen," Sam said.

The two men found a dry riverbed which allowed them to move without being seen from the makeshift fort. The wind rustled the leaves and the weeds, creating the only sound in what seemed like a lifeless world. No birds or other wildlife stirred or made noises of any kind. An occasional disturbance would reach them from the direction of the camp, but it was obvious they were trying to be as quiet as possible.

Sam brought them to a halt when they were almost in a direct line with the entrance. They waited in the trees, studying the layout and listening for the unknown.

Sam's heart rate increased and his palms turned sweaty. "Well." He swallowed.

"Good luck. I'll cover you as far as I can without being spotted," Sundance promised. "Be extra careful. You know how crazy these drums make people."

Sam climbed out of the riverbed and up a small hill towards the fort. When he reached full view of the structure, he raised his hands above his head and started forward slowly.

It wasn't until he was within fifty yards that he could make out all the weapons pointed at him. There were at least a dozen assault rifles trained on him as he continued to take one slow step at a time. "I come in peace," he shouted when he was within thirty yards of the gate.

"That's far enough," a voice commanded through a megaphone. "Either turn around now or lay down on the ground. If you attempt to come any closer, you *will* be shot."

Sam kept his hands in the air while getting into a kneeling position and then brought them down to lie on the ground.

The instant he was flat the gate flew open and several four wheelers zipped out of the gate, along with about a dozen armed men. The vehicles created a dust cloud as they circled him, their engines breaking the tense silence.

"Hands behind your back," a man screamed when the group reached his location and everyone pointed weapons at him.

Boom! Boom! Boom!

Sam placed his hands behind his back and a man tied them together while driving his knee painfully into Sam's spine. Once he was secured, a couple men stepped forward and lifted Sam off the ground.

"I come in peace," Sam repeated.

"Shut up." One of the men punched him hard in the gut, causing Sam to double over in pain and gasp for air. "We'll ask the questions. You wanted to come inside, well that will be under our conditions. If we don't like your answers, we will either expel you or kill you."

"Aren't you glad you approached the gate," another said and chuckled in his ear before a hood was pulled over his head and the world went dark. "If your friends want to see you again, they better stop pounding on those drums."

Sam felt like a sack of potatoes. His captors didn't seem too concerned with how well they treated their prisoner. He was bumped, kicked, and shoved. With his hands bound behind his back, he had no way to break his fall. Every time he stumbled he hit the ground hard. Then someone would immediately yank him back to his feet.

They made him march blindly for what seemed like several hundred yards before they removed his hood. He stood in an otherwise darkened room, with extremely bright lights blinding his vision. Sam couldn't tell how many people were in the room. Only shadowy outlines danced occasionally at the periphery of his vision between the lights.

"Who are you? What reason do you have for approaching our walls?" a deep voice roared at him. "And what's with the war drums?"

"My name is Sam. I am here to help you," Sam stated boldly. "I am not connected to those drums."

"Here…to *help* us."

A roar of laughter told Sam there was a large crowd gathered in the room.

"What makes you think we need your help?" the same deep voice asked. "We are well protected and well informed. We know about your group of men down in the riverbed. And I'm sure your army is nearby. What is your real purpose here?"

"We came to help you. You are in extremely great danger," Sam stated. "If you last the night, you will need to head west. There is a well-organized society in the Rocky Mountains. You will be safe with them."

Boom! Boom! Boom!

"Really? We just up and leave with twenty-five hundred people and supplies. That sounds like a ploy to get us out in the open so you and your people can slaughter us and steal our property." A female voice spoke this time.

"I guarantee you. We are here to *help*. We only stand a real chance if we join forces," Sam urged. "You are vastly outnumbered and you are not as well informed as you think you are. You have been cut off from the real news."

"We have our sources," a different man interjected.

"What sources? Those news broadcasts? They are lies and propaganda meant to trick you into thinking you are safe. I've been out there. I've seen what's coming tonight and it isn't anything you can defend against." Sam spoke more confidently than before.

"This is just another con artist trying to trick us into losing our possessions or worse," another bellowed. "Toss him over the wall or slay him, but I don't want to hear any more lies."

The crowd volume in the room continued to grow with everyone trying to speak on top of each other.

"Give me a chance to prove myself," Sam shouted above the din, bringing silence.

"And how do you plan to do that?"

"By fighting with you tonight. My men and I can keep you alive if you listen to me," Sam informed them.

"We don't need this fool. We have already withstood several assaults in the past and against great odds," one argued.

The roar of the crowd started to build again. The tone and the comments were not in Sam's favor. Slowly and steadily a chant began and continued to grow. "Throw him out! Throw him out!"

"This battle will *not* be like any other," Sam yelled as loud as he could.

"How?" The crowd roared together.

"What do you know?"

"Throw him out!"

"The things you are about to fight will not be only *human*!" Sam shouted again. "They will not spare women or children."

The chant changed to laughter and calls of "You're mad! You're crazy!"

"You won't be dealing with conventional weapons," Sam continued to holler above the mocking throng.

Boom! Boom! Boom!

"QUIET!" a loud deep voice shouted above the crowd and the roar disappeared. "What sort of weapons are we facing?"

"Magical weapons," Sam spoke in a normal voice.

"He's out of his mind!" The roars and chants returned, more raucous than before. "Throw him out."

"He's wasting our time. This is some kind of ploy."

"I can prove it," Sam shouted again.

"He's trying to trick us. He's a devil. Toss him out."

"QUIET!" the same deep voice shouted again. "Before I came to you, I was in a battle that matches his description. Creatures stormed out of the dark and slaughtered us. We managed to kill a few but we were outnumbered and outmatched. The battle was over quickly. It was only blind luck that I survived. The other few survivors were carried away."

"I and my men can help you. It will not be easy but if you want to survive you must do as I say," Sam affirmed.

"You said you can prove they will fight with magical weapons. How?" another questioned.

"Like this. *Izginem se.*" Sam disappeared right in front of them.

"Where did he go?" Several gasped.

"I told you he's a devil," others exclaimed.

"Do you really think I'm *your* prisoner?" Sam spoke from a new section of the room, turning the heads of the crowd. A few seconds later he spoke again, "I *am* here to help. Otherwise, I could leave at will on my own power."

He used a spell to untie his bindings and slipped into the bleachers until he was standing by the man who supported his story. "*Prikazim se!*" He reappeared.

Most of the people in the immediate area where Sam showed himself, scrambled away from him in fear. The man who had supported Sam's claims jumped a little but remained where he was.

"How did you do that?" the man asked.

"Magic. It's real and I can teach you how to use it. My name is Sam and I am *really* here to help." Sam extended his hand.

The man eyed it for a moment, then accepted it. "I'm John."

Boom! Boom! Boom! The drum beats grew louder and stronger.

"Don't trust him. It is the power of the devil that is going to fight devils," a woman shouted in a shaky voice.

"Have you not heard a house divided cannot stand? How could the kingdom of the devil stand if I destroy his followers with his power?" Sam reasoned. "Those drums will continue to increase as the enemy approaches. If you want my help, we need to start preparing now. Otherwise, my men and I will leave you to your fate."

"Why would you help us?" one questioned. "Don't get me wrong. I want your help, but why?"

"Because you are needed. There is a bigger war being waged. We can't win without the help of people standing for good."

John rose to his feet and waved his arms, silencing the crowd. "All in favor of accepting help from Sam and his men, say 'aye.'"

There was a loud chorus of "ayes."

"Those against?" John asked.

A small spattering of "nays" returned.

"The ayes have it," John pronounced. "Now, Sam, what's first?"

"Send someone to retrieve my men from the riverbed. We also need to gather all the lights you can find. We need to make this place look like a tree on Christmas morning," Sam ordered.

"Won't that give away our position?" a man questioned.

"Yes, but what chases away darkness better than light?" Sam smiled.

"What else do we need to do?" John asked.

"Do you have maps of the surrounding areas, and what kind of supplies do you have, especially weapons? We need to set up a planning area. I may be able to bring in additional help," Sam responded.

"How? More magic?" the people questioned curiously.

"Not exactly, but it may seem that way." Sam smiled, trying to ease people's fear of the unknown.

"What do you need maps for? Offense?" a short stalky man asked.

"Anyone who tries to go on the attack tonight will be lost, but we might be able to lay down some traps."

Boom! Boom! Boom!

"Do your people make regular runs outside the camp on four wheelers?" Sam questioned.

"Yes," John responded.

"Start sending people out on regular patrols and mock errands. We need to create a lot of dust. That should allow us to set some surprises."

Within a half an hour, Sundance and the others had been brought inside the fort, and had set up an operations center in the area where Sam was questioned. Plus, they had designated a spot to open the gateway.

"Why aren't we just taking these people out?" Sundance asked.

"Unfortunately, we aren't the only battle going on at the moment. Access to the gateway is tight right now. There are missions being run through it non-stop. When we have a window, they will bring us through. Plus, always running from your enemy isn't a good thing. *And*, reducing their numbers is always a positive," Sam advised.

"I can't argue with that, but there are women and children here. Maybe we need more gateways?"

"There are plans for that as well." Sam patted Sundance on the shoulder.

Boom! Boom! Boom, sent shockwaves through the air. An occasional inhuman, hair-raising scream joined the chorus of drums, which added even more tension to the situation. By now everyone pretty much ignored the drums, rushing about to get things done, when the scream stopped everyone in their tracks.

"How much fuel do you have? Or is there a supply nearby?" Sam questioned after a group stood around studying several maps for a while.

"I'm Mark. We have a good supply but are trying to ration it. We understand we may need to flee when our other supplies run low," said a short stocky man who introduced himself while adding the information.

"We're going to need all you have," Sam reported. "You aren't going to need it after tomorrow, and we have a faster way of getting everyone out of here. We just need an open window."

"How are we going to leave without fuel?" John questioned. "I don't think we can spare any at all."

"Your lives depend on sacrificing everything tonight. You'll understand more tomorrow, I promise."

Sam and his men spent the last few hours before sundown preparing the people of the small fort for the coming attack. They faced resistance to using the fuel and to rerouting all of their electrical wiring to place almost every available light around the walls and on the rooftops of the make-shift fort. The drums and high-pitched screams continued to grow in volume and frequency, generating fear among all the inhabitants of the camp.

After positioning his men, with their futuristic weapons, at key locations along the wall, Sam and Sundance joined John and a few of the other leaders on the top of a tower inside the perimeter.

Boom! Boom! Boom!

Boom! Boom! Boom!

"Do you think we'll make it?" John questioned with a grim expression.

"With a little luck, we just might," Sam responded.

"A little luck and an open gateway." Sundance squinted into the setting sun.

"And this gateway is, again?" John asked as the sun sank behind the hills.

"A machine that can transport us anywhere in the universe in no time at all. We can move all of your people out of here in about a half an hour," Sam replied.

In the fading light along the horizon, coming from every direction, dark twisted shapes of varying sizes massed. The drums continued to pound out a steady beat and the high-pitched screams grew in strength and number. A constant chatter of excited creatures and men matched a strange dance coming from the dark shadowy figures. Several of the monsters circling the compound were massive, while others flapped bat-like wings to rise into the air before descending to the ground a few seconds later.

The drum beats began to increase to a steady, Boom! Boom! Boom…Boom! Boom! Boom...Boom! Boom! Boom! The twisted forms of the surrounding army began to stamp their feet and beat their weapons in unison with the drums, creating a roar like thunder over the entire area.

"Should we turn on the lights?" John questioned, his eyes darting nervously around the awaiting doom.

"Not yet. We want to hurt them. Darkness hates light. Wait until they are upon us for it to have the greatest impact. If we turn them on too soon, they will use weapons or magic to try to destroy them. But, when they are blinded, they are easy targets." Sundance cocked his weapon and positioned it so it was resting on a rail while he sighted it on a section of the enemy.

Sam glanced at the ever darkening sky. "Dark of the moon. Their favorite time."

"I like ruining that for them." Sundance grinned.

Dusk slowly changed into night and the beat and screams continued to send a shockwave of fear over the camp. When the night grew so complete that the shapes of the twisted creatures and men were barely visible, the drums stopped. Dead silence settled over the area for a few moments, then a hair-raising scream propelled the surrounding army forward.

The black mass rushed forward with a reckless frenzy. They raced over the fields like flood water. Many among the surge launched themselves into the air and advanced quickly towards the camp.

"WAIT FOR IT!" Sam called to John above the roar from the oncoming attackers.

John held a shaky finger against the switch to turn on the lights. "There's so many of them."

The twisted forms welled up like a massive wave, and seconds before it crashed upon the camp, Sam screamed. "NOW!"

2

A Horrifying Discovery

Puffing for breath, Max and Cindy ducked behind the safety of the thick jungle vegetation. Max peered through the tangle of plants and trees for any signs of pursuit, following the path he and Cindy had just used. He shifted his baseball cap quickly back and forth, to scratch an itch created by the ring of sweat forming a perfect circle around his head.

"They're coming. I can feel it." Cindy breathed heavily, while wiping a few loose strands of hair out of her blue eyes. Her face was blotchy from the hot and humid jungle, almost matching the red of her lips.

"Yes, but there's something else out there." Max, a tall boy of seventeen with thick brown hair, continued to scan the area.

"I don't detect anything else," responded Cindy, a slender girl with long blond hair.

"Whatever it is, it isn't magical. But it is hunting us and there are more than one."

"Animals? How do you know?"

"I saw several of them in a holding facility when I entered the perimeter, before we reunited. They looked like some kind of raptor. I'm willing to bet there are several loose in here." Max threw Cindy a worried look.

"They must have imported them. Are you sure you didn't trigger an alarm?" she whispered.

"Are you?" Max shot back. "They have some pretty tight security measures on this place. It took months for Grandpa to find this location.

It is the enemy's main military compound and prison. If we're going to help win this war, we need to destroy this command center."

A rumbling noise somewhere near their position froze them in their tracks. It started softly but grew louder before silencing. They glanced skyward and to the west of their location, only to see an empty blue sky.

"That sounded like a ship. And it just arrived from somewhere. It was coming from that direction." Cindy pointed. "I think it landed."

"Yeah, but I…wait. Remember how that ship Brian captured had a cloaking device?"

"And our intelligence indicates they were constructing more of them."

"Not good. We don't want to be spotted from the air." Max looked up once more.

"Well, let's not become stationary targets for *raptors* or *airships*." Cindy started through the thick jungle foliage once more.

Max followed her lead while continuing to search for the 'unseen.' Both he and Cindy sent out their magic to detect things that might be hidden around them. The two had acquired this unusual ability as a side effect of the zombie spider's venom, which had been injected into them a couple of years earlier.

Cindy worked around a large tree when her hands shot out and caught onto a small tree next to her to keep from falling into a camouflaged pit. Max sprang forward and grabbed her by the back of the shirt to prevent her from tumbling forward into the hole.

"Thanks." Cindy's red face had turned white and she visibly trembled. "I was so busy looking for those creatures you mentioned, I wasn't watching where I was putting my feet."

"What is it?" Max tried to peer through the mass of vines, branches, and leaves covering the pit.

"And how big is it?" Cindy regained her composure.

"Look at the way it sags, kind of like a net." Max made a large circle in the air with his finger tracing the rim of the hole. "I'd say it is at least sixty yards wide."

"There is air moving through it. See the way the leaves rustle." Cindy pointed out.

"It's empty or its depth is greater than my senses because I can't detect anything in it." Max grabbed a vine and leaned out over the pit as far as he could. He took a deep breath through his nose. "There is a slight stench." He pulled himself upright.

Cindy glanced around the area. "What do you want to do? We're supposed to meet Sky in a few minutes. This jungle is so thick, I don't know that we would be able to find our way back to it."

"We could chance a radio call." Max knelt next to the pit, searching for holes in the covering.

"Are you really that stupid?" Cindy rolled her eyes. "You said it yourself, this place has some high tech security. They could be on us before we knew it."

"I know. I just want to know what this is. Something tells me it's important." Max used a long stick to try to nudge some leaves out of the way.

"Careful idiot. It might be wired too."

"*Remember?* Grandpa said that once we were inside the wall, we shouldn't have to worry about any more security devices?"

"The operative word being *shouldn't*. And, Grandpa didn't know about this hole, so it doesn't mean there aren't any sensors."

"I still think we need to explore it. What if the stuff above ground is just a decoy?"

"I wish we could send a message to Sky." Cindy held a compass out in front of her, turning until she found the desired direction, and then shot a glance in that direction.

Off to their right, a strange animal call seized their attention. They both stared in the general direction of the sound, while drawing their weapons.

"That's close," Cindy commented, her chest heaving and her rapid breathing indicating her shock.

Another call answered the first, but this time to their left.

"They know we're here. If we start blasting away at these things, someone's bound to notice. This pit may be our best route." Max nodded toward the hole.

Cindy spun to meet his gaze. "I have an idea. Maybe if I send a spell toward the area of Sky's path, she may pick it up."

"Do it. Send several but nothing that will give her or us away." Max got down on his stomach and slid the top half of his body over the pit. He'd reached out in order to make a hole, when he discovered netting just under the jungle covering. "There's some sort of mesh here and I can't tear it." Max tried to create an opening, without success.

On the opposite side of the pit, a raptor-like beast with reddish skin and a strip of fur growing from the crown of its head to its tail, like a

Mohawk, emerged from the trees. The creature's yellow cat eyes locked on Max and Cindy while it roared with apparent delight. The thing leapt out into the middle of the pit, landing in the sagging mesh. The loose covering sank under its weight. The vegetation growing all over it proved to be too unstable for the beast to remain upright. It clawed, kicked, and thrashed about wildly in an effort to gain footing on the wobbly surface.

"So much for alarms." Max leveled his weapon at the beast.

"WAIT!" Cindy pulled Max's arm down. "He's making us a hole. Let's give him a minute and then use magic to move him."

"Finally, a good idea." Max climbed to his feet. "Together?"

"On the count of three. One – two – three."

Together they cast a spell that lifted the creature out of the net, transported the beast barely above the tree tops, and deposited it several hundred yards away. They had barely released it when a call from behind startled them.

Max spun on his heels and extended his arms. "*Premakni!*" The spell slammed into the midsection of the advancing monster, throwing it backwards into a tree, knocking it senseless. "Go!"

Cindy scrambled out onto the mesh with Max right behind her. They struggled to move very quickly across the swaying, sinking surface.

"Even if this leads nowhere, as long as Sky gets the message, she will clear the place of these creatures by the time we get back." Cindy reached the rent created by the beast, sent a small fireball into the pit to see how deep it was, and discovered they were only about ten feet from the bottom. She climbed down and then hung from the net for a second before letting go.

Max followed her example and used his body length to eliminate some of the distance before dropping to the bottom. He landed hard, falling onto his knees. The first breath of the air in the hole stung his lungs. "Whew! It's not a slight stench down here."

"Nope, it's horrible." Cindy covered her nose and mouth with a cupped hand. "What do you think it is?"

"I don't know but I have a bad feeling about this."

It took a moment for their eyes to adjust to the dim light.

"There's a tunnel." Max pointed to a section of the pit wall which was darker than the rest. He dug in his backpack and took out a flashlight.

A couple of calls from the strange creatures above drew their attention for a moment before they started down the tunnel.

Max used the flashlight to see the tunnel was wide and tall enough for two semi-trucks to drive side by side the length of it. The floor was hard packed dirt with only the occasional hole or rock along its surface. The wind, which had only been a slight breeze above, grew so strong Max had to pull his hat lower on his head to keep it from flying off.

Breathing through a small gap in his bent elbow, Max said, "I think it smells like…burning flesh."

"It's also getting a lot hotter and the slope is becoming steeper."

"Yeah, and do you hear a soft hum?"

"Yes."

They continued down the tunnel where the air movement, which had only been a gentle breeze at first, began to increase with each step forward. The downward angle of the tunnel increased to where they were leaning backwards like they were climbing down a hill. Max and Cindy began to cough as the already putrid air was now heavy with smoke, stinging their eyes and lungs.

"I can taste this nasty stuff in my mouth," Max complained, coughing several times.

"I'm not sure this was a good idea." Cindy ripped a strip off the bottom of her shirt and tied it around her face.

"Good idea." Max followed her example.

They had walked for about a half mile when the hum grew to a soft roar. The sound of large fan blades chopping the air indicated the source of the wind. Sweat streamed down Max's and Cindy's faces as the heat increased to an uncomfortable level.

With the aid of his flashlight, Max located the large machine about thirty yards ahead.

"For as big as this thing is, it's not putting out much wind," Cindy commented.

Max approached the back of the fan with caution. "I don't think there is any air flow, like something isn't open."

Small lights springing to life, about two hundred yards on the opposite side of the equipment, forced Max to douse his light and pull Cindy to the side of the tunnel. They remained by the wall for a few moments before carefully poking their heads out for a better look.

Cindy's voice mumbled something completely inaudible, fearing discovery, but the spinning fan drowned out everything.

"What? There's no chance they can hear us with the fan pushing air in our faces."

"I said, what do you think is between us and those lights?"

Max poked his head out to get a better look through the fan. Some kind of platform with a metal door in the side of the pit, surrounded by four lights on stands, met his gaze. Between them and the platform the ground glowed. "I don't know, but whatever it is, it's casting a reddish hue over everything. And there is a black flag with white writing hanging on the platform."

Cindy moved around Max for a better look. "I think they are live embers from a fire."

"I think you're right. That would account for the heat and the smoke."

"Did you bring the night vision goggles?" Cindy questioned.

"Ah...nope."

"What were you *thinking*?"

"I *thought*, what would Cindy bring?" Max joked. "We weren't supposed to be here at night or...in a tunnel."

"Some boy scout you are. Geez!" Cindy exhaled loudly.

"I never claimed to be a boy scout. I'm a girl scout. I scout for girls."

"Not very good at it, are you?" Cindy taunted before elbowing him in the ribs.

The clunking of gears turning and the grinding of metal on metal, broke through the sound of the equipment and startled Max and Cindy into ducking back against the wall. Directly between their positon and the platform on the opposite side, a hole opened in the ceiling and continued to grow until it was about thirty yards wide. The light streaming through the hole was blinding. Max and Cindy held a hand in front of their faces as they tried to view what was happening. The wind from the fan gained in strength as the opening allowed air in the system to flow freely.

Another loud clank and the hole stopped expanding, and then shadows began flickering against the blinding light as twisted shapes tumbled through the hole. Eerie wails and screams mingled with rushing wind and the embers which had been glowing slightly sprang to life, with flames stretching forty feet into the air. A wave of hot, smoky, foul air flooded the tunnel where Max and Cindy hid. The increasing temperature forced them to cover their faces and retreat into the tunnel.

The scorching heat drove them over a hundred yards back up the tunnel. The crunching metal sound and the extinguished light indicated the hole had been closed. The wind and the heat slowly retreated enough for Max and Cindy to breathe safely again.

They stood panting, staring back down the shaft.

"Were those...*bodies*?" Cindy questioned in a horrified tone.

"I think so." Max fought a nauseating feeling in his gut. "We should have known. They're committing genocide and disposing of the dead."

They remained silent, trying to process what they had just witnessed.

"I'm...sure those were *bodies* and I think they went into the pit *alive*. Did you hear the screams?" Cindy stammered, her bottom lip quivering.

"I have a very bad feeling," Max added.

"You have a bad feeling about what?" Sky's spoke out of the darkness, scaring Max and Cindy.

"Sky." Max jumped and then patted his chest as his eyes locked on the slender form of the pale blond woman dressed similar to a ninja. "You about gave me a heart attack."

"What did I teach you about letting your guard down?" Sky put her hands on her hips like a scolding mother. "And what's that horrible stench?" Sky covered her nose and mouth with her hands.

"I thought someone *as* observant *as* you would have noticed the smell before you made your way halfway down the tunnel." Max coughed on the smoky air.

"It's all about focus. When I detected your spells, I thought you were in trouble. My attention was on possible danger, not the air," Sky stated.

"Yeah, yeah." Max teased.

"So, what's horrible?"

The momentary relief of meeting Sky disappeared, swallowed up in the awfulness at the end of the tunnel.

"We think they are...destroying...people." Cindy sniffled.

"What?" Sky responded, her voice echoing off the walls.

The cranking of metal started once more. Max spread his arms wide. "Let's get out of here before the next wave of heat."

They didn't make the surface of the pit before another rush of hot, foul, smoky air mingled with fleeting, painful cries whipped past them.

Max tried to hold his breath until this new round finished but was unsuccessful. He gagged and coughed the same as the others after inhaling the hot, tainted air.

"What do you mean, they're destroying people?" Sky asked when they reached the surface.

"We aren't sure, but it looked like they were burning...*people while they were still alive.*" Max shot a wayward glance at the pit. "Didn't you hear the faint sound of screaming?"

The roar of spacecraft engines caught their attention once more. They stared in the direction of the rumble until it finally stopped.

"What do you think they're bringing in? More people?" Cindy questioned.

"Are you sure they're not taking stuff out?" Sky raised a skeptical eyebrow up her forehead.

Max used his hand to trace the direction of the tunnel to the possible location of the furnace on the surface of the jungle. "I think the ships are landing near the spot where they were dumping the bodies."

"Are you sure they were bodies?" Sky eyed both Max and Cindy for a moment. "And those screams could just be echoes from the grinding metal."

"What does the air smell like?" Cindy nodded to the pit.

"It's definitely worth checking out." Max added.

"I hope that's not what's been happening to the tribes and camps from other worlds." Sky's face reflected concern and disgust. "Come on." She started marching in the direction Max had indicated.

"*Wait!*" Cindy brought them to a stop.

"What?" Max and Sky stopped to look at her.

"What about those raptors?"

"What raptors?" Sky winked and then started walking the line of the tunnel.

Max flashed Cindy an I-told-you-so look before following in Sky's wake.

They walked in silence, picking the easiest path they could through the dense jungle vegetation. While in route, the rumble of another ship arriving indicated they were heading in the right direction.

The closer they drew toward their desired destination, the more a sense of dark magic began to grow in Max's mind. His strange senses and a couple of worried looks from Cindy told him he wasn't imagining his impressions.

"Psst, Sky," Max whispered to get her attention. "There's magic ahead. Be careful."

Sky gave a quick nod, drew a laser pistol out of a holster on her hip, and inched her way forward. She took them at an angle towards a massive tree. A faint trace of voices wafted in their direction, carried by a slight breeze.

Before they reached the large tree, Sky waved them into a crouch. Barely visible above the tall jungle grasses, a sizeable valley with flattened grass bobbed into view with each step forward. While scurrying in this hunched stance, Max couldn't see who was creating the conversation, which had grown in volume as they drew closer to the speakers. He and Cindy quickly filed in after Sky, who had ducked behind the massive tree.

"What is this place?" Max questioned. "I thought our targets were still a couple of miles beyond this point."

"They are. This wouldn't look like anything special from a satellite. We don't have any intel on this location or what it is used for." Sky stared around the tree. "If it *is* what you saw from inside that tunnel, this is an important find."

"If it's what we think it is, it needs to be destroyed and will change the nature of our operation here." Max watched the area intently.

"But why are they using it? I mean, they've been pretty much advertising their murderous ways for several years now through social media," Max reported.

"That's a good point. It might be because, with the collapse of or destruction of all the civilized societies, they no longer feel the need to advertise. Their 'submit, join, or die' mantra has swelled their ranks," Sky added.

Cindy checked her watch. "Well, I hope we find out in a hurry. We are already late for our other task."

"Our other job was a surprise as well, so no one but us will miss it if it doesn't happen," Sky commented.

"I don't think we will have to wait long." Max glanced skyward toward the roaring of spacecraft rockets.

The thundering engines continued to grow with each passing second. The trees and plants rocked back and forth violently from the wind created as the invisible craft hovered over the small clearing and then set down. The turbulence forced Max, Cindy, and Sky to cover their faces to protect their eyes from the dust and small flying particles.

A moment later, after the invisible ship had landed, the engines stopped, bringing a cessation to the small tornado. From out of the trees, a group of armed soldiers with faces hidden behind masks, wearing uniforms indicating a combination force of multiple races from across the galaxy, formed a line with their weapons aiming at the right side of the valley. As if a gateway had been created in midair, a door to the cloaked ship opened several feet above the ground, exposing a tight-knit group of prisoners who began descending the invisible ramp.

The prisoners who exited the ship also appeared to be a group of many races. They were battered and bruised, indicating mistreatment at the hands of the enemy. They all wore tattered gray clothing and didn't appear to have been able to bathe for some time.

"They must have suffered a great deal," Cindy groaned.

"There are *dijinnies* among them!" Sky poked her head farther out from behind the tree for a better look. "That guard, carrying that box, must have their dars."

"What are they doing with prisoners all the way...?" Even before he finished his sentence, Max's gut squirmed uneasily and the whole area seemed to darken with a heavy depressing sensation.

"Oh no!" Cindy gasped and then clamped her hands over her mouth after realizing that she had spoken too loudly.

Everyone ducked back behind the tree, holding their breath in case the soldiers had noticed her outburst. Not hearing any indication that the enemy had noticed Cindy's involuntary outburst, Max, Cindy, and Sky returned to observing the situation.

"We can't just let them slaughter *those* people," Cindy moaned.

The guards taunted the prisoners while escorting them towards the center of the field. The enemy pushed and kicked their victims to keep them moving. One even opened fire, spraying the area above the prisoners with machinegun fire. The prisoners screamed and dropped to the ground, terrified.

One of the tall, lanky, zombie-like men whom Max had fought when he met the Vice President last year, stepped out of the jungle.

"I say we make them fight to the death," one of the guards commented, and the others laughed and voiced their agreement.

"That would be more fun than just flipping the switch," another added.

Max, Cindy, and Sky exchanged worried looks.

"We can't just let them *die*." Max held up his weapon and cocked it.

"How do we want to do this?" Cindy questioned.

Before Max or Sky could answer Cindy's question, the zombie-like man cast a spell which pushed the prisoners into the center of the valley. The soldiers laughed while debating about forcing groups of prisoners to fight each other to the death. The complete lack of humanity displayed by the guards ignited Max's anger.

The prisoners have to be over the pit. There must be someone who controls the opening to the furnace below. Max scanned the area, searching for the one who would send them to their fiery grave.

After several minutes of the soldiers tormenting the captives with vocal threats, a large Trog was seen pushing and shoving his way into the clearing. "All right, all right, back up. Ya've 'ad nough fun. We 'ave ta dit ready fer another shipment." He waved the guards back with one massive hand while holding a small remote-like device in the other.

Once the troops had moved away and only the prisoners remained in the middle of the valley, the Trog chuckled wickedly. He held the remote out in front of him and extended the index finger on his opposite hand in a taunting manner.

The prisoners wailed, sensing what was about to happen. Several inched their way forward but were driven back with machinegun fire tearing up the ground in front of them. They screamed and huddled together in a tight knot.

Max's heart thudded rapidly against his chest and ears. *Do something!* Max sprang around the tree, took aim with his weapon and dropped the Trog with the remote.

Sky also sprang out and eliminated the zombie-man with another blast.

3

Into the Water

"So much for a plan." Cindy joined Max and opened fire, targeting the soldiers.

"*Pridi,*" Max called, and the remote flew from the Trog's dead hand into Max's. He dropped the remote into his pocket and refocused on the fight.

The captives dropped to the valley floor to avoid being hit in the crossfire, while the soldiers scattered, returning wild shots.

"Get the prisoners *out* of here!" Sky raced after the retreating troops.

The cloaked ship's engines sprang to life, creating hurricane-force winds which whipped across the area. The trees around the valley rocked back and forth wildly from the thrust of the spacecraft's rockets.

"*Stop* that ship. I'll get the prisoners," Cindy screamed.

Max spun around and opened fire on the cloaked craft. The laser blasts from his futuristic weapon bounced off the invisible ship. "*Prikazi!*" To Max's surprise, his desperation spell worked, and the cloaked aircraft slowly rising off the ground appeared in the form of a large chrome saucer.

With the ship now visible, Max targeted the craft's engines underneath, but its shields continued to deflect all his attempts. Max's mind raced for a solution to bring it down.

Cindy had reached the prisoners and given them cover while they crouched down and scurried towards Max's position. Sky attacked the guards with such ferocity, they began retreating from her advance.

"*Premakni*! *Premakni*!" Max's spells bounced off the massive ship, the same as his gun fire.

As soon as all the prisoners had made it into the jungle behind Max, Cindy joined Max's efforts to destroy the enemy ship rising into the air. They fired their weapons and cast spells to knock it out of the sky, without success.

"How did you make it visible?" Cindy questioned.

"I...wait! Stop trying to move it by force. It's too big. Send spells to turn off the engines. *Ugasni*!" Max called out and Cindy copied him.

The roar of the spacecraft and the turbulence shaking the trees around the valley suddenly stopped. The ship, which had been level and climbing steadily higher, rotated into a vertical position and then dropped to the ground. It smashed into the jungle floor with crunching metal, throwing trees, plants, and dirt in all directions.

"Stay with them," Max shouted and nodded to the rescued prisoners and then bolted towards the downed craft.

"Max! Wait! We need to get out of here before more ships arrive," Cindy screamed after him.

Somewhere in the back of his mind Max registered Cindy's argument, but he was already on his way. *We need to get information on their ships and where they come from.* He bounded through the jungle holding his weapon at the ready, closing the distance between him and the spaceship.

The massive gray saucer remained in a vertical position with the aid of the thick jungle trees. The front of the vessel had been crushed by the impact, and steam rose in steady streams from both sides.

Max paused a moment to consider how he was going to get inside, then tried, "*Odpri*!"

Ten feet off above him, the sound of gears and motors attempting to work created a horrible grinding noise, which rattled the trees surrounding the ship. After a few moments a small opening appeared where the sound originated but then stopped, followed by a pillar of black smoke.

Must have been damaged by the crash.

"Max, there's another ship coming in," Cindy's screams reached him through the hissing and rustling of the trees around the crash site.

A moment later, the roar of engines grew louder and louder.

"Let it land," Max yelled, hurrying back towards the valley. *Hopefully they aren't aware of what's happened and don't spot the crash.*

Max rushed through the tangled vegetation towards the area where he figured the ships would land. Before he could make it back to the clearing, the engines of the landing vessel almost swept him away in a tornado of air. The wind forced him to take cover behind a large tree.

"*Prikazi*," Max shouted the moment the rockets started to ebb and the landing craft appeared at the edge of the valley.

Max raced forward through the jungle as the doors to the ship opened and a ramp descended to the ground. A few unsuspecting guards had escorted a new group of prisoners out of the ship when Max attacked.

"*Premaknite!*" Max screamed with fury. His spell blasted the leading soldiers off the ramp and through the air.

The captives inside the ship froze on the ramp, unsure what to do. Machinegun fire from inside the ship forced them out in a rush. They leaped from the sides of the withdrawing ramp in an effort to avoid being shot. The ship's engines ignited and the ramp started to withdraw.

"*Ugasni!*" Max called and the engines stopped. "*Odpri.*" The ramp extended back to the ground.

Gunfire continued to spray out the door, forcing Max to keep clear of the opening. Chancing a peek, Max popped his head in and out of the line of fire for a brief moment. The horrific scene of several lifeless bodies lying on the floor of the ship caught his attention. *Murdered.* Max clenched his teeth.

"We need to hurry." Sky appeared next to Max, nearly stopping his heart once more. "Before…"

The roar of approaching crafts demanded their attention.

"Sounds like an army is coming." Max swung his weapon around the opening and fired several wild shots into the ship.

"By land and air. I don't know how we are going to get these people out of here." Sky ducked under the ramp to take up a position opposite Max.

"I hope Cindy is already moving them through the gateway." Max fired some more random shots.

"Me too. Do you detect any magic inside?" Sky questioned.

In all the commotion, Max hadn't thought about determining the strength of their enemy. He quickly sent out his feelers which returned the answer quickly. "NO! They're just soldiers. I think they were as surprised by us as we were by them."

"Then let's smoke them out." Sky held a large fireball in the air above her hand and Max followed her example. "Don't just send it wildly into the ship. Remember your lessons. Use it to flush the enemy out."

"But I don't know the layout of the ship." Max flashed Sky a confused look.

"Neither do I. You just have to listen to what your magic is telling you. How about this? I will tell you what to do." Sky sent her spell into the ship.

Max took a calming breath and closed his eyes before sending his fire into the ship. It took a great deal of effort for him to maintain the structure of his spell as it collided with a back wall.

"Move it slightly to the left after you hit the wall and then increase its size while holding your position. I will drive them through the ship but you have to keep them from being able to run in circles." Sky's right hand danced around in the air.

Following Sky's orders, Max positioned his flames so that he blocked a hallway to the left of the main entrance. *Rasti*! In his mind's eye, Max used magic and his will to expand the size of the fire. His heart raced from the effort, and sweat formed across his forehead. Even his breathing increased as if he were performing an intense exercise.

"Hurry," Max called.

A moment later, a half dozen screaming men raced out of the ship, dressed in black garb, with scarves wrapped around their faces and a raging fire chasing after them.

Max released his spell and raised his weapon to fire. Before he could attack, Sky's fire engulfed the fleeing enemy troops.

"*Premakni*." Max launched the victims into the jungle.

"Cindy, is the gateway open?" Sky called.

"No. There is too much traffic using it right now. We're on our own for a while." Cindy raced toward them with a pack of freed prisoners on her tail.

Out of the south, two jets zipped overhead with a ground shaking sonic boom. They flew past and then banked hard, preparing to make another pass.

"Into the trees." Cindy waved her arm frantically to the people behind her.

Sky handed the dijinnies their dars. "You're free. Now, we need your help to win this battle."

"Here they come." Max opened fire in the direction of the guard shack as several attack Humvees sped out of the jungle and into the middle of the valley.

The vehicles formed a semicircle, setting up a wall as troops poured out of the transports and began returning fire. Max used the ramp from the strange ship as cover while launching counter fire. Mingled with his, Cindy's, and Sky's weapons fire, they also cast spells to hammer the enemy.

"Stop those jets," Sky ordered the dijinnies, while pointing skyward at the incoming planes.

Before the dijinnies could respond the jets opened fire, forcing everyone to take cover. The rain of bullets ripped through the jungle, wounding several of the prisoners, while killing others.

"We need some cover," Cindy screamed.

"HEY." Max patted his clothing and felt the bulge from the remote he had deposited in his pocket. He yanked the remote from his pocket and pushed the button.

The center of the valley opened up beneath the unsuspecting soldiers and their vehicles. Screams issued from the doomed combatants as the majority of them and all but one of the Hummers dropped into the fiery pit. Those who managed to make it safely off the trapdoor became easy targets after losing their cover. Max, Cindy, and Sky made quick work getting rid of the exposed troops.

With the ground forces out of the picture, they turned their attention to the jets. The speed of the aircraft made it difficult to hit them with their weapons or spells.

"There's no way we will get out of here, even with the gateway, if we can't stop those jets from hammering us," Cindy screamed.

"We need...everybody into the ship," Max ordered while trying to hit the jets with his laser gun. "*Zachni.*" The ship sprang to life.

Max, Cindy, and Sky waved everyone under the ship until they could make their way to the ramp. Max's idea worked, as the ship's shields deflected the bullets and heat seeking missiles fired by the circling crafts.

"Now what?" Cindy hollered after the last of the prisoners had made it safely into the ship.

"With this shield we could hold them off until we can move them through the gateway," Max suggested.

"That could take a while and in the meantime, they could send in something or things nastier than these jets," Sky responded.

"We could try to fly this thing out of here." Cindy fired off a few attempts to hit the aircraft, but it was useless.

"It appears to be designed with humans in mind because of the soldiers who came out of it." Max raised his eyebrows and shrugged his shoulders.

"It's worth a try," Sky agreed. "I'll watch the door. Go take a look."

Max and Cindy raced up the ramp and into the craft. They ran into the pack of prisoners all huddled together, waiting anxiously just inside the craft.

"What are we going to do?" Some of the prisoners questioned.

"What can we do to help?" others asked.

"Where's the main deck?" Max asked, and most of the prisoners pointed to the hallway branching to the left.

"On the opposite side of the ship," several stated.

Max and Cindy hurried through the prisoners, who followed in their wake. The inside of the ship was also set up in a circular layout. They passed glassed-in cells as they raced around a curved hallway which opened on both sides as they reached the main deck. To their right was a small area with holographic charts of galaxies and worlds, and on the left were several computers and a pilot's chair facing a large glass windshield.

Max slid into the pilot's chair and glanced down at the controls. "The instructions *are* in *English!*"

"What?" Cindy leaned over him while staring down at the controls. "What does this mean?"

Max met her gaze. "I don't know. Go get Sky. Everyone find a place to sit." Max hit the control to close the door but nothing happened. "Wha...Oh. *Zakluci!*"

Taking the controls in front of him, he slowly lifted the craft off the ground.

"Are you sure you know what you're doing?" several of the prisoners questioned.

"No! But do you have a better idea?"

"Have you flown before?" others asked.

"Yes!"

Cindy returned with Sky and hovered around the command chair.

Missiles continued to explode against the ship's shields, but only a bright flash in the front glass shield or a dull thud were noticeable.

"Do we have weapons?" Cindy hopped around to the other stations near the main chair, looking at each control panel. "Yep!" She plopped onto a chair to the right and slightly lower than Max's.

"What do we have?" Sky moved over by Cindy.

"All kinds of stuff. Missiles, lasers, you name it." Cindy's fingers danced over her controls, bringing different forms of weapons across her monitor.

"Do it fast before they figure out how we brought a ship of theirs down and captured another, and that magic can affect it," Max ordered while lifting the craft higher into the air.

"Missiles." Cindy pressed the launch button and four rockets took off after the attacking jets. They left trails of smoke that arced and rose into the air after locking in on their targets.

The aircrafts tried several maneuvers to avoid the deadly pursuers, but in a matter of seconds two large explosions eliminated the jets.

"So, where to?" Max questioned while raising his eyebrows.

"*Grandpa's*," Cindy said.

"What are you thinking?" Sky asked Max.

"Well, I noticed there is an autopilot and it seems to already be programmed. This ship could take us right to where it came from." Max motioned to a monitor in front of him.

"Hey, normally I'm as adventurous as you are, but that could take us *right* into the heart of the enemy!" Cindy widened her eyes, pursed her lips and waved her hands wildly. "That's not exactly rescuing these people, is *it*?"

Max fought to suppress the smile creeping at the corners of his mouth. "When have *I* ever endangered anyone?" Max spurred her on.

"All right you love birds. Enough flirting. You're going to make our passengers sick. You're already turning my stomach." Sky laughed.

"Well?" Both Max and Cindy stared at Sky.

"We don't want to go back there." A few of the passengers pleaded.

"We could drop them off first." Max twisted his hat back and forth on his head to scratch the sweat line before sending the ship forward. "*Izgini!*"

"What was that for?" Cindy questioned.

"I just reactivated the cloaking device. We need to spread the word that at least some of the enemy's ships respond to magic." Max flashed a mischievous grin. "I figure it might be safer if *we're* cloaked."

"No! Really!" Cindy crossed her eyes.

"So, where to? Grandpa's or the mountains?" Max questioned as the land below them changed to the solid blue of the Pacific Ocean.

A loud beeping sound issued from one of the computer stations on Max's left, drawing everyone's attention.

"I don't like the sound of that," Cindy commented.

"Stay with the weapons' controls." Sky plopped onto the seat in front of the signal. She stared at the monitor for a moment. "We have ships coming in. Get us out of here."

Max pushed the thrusters to their limit and angled the ship upward. The resulting g-forces pulled him back into his seat.

Laser blasts started flashing all around them. Every few seconds one would connect with a loud bang and rock the craft.

"Whatever they're using is impacting our shields, and it doesn't appear the cloaking device is hiding us from them," Cindy reported, trying to work the weapons.

"NO! Head back towards the ground. Make them worry about more than just trying to shoot us out of the air. Have you learned *nothing*?" Sky barked.

"Try turning off their engines with magic." Max took the ship into a steep dive while zigzagging back and forth.

"We're traveling too fast," a couple of dijinnies responded.

"We need to slow them down," Max stated as the North American continent started to fill up the windshield. "Hold on." Max took a sharp hundred and eighty degree turn that took them within several feet of hitting the ground.

"Please don't try to impress me." Cindy fired the laser cannons at the trailing ships.

"Well then you're not going to like my next move." Max adjusted the controls on his main panel.

"What are you planning?" Sky questioned.

"Let's just say, I hope the English describing these controls is correct." Max closed his eyes and turned the ship at an angle, heading into the ocean. The vessel skipped off the surface of the water like a stone.

"Are you sure the ship can do that?" Sky shrieked. "If so, you have to slow down. At this speed that water will be like cement."

Max put on the brakes and the three trailing ships zipped past them. Adjusting the controls, Max dove into the water. The outside scene went from light to dark in a matter of seconds. The only light in the cockpit issued from the computers and controls.

Max made a few more changes and the ship started to move through the water like a submarine. He traveled just under the surface to where the other ships should be preparing to enter the water. "Once they're in the water, we'll use magic to turn off their engines. They should just sink like a rock."

"Magic doesn't travel through water like it does in the air," Sky stated.

"Uh oh."

"Don't worry. We can lay it down like a trap. They will just need to move through it," a dijinnie behind them stated. "I've done it before."

"They're in the water," Sky reported.

"How many?" another dijinnie questioned.

"Three of them," Sky answered.

"Turn the ship around," one of the dijinnies ordered.

"I'm going to try something, so hold on." Max spun a dial on his chair. The deck, minus the room with the charts behind them on the opposite side of the hall, rotated around to the back of the ship. Max hit the thrusters and the ship started moving in the opposite direction.

"Don't do that again." Cindy looked a little peaked and put a hand over her mouth.

"Stay on this line," a dijinnie said.

"You got it."

"Whatever you're going to do, do it quickly. Torpedoes in the water," Sky reported, staring at her monitor.

The prisoners, who had been left on the other side of the ship when Max rotated the deck, filled the hallway behind them.

"We're on it." The dijinnies formed a circle and started muttering in quiet voices.

A few moments later, an explosion rocked the ship and then another.

"Torpedoes destroyed," Sky reported.

"I wish I could see what was happening." Cindy exhaled the tension she had been holding.

"Yeah." Max wiped his brow with his hand. His body tensed while he worked the controls.

"I can hear the other ships," said one of the rescued prisoners.

"So can I," others added.

Everyone in the ship held their breath and strained their ears. Mingled with the ships jet propulsion, a strange chatter like frantic conversations penetrated the ship.

"The first ship should reach the trap…now!" a dijinnie said.

The volume to the chatter increased, and then what seemed to be screams of terror filled the hulls of the ship. The same scenario played out twice more, leaving an empty feeling in the pit of Max's stomach. The terrified cries reminded him of those he had heard, mixed with the noise of the fan, down in the tunnel.

No one spoke for several moments while Max continued to drive the ship through the water.

"Let's get out of here." Sky broke the silence.

"Yeah." Max had angled the ship towards the surface when the lights went out and the ship's engines died.

4

Tunnels and Traps

"Are you sure they went this way?" Joe, an elderly man who resembled Mark Twain wearing a ski cap, peered through binoculars at a snow capped pyramid sticking out of a dense, tall, pine forest. The dim light from the cloudy day didn't hamper his high-tech binoculars, which made everything appear as if it were high noon on a sunny day.

Yelka, a short woman with tan skin and pointed ears, breathed warm air into her cupped, gloved hands. The cold wind whipped her blond-gray streaked hair around her face. "Yes. That is their temple. But whether they're here or not is another story. The enemy has grown extremely powerful and I *am* very worried."

"Me too. I'm getting too old for this." Joe lowered the binoculars, and then looked over the edge of the cliff in front of them. A slight dizzying, nauseating sensation swirled in his gut at the sight of the two hundred foot drop off.

"The end isn't that far away." Yelka patted his arm.

"Yes, but this cliff is in our way."

"I wasn't speaking of that end."

Joe flashed a sad, understanding expression.

"And there is always a way, if you learn to see." Yelka smiled, stepping behind Joe and rotating his body so that his right shoulder was nearly parallel to the cliff face.

Joe's jaw dropped as a strange, steep staircase cut into the cliff face came into focus. "I'm not sure that is all that comforting." He chuckled.

"Yes, but this scary set of stairs is a little more special. You need to look just a little harder. There is a groove carved all along the steps that makes a nice hand rail." Yelka pointed at the strange handle near the start of the stairway.

"Okay, that makes me feel slightly better." Joe winked and made his way to the top of the cliff and the start of the steps.

"Let's just hope nothing dreadful has happened to the Kannels. They were truly the best society I have ever encountered." Yelka followed Joe to the flight of stairs.

"And you think they can help us?"

"They know more about reading the signs than anyone I have ever met. The only problem is we must pass a test to abide in their presence."

"Let me guess." Joe paused on the stairs to glance back at her. "The test isn't easy?"

"And will not be anything we will expect either."

"Terrific."

They were about halfway down the staircase when something out in the forest caught Joe's eye. He froze mid-step for a moment and then rocked back up onto the step behind him. In a small clearing a couple hundred feet from the temple, rising out of the forest, lifeforms dressed in black moved about.

"It looks like they've set up camp," Yelka commented in his ear.

"Disappear." Joe cast the invisibility spell, as did Yelka.

While holding the stone rail with one hand, he fished out his binoculars with the other. "They have a regular war camp down there with tents and weapons and...*Hudich*!" Joe caught sight of a tall figure cloaked in black with a skull-like face and red rat eyes.

"*What?*"

"That *must* mean they think the Kannels are here as well. But why would he want them?"

"Do you really not know the answer to that question? He is evil and anything good he wants to destroy or pervert. It could be a sign that he's concerned about The One and is trying to destroy anything to do with him."

"We better warn Jax and his men. They shouldn't have left yet. I don't want them to come in blindly." Joe took out his communicator.

Yelka grabbed his elbow. "Tell them just to hold back. If they are discovered, Hudich will know we are here as well. We have a better chance of getting in alone."

"Good point." Joe typed his message. He waited just a moment and the response returned. "They will hold at the gateway. Well..." Joe returned to checking the area with his binoculars. "If they have a camp set up down there, I'm willing to bet they have established some kind of perimeter around the temple."

Joe searched for more of the enemy. "The forest is too thick. It was blind luck that, in this storm, we hit an exact opening in the trees to see that camp."

"Let's get out of their line of sight so we can conserve energy. I'm willing to bet they don't know about these stairs, so we are probably approaching from the safest direction."

"Agreed." Joe started down the stairs once more.

After they had descended until they could no longer see the camp, they released the invisibility spells to conserve energy. Before they could reach the bottom, the heavy dark clouds began to release moisture in the form of thick, wet snowflakes. The sudden storm, combined with the wind, limited their visibility.

"Hopefully, the snow will cover our tracks." Joe put his foot into the existing snow pile and sank in a few inches.

"Well, we definitely shouldn't attempt using any magic with Hudich nearby. He would detect us in a heartbeat," Yelka commented.

"I think we're going to have to chance it. Like you said, I don't think they are patrolling this side because of the cliff face. I will use the thermal imaging setting on the binoculars every now and then to spot any possible threats." Joe took out the field glasses and made an adjustment before putting them up to his face. "Nothing." He then put them back and pulled his hat lower over his ears before putting on some gloves.

Yelka slung a scarf around her neck and tightened her jacket as they stepped off the stairway.

They started forward with their heads bent against the heavy snow. The storm also muffled the scrunching of the snow beneath their feet. They paused every thirty feet or so for Joe to check for heat signatures with the binoculars. He also kept them on course with his compass.

"We've got something. A couple of somethings." Joe reported, when they were within two hundred yards of the pyramid.

"Where? I don't see them in all this snow."

Joe handed the binoculars to Yelka. "One is to our right about forty yards away. The other is a little farther to the left."

"Do you think we can go between them with this storm?" Yelka asked.

"Or we could take the one on the right out. He's farther from Hudich." Joe glanced at her and shrugged his shoulders.

"I don't know. Any misstep could give us away."

"Yes, but they might be using thermal imaging as well. Hudich has been wising up to modern technology." Joe drew his laser weapon and adjusted it to stun. "Better to knock him out."

They made a right turn and began traveling parallel to the soldier on their right in order to stay on his flank. The storm had increased to almost whiteout conditions. They traveled with their heads down to avoid getting snow in their eyes. Every few feet they would look up, to avoid any trees or obstacles in their path.

"I think we should work our way forward now. It appears the sentry is facing the pyramid." Joe handed the binoculars to Yelka.

"You should be in good range by that tree several yards ahead." Yelka passed the binoculars back.

After reaching the tree, Joe used the binoculars to locate the guard in the storm. While holding the binoculars to his face, he took careful aim with his firearm and squeezed the trigger.

"He's down."

They hurried to the fallen sentry to secure him, in case he woke up before their job was finished.

"He's human," Yelka commented in surprise as she bound his feet.

"And a member of ISIS, the enemy of all things good." Joe pulled a small version of the Islamic state flag out of the man's jacket. "It is Hudich's political system of choice, with millions willing to commit horrible acts in the name of religion."

"I don't know how we didn't see how his followers had been pushing militant Islam throughout the universe for decades, to control the masses."

"It was a brilliant move. While we focused on Allan and his top followers, they were building evil armies behind the scenes."

They hauled the man under the branches of a large tree to keep the storm from completely covering him. After checking the thermal imaging to see they hadn't missed any other guards, they hurried to the temple.

"I expected something already." Yelka tried to peer up as the storm obscured the structure in front of them.

They walked the perimeter of the pyramid, searching for some kind of entrance, without success.   Every so many paces, they would push on a strange rock protruding from the black surface.

"Maybe they're not here," Joe suggested.

"This is the only place I know they could be. I say we climb the stairs." Yelka pointed to large steps on the side of the structure.

"It looks like it's our only option."

They made their way around to the side of the pyramid, where the stairs climbed up the center of the structure. The steps were wider and taller than normal ones on earth. Joe's long legs didn't have much trouble with the difference in size, but Yelka was forced to use her hands to climb, making it a slow process. The snow packed on the surface made each step a slippery nightmare.

With each new step the snow, which had been falling heavily, began to diminish in its ferocity. At first, the top of the temple grew visible, and soon the treetops below them started to appear.

"If they spot us, let's not hesitate to use magic to get to the top," Joe recommended.

"They won't spot us. There is already magic at play. I can feel it. And it might not protect us from unwanted eyes, but to launch an attack against this structure would be a very bad move on their part." Yelka stretched out her hand for Joe to assist her up the next step.

"Yes, but remember that's Hudich down there. He might be willing to attempt it."

"Even he knows enough not to assault your house. Whatever is protecting this temple is stronger than what we created to protect your place."

"Excellent observation." Joe glanced out toward the forest, noticing the low clouds had risen, exposing most of the forest to view.

"This magic will not stop them from following us though. It isn't built to keep them out, but to protect itself. So keep moving," Yelka ordered.

Loud horns rang out, drawing their attention as they continued to climb. They glanced around, searching for the source of the noise. The storm and clouds continued to block Hudich's camp from view, but a section of the forest on the opposite side of the temple had opened enough for a sentry to spy them on the stairs.

More alarms followed the first, until the entire forest was alive with blaring horns. The volume and tone vibrated the snow resting on the pyramid.

Small flashes of light erupted in the air just yards away from the surface of the pyramid, Joe, and Yelka. Even though the magic protecting the structure blocked all attempts from Hudich's followers attacking them, the unnerving bombardment drove Joe and Yelka up the stairs at an accelerated pace.

Joe's heart pounded in his chest and sweat formed along his brow and down his back. His and Yelka's heavy breathing rose in steady clouds of steam above their heads. Even though it felt like they were working harder, the slippery surface didn't allow them to climb any faster.

"They're coming." Joe glanced down the steps.

Hudich's followers rushed through the trees, closing in on the temple. Before Joe and Yelka could reach the top, Hudich suddenly appeared at the bottom of the steps. He paused for a moment with outstretched arms and his head down. Then meeting Joe's gaze, Hudich started up the stairs.

"He's coming and he's moving fast," Joe warned.

Joe's legs shook from the exertion of climbing when they reached the top of the temple. In the center of the flat twenty-foot wide surface was a hole with a spiral staircase leading down into the building.

"Oh great, more stairs." Joe panted, resting with his hands on his knees, staring down into the black hole. He swung his pack off his back and fished out a flashlight.

"Well, we can't wait for Hudich to catch up to us." Yelka snatched the light from Joe's hand and took the lead.

"That might not be a safe position. If I fall, I'm going to take us both out." Joe tried to make light of the situation, while they began hurrying down the steps.

They scurried as fast as their tired legs would carry them, around and around the spiral staircase. Even though Joe couldn't see Hudich, the image of him giving chase pressed down upon them as if the tunnel were closing in on them.

"There's a light up ahead." Yelka switched off the flashlight.

Joe squinted into the darkness and a faint light appeared around the outline of Yelka's silhouette.

"JOE!" Hudich's voice echoed through the small tunnel, spurring on Yelka and Joe.

They reached the bottom of the stairs where a small room bathed in flickering torchlight met them. Straight ahead was a long arched hallway lined with torches mounted in wall brackets.

They paused for only a moment and then Joe moved to the front as they raced into the tunnel. Fear of what was coming up behind them drove them forward at a more reckless pace than normal. Joe's eyes remained fixed on what appeared to be a room at the end of the hall, growing larger by the second.

The sight that greeted Joe's and Yelka's eyes brought them to a dead stop. They entered a massive room filled with all manner of imaginable riches. Gold, silver, jewels, statues, and artwork littered the room. It reminded Joe of a scene right out of a treasure hunting movie after they had just solved the final clue to some map and found the mother lode.

The room was the size of a football field and the treasure stretched from the floor to the ceiling. Piled on shelves and desks and on top of more treasure, the shiny objects reflected the light from the torches, making the room appear as bright as noonday. Trails wound their way around and through the treasure.

"Joseph." Yelka nudged Joe with her elbow and nodded towards a person in the center of the room.

In the middle of the room an elderly humanoid man dressed in long red robes sat at a table. Two glasses and a crystal pitcher filled with a purplish liquid rested on the table. The person was several feet taller than a normal human. He had long, flowing, silver hair and a beard, dark skin, and a wiry frame. He eyed them curiously, without saying a word.

Joe glanced around to see if he could spot any other strange beings, without success. "Let's get this over with before Hudich arrives."

They made their way through the treasure to the person sitting at the table. Joe's attention continued to jump from each new tower of treasure to make sure they weren't walking into a trap. The old man at the table didn't move, just sat silently and watched them approach.

The closer to the table Joe and Yelka drew, the more cautious they became. Their steps were slower and their muscles tensed from fear of the unknown.

"How do you do?" the man spoke softly, startling Joe and Yelka.

Even though the man's gray hair hinted of great age, his smooth features appeared to be those of a much younger man. His eyes were large, with bright baby blue pupils that gave one the impression they were seeing more than just the surrounding environment.

"You speak English?" Joe questioned with a puzzled look.

"This is my first attempt." The man smiled.

"How did you know? Learn? How…" Joe stammered.

"By reading your minds and listening to your conversation," the man answered.

"I'm Joe and this is Yelka." Joe motioned to himself and then Yelka. "But I suppose you already know that."

"Yes. I'm Zenos."

"And you already know why we've come?" Yelka stated more than asked.

"I do." The man twirled a hand through the air and the pitcher on the table poured some of the purplish liquid into the two glasses.

"I take it you aren't just going to give us what we want?" Joe raised his eyebrows as he eyed the glasses.

"Is anything worth it when it is just free?"

"No, not really." Joe shook his head.

"What will this liquid do? As I'm sure you mean for us to drink it?" Yelka questioned.

"It will test you. You will see the things you desire and…more."

Joe picked one of the glasses off the table and peered through the clear liquid. "I suppose it will not harm us?"

"It is *not* poison. But, it may harm you."

"How?" Yelka asked.

"There is only one item that may be taken from this place. I am the last of my people and remain to protect our secrets until such time as one worthy to retrieve them arrives."

"And if one isn't worthy?" Joe asked.

Once more the old man waved his hand through the air and the treasure disappeared. Instead of gold and jewels, skeletons littered the room. Piles of skulls and dead bodies rose into the air, forming tall pillars. A suffocating wave of decay forced Joe and Yelka to cover their faces to avoid the sickening odor. Swarms of flies buzzed around the room, giving the place an ominous shadow.

"Since you obviously can read our minds, you then know that I think this is some sort of illusion," Joe commented while breathing through the sleeve of his coat.

"Yes, but you aren't totally sure and that is the desired effect. Now, if you will drink, we may begin."

Joe passed the glass he had been holding to Yelka and then retrieved the second one off the table. They paused for a moment.

"To your health," Joe chuckled and they clinked their glasses together before downing the purplish liquid.

The second they lowered their glasses, Hudich entered the room.

5

The Signs of the Times

Hudich stood at the entrance, dark and menacing. His red-rat eyes seemed to be taking in the room before glancing at Joe, Yelka and Zenos. Joe dropped the glass in his hand, which shattered on the floor.

"He *cannot* see you," Zenos stated flatly. "However, I sense he is searching for the same thing you are. Interesting. Most who enter here are seeking riches. It is rare that someone is hunting for the true treasure here. And now, one after another, even different beings are after the same thing. I can see that the information in his hands would cause greater pain and suffering. I suggest you hurry."

The dead bodies and putrid air vanished slowly from all around them. The image that met their eyes now was a room full of books, scrolls, charts, stone tablets with writing, and other record keeping devices.

"And we can't touch the wrong item without suffering death?" Joe questioned.

"You may touch whatever you want, but whatever your heart accepts is considered the chosen item. So be cautious. The elixir you just drank is meant to test your convictions. Everything you look at will seem to have great importance. You must not be fooled by deceptive information."

"What happens to Hudich if we remove the item first?" Yelka asked.

"I will no longer have any reason to stay. You and the item will be safely removed from this place because it is my job to protect it within the walls of this temple. Hudich will no longer be faced with the temptations and be free to leave. I don't think you will be free to leave if he finds it first, as the siege outside will still be waiting for you." He then motioned to the maze of information in the large room.

"I suggest we stick together. Two minds should be clearer than one. The things that tempt us might be different, so if we don't both agree, we might be safer," Yelka suggested.

"Good point." Even as Joe made this last comment, a euphoric feeling spread through him. All his fears, anxieties, and desperation vanished as if he didn't have a worry in the world.

"Now. What are we here for?" Yelka questioned.

"Something about information but I'm not really sure," Joe replied in puzzlement. There seemed to be a small voice somewhere in the back of Joe's mind trying to make contact but he couldn't quite discern what it was saying. He shook his head as if shooing away annoying insects. "I do have this feeling that it is something important."

"I have the same feeling. Let's start looking and maybe we will remember what it is." Yelka took him by the hand and they headed towards a table covered with stacks of books.

Joe snatched a book from a pile on the table and began flipping through its pages. What he saw sent of wave of surprise through his whole body. There, on the page in front of him, stood the diagrams for building the perfect gateway. One that could create two portals at one time so they could move from one world to the next without having to stop in his attic. *This cannot be. I've wanted to figure this out for so long. Who figured this out?*

"I've been looking for this all my life." Yelka examined the pages of another book.

"Me too. But how did this information get here?" Joe glanced around the room full of books and other items used for the storage of data. "Did we hit the mother lode of knowledge?"

"I still can't believe it." Yelka exhaled. "I don't understand it."

What else could they have information on? Joe placed the current book in his hands where he could find it again and picked up another from the table.

"No way," Joe said so forcefully Yelka looked up from the book that had been dominating her attention.

"What?" Yelka questioned.

"This books contains schematics on how to block magic with technology."

"I didn't think that was possible." Yelka shook her head. "This is very odd."

"What is?"

"We both seem to be finding things we have wanted for a long, long time." Yelka eyed the piles of books and scrolls around them.

Once more, Joe had the feeling that some annoying insects were buzzing around his ears, creating a dizzying affect. A wave rolled down his vision as if it were a projection of some kind. He shook his head from side to side and the cluttered room came back into focus.

He's going to kill me!

"What?" Joe gasped looking at Yelka.

"How?' Yelka stared at Joe.

"You just said someone was going to kill you," Joe stated.

"I thought that was you."

"Then?"

I can read his intentions. I will not be able to stop him.

Both Joe and Yelka began glancing around the room, trying to find the source of the voice. Only the room full of books and records met their gaze.

Once I am dead, the spell will be broken. Hudich will find you!

"Hudich." Joe shook his head again to clear his thinking. "Why are we here?" He looked at Yelka.

"We were…are after information." Yelka let the book she held in her hands slide out of her fingers to land on the ground. "Hudich!"

"He's here." Joe peered around trying to find his enemy, but to no avail. Again, a wave washed down his vision. "We're…under a spell."

"We drank that liquid." Yelka placed her fingers on her lips. "It was the potion. This *isn't* real."

"None…of this…*is* real?" A couple more shapes flowed down his vision as if he were watching a TV and the signal was losing power.

You need to hurry. He is going to act.

"We came for the book of prophecy." Joe stated so loudly it caused him to flinch. "These are just a distraction." Joe waved at the room and all the books, scrolls, and other items began to dissolve or distort.

Joe's attention jumped around the room while trying to fight the spell, causing him to see things that weren't there. The picture in front of him continued to twitch and fade. For one brief moment, a vision of Hudich eyeing a glass of purple liquid flashed and was gone.

"There." Yelka pointed to a small table with a large leather bound book in a corner of the room. "That is the only object that isn't changing shape based on the fading spell."

Hurry!

The quiet warning spurred Joe and Yelka across the room. At first Joe followed the paths laid out in the room between tables and shelves according to the piles of information, until Yelka made a beeline straight for the book on the table.

"This other stuff isn't real." Yelka stated, walking through images of junk created in their minds by the potion.

A cry of pain echoed off the now almost empty room, freezing Joe and Yelka in their tracks. The spell which had clouded their minds only moments before ended. Hudich stood over the old humanoid, holding the hilt of a dagger buried in the man's chest. The man's eyes briefly locked with Joe's and Yelka's as he laid sprawled backwards in his chair.

Hudich followed the man's line of sight to spot Joe and Yelka rushing across the room.

"*Pridi*!" Yelka screeched and the book zoomed off the table and into her outstretched hands.

Joe drew his laser pistol in mid stride and opened fire at Hudich. Laser blasts bounced off Hudich's protective spells and ricocheted around the large stone room. The gunfire shattered the stone structure wherever it impacted, creating a storm of dust and small rock chips.

"Head for that door." Joe nodded in the direction of an open doorway to the left of the table where the book had rested, while continuing his attack.

"We don't know where that leads…"

A loud pop echoed off the walls and a large crack in the floor threw Joe and Yelka off their feet from Hudich's counter curse. Joe and Yelka threw up a protective spell, but the force of Hudich's rage pushed their shield backwards, sending them sliding across the floor.

Joe held down the trigger to his laser pistol while Yelka cast a myriad of spells, all the while scrambling for the open doorway. The battle threatened the stability of the structure of the room. Large chunks of the ceiling crashed down onto the floor, creating more obstacles for Joe and Yelka to avoid.

They finally ducked into the dark doorway and sprinted down a long dark hallway. Yelka conjured a small ball of flame to light their way.

Every ten feet or so, Joe would fire a shot back down the tunnel behind them.

"Stairs." Yelka warned.

They shuffled down the spiraled stone steps for what would equal several stories as they completed three full circles. When they reached the bottom, they encountered a junction which ran in three different directions.

"Which way?" Yelka said, panting.

Joe stuffed the book into his backpack and took out a flashlight and a compass. He used the latter to figure out the directions of the different tunnels. "That way. The gateway is in that direction. And douse your light. With the flashlight shining in only one direction, it will be harder for Hudich to see us." He pointed to a tunnel on their right and Yelka took the lead.

"We don't even know where these things lead or if there is an exit at the end." Yelka started forward.

"We just need to create some distance so I can have Rachel open the gateway and give us an exit." Joe gasped for air. A sharp stitch built in his side and his lungs burned. "I'm just hoping that this structure allows it."

"WHAT?"

"Some of these ancient buildings are quite ingenious. They hold electromagnetic energy that could interfere with our communicators and possibly the gateway. Many hold..." An alarm in Joe's head went off shooting such a powerful jolt through his body that he actually flinched. "STOP!"

Yelka's chest heaved with each breath as she spun to face Joe. "Are you crazy? Hudich is going to be coming up behind us at any minute."

"Yes, but death could be waiting in front of us as well."

"What do you mean?"

Joe pulled her behind him and started forward cautiously, using his flashlight to check the path ahead thoroughly. "A lot of civilizations protect their sacred sites with booby-traps to keep people from stealing artifacts or disturbing tombs."

"But we were able to enter safely from the top." Yelka glanced over her shoulder every few seconds, expecting to see Hudich coming up behind them.

"Yes, but we were led to that room where we were supposed to make a choice, which had life and death as its options. Hudich interfered. I would be willing to bet that entrance is now sealed."

"While you look for traps, I'll try the communicator." Yelka took out her device and started typing a message. "You were right," Yelka said in a dejected voice. "I can't get a signal. I even tried Jax—and nothing."

"I think this wall comes down." Joe put an arm out to stop Yelka from walking forward, while following the outline of a doorway with the flashlight.

In the ceiling above them, there appeared to be a thick stone slab that could be lowered. The side walls had six-inch deep grooves which would secure the stone in place once it had descended from overhead.

"So how do we trigger it? And, do we want to?" Yelka asked.

"That's the million dollar question. Is it built to keep us out or in?"

"Shhh." Yelka warned.

The faint sound of shuffling feet echoed softly through the hallway. Joe and Yelka exchanged a worried look. Joe pointed to his mouth while shaking his head and then motioned to the hall in front of them.

The flashlight beam jumped from the floor to the ceiling to the walls while Joe searched for any sign of a trap. Once more his arm shot out to stop Yelka from moving forward. He waved the light over several small holes about a foot off the floor, spaced about a foot apart. The wall on the opposite side appeared to have matching holes.

Joe leaned in close to the first hole. Holding the flashlight only inches away. A small stream of particles like dust appeared to be traveling between the holes across the hallway. The flashlight reflected off the particles, making them glow.

"There is magic here." Yelka whispered, standing with the palms of her hands extended towards the hallway in front of them.

"I think something will happen if we break these streams," Joe commented in a hushed tone. "And I don't think it will be something good. You better get out your flashlight so that you can see where you are stepping."

Yelka nodded and then retrieved a flashlight form her backpack.

Taking a deep breath, Joe stepped over the first and placed his leg between two of them. Then, carefully, he moved his second one so that he stood between two of the dust-like beams. He proceeded to the next section, turning his feet sideways while lifting them over the streams.

Joe paused mid-step when a tingling sensation spread through him. "What was that?" he whispered.

"Hudich. Just found us. Go!" Yelka pressed and they started to move over the small hurdles as fast as they could.

"JOE!" Hudich roared, rushing down the hall towards them.

"We're not going to make it." Yelka shined her flashlight forward to see the small holes extending as far as her light would go.

A shockwave slammed into Joe and Yelka, lifting them off their feet and throwing them forward through the hall. They crashed down against the hard stone floor, skidding and bouncing several feet through the strange magical beams.

Stone grating against stone filled the hallway and a strange clicking issued from the floor.

"Eek!" Yelka squealed, jumping off the floor and shaking her hand in the air. The snap of her hand sent a small black object flying out of sight. "Something bit me."

Joe also leapt to his feet and started swatting small black creatures swarming all over him, inflicting vicious, painful bites on any exposed skin on their faces and hands. Even in the darkness of the underground tunnel, a shadow closed in on the light, stirring twangs of panic in Joe's mind. His heart pounded against his ribcage and his mouth grew dry.

An explosion of sparks flashed in a strange pattern behind them, where Hudich's spell smashed into the sinking stone slab.

Joe snatched Yelka's hand and jerked her forward, their feet crunched on the now critter covered stone floor. "Run! We have to make the other door before we are sealed in here and devoured." Joe's flashlight bounced around the hall, revealing countless black things chasing after them.

Yelka sent a wave of fire down the hall ahead of them in an effort to destroy the small attackers, but they kept springing forth from the ground and taking flight. Joe squinted his eyes and raced into the surging pests. The grating stone sound grew deeper and louder.

"There it is. Get ready to slide," Joe screamed and pulled Yelka down to the floor. He stuck his leg out in a baseball slide. The small black pests smashed under his weight, creating a slippery surface that propelled them under the door only moments before it sealed.

Once more, they sprang to their feet and began smashing the biting things, as a small army of them had made it through the door.

"Ouch! Die!" they both yelled while killing the blood thirsty creatures.

It took them several minutes to wipe out the remainder, which left them standing with bite marks all over their hands and faces.

"It's a good thing we were wearing winter clothing." Yelka stretched the bottom of her coat forward to reveal a tattered piece of garment.

"Yeah. We might not have made it out of there." Joe put his hand on the stone slab. He pointed the flashlight at his coat and then swatted it with the palm of his hand. Thousands of small feathers flew out of holes created by the black things. The feathers drifted slowly in the air, reminding Joe of the storm outside.

"That was close." Yelka watched the falling feathers with wide eyes and took a deep breath. "Now, if this tunnel has an exit we should be past the danger. I don't think Hudich will get out of there very easily."

"Hudich may be trapped for a bit, but we might not be out of danger even if this tunnel has an exit." Joe pointed his light down the tunnel to see no end to the long dark structure.

"What? Why?"

"These types of places usually have more than one trap." Joe shot her a concerned look.

They started forward once more, going slow and constantly checking for hidden dangers. The hallway ran in a straight line for several dozen yards before opening into a dimly lit room about the size of a gymnasium with a high ceiling. The soft light filtered in through several shafts positioned across the roof, which also gave the room a slight chill. Their breath appeared in small puffs of smoke.

"I wonder what this room does," Joe muttered while they stood in the hallway, peering inside.

"Again, there is magic at work here." Once more, Yelka stood with her arms and palms extended towards the room.

"Can you tell what it's doing?"

"I don't think it is part of the trap, but more of a protection for it. I wouldn't be able to use magic to disable whatever it is."

"Hmmm." Joe slowly extended the tip of the flashlight into the room.

The moment the flashlight passed into the room, the clunking of gears rumbled the ground under their feet. Several evenly-spaced round cylinders rose out of the floor all over the room and began spinning. A dart flew out of one of the cylinders and shattered the flashlight Joe was carrying.

"Ahh!" Pain erupted in Joe's hand as fragments of the shattered flashlight exploded backwards against his skin. "This doesn't look good." Joe shook his hand to ease the throbbing.

"Well, they may have figured out a way to block any magical solutions. Aren't you the one in love with technology? I say we try a gun."

Taking a step back to keep well within the hall, Joe drew his gun. He adjusted the setting to increase its power, leveled the weapon, and fired a shot at one of the spinning pillars. The blast destroyed the cylinder in a cloud of dust. Several whistling sounds filled the air as darts flew in the direction of the destroyed stone pieces.

"That's promising," Yelka commented.

The grating of stone on stone echoed down the tunnel once more from behind them, drawing their attention. Whirling around, Yelka shined her light on a solid stone object pushing its way down the hall towards them. It filled the entirety of the hall, pushed by some unseen force rapidly closing the distance between them.

"Start shooting, before we are forced into the room," Yelka screamed.

Joe focused on the next pillar and squeezed the trigger. The stone closing behind them seemed to respond to the destruction of another pillar by gaining speed.

"It's coming faster," Yelka screamed as Joe destroyed a third column.

After Joe disintegrated the forth spinning pole, the stone at their rear slammed into them, forcing them out into the room and sealing the tunnel behind them.

6

Messengers, Warnings, and Battles

"What did you do?" Cindy shrieked when the ship died.

"I didn't do anything." Max's hands flew over the controls in a desperate effort to restart the craft's engines. "*Zachni!*" He attempted a spell to get the ship going.

Several loud pops and clunks drew momentary silence from everyone aboard the craft.

"It's the pressure. We're sinking." Sky stepped toward the front windshield to look up at the surface.

Everyone but Max and Cindy rushed to get a look through the front window. Max continued to try to ignite the ship's engines amid the ever-darkening cockpit. The water pressure continued to squeeze the ship, creating nerve-racking thumps that vibrated the entire ship.

"What are we going to do?" Cindy questioned in terror.

"Try your communicator," Max ordered, still messing with the controls.

"They're not responding," Cindy complained after several moments.

The disturbing sounds of the hull giving way under the rising pressure continued to increase, along with the growing darkness.

The intensity of the situation increased, giving Max a drowning feeling. He could barely make out the shadows of the people standing by the windshield. His pulse pounded in his temple, giving him vertigo, and the tilting ship did not help.

"We're going to die," one of the prisoners cried.

"You've killed us," others shouted.

"Shut up!" Sky barked. "If it wasn't for us, you'd already be dead."

"Maybe if we use magic?" a dijinnie suggested and the few dijinnie prisoners on board attempted to keep the craft from sinking, without success.

"We can't find anything to lift it with. The water is very deep here. There is nothing for us to leverage the ship against."

Cindy reached out and took Max's hand. "What are we going to do?" Her voice shook.

Max could feel her trembling and gave her hand a squeeze. He could barely make out her outline in the ever growing darkness. Max felt himself pulling Cindy towards him, and in the darkness their lips met. All the fear and anxiety of the situation vanished in that instant. A sense of exhilaration and excitement rushed through him, sparking a desire to never let her go.

"There's a light out there!" one of the prisoners called, snapping Max and Cindy apart.

"You're imagining...Hey, she's right. I see a small light as well."

"And it's getting bigger."

"What is it?"

"I don't think we're sinking any more either," Sky observed, shooting a glance back at Max and Cindy.

Out in the dark ocean water a small spark danced for several moments before slowly growing in size. The closer it drew to the ship, the brighter it got, with rays of light extending and receding randomly all around its circumference. The light appeared to be whiter than anything Max had ever seen in his life.

"Wow, that's bright," someone stated, and the light source grew so large it filled the entire windshield, picking up speed.

"It's going to hit us," another prisoner panicked, while there was a mad dash to scramble away from the windshield.

In a desperate act to protect himself Max flung his arms in front of his face and turned his head. Cindy grabbed his arm to brace for the impact when the light passed right through the glass to hover in the air in the center of the cockpit.

Max peered through the fingers on his hand. To his surprise he could look at the light, although brighter than the sun at noonday. He couldn't remember seeing anything so beautiful. He lowered his hands.

"What is it?" Cindy whispered at his side.

"I am here to help you. I am a messenger," a soft voice spoke from amid the ball of light. It was the strangest voice Max had ever heard. It seemed to penetrate his very being, causing a burning in his chest.

"We sure need it," Cindy commented.

"I don't think he is just talking about pulling us out of this mess," Max responded.

"That is correct. Events are turning against us as the forces of Hudich are growing exponentially, while our numbers are dwindling through deaths or desertion. We need a beacon, a light on the hill for the rest of the worlds to look to for hope. The One needs your help before he comes to set things right."

"What do you need us to do?" Sky questioned.

"To retake control of the United States of America. To reestablish the constitution and free the people, as was initially intended."

"That's the light on the hill?" Cindy asked in amazement.

"Yes, it was, and needs to be again. It was the last safe haven for people seeking freedom. It is necessary to become that place once more. It gave hope to billions. It is a precious commodity that has been taken from everywhere by Hudich and his followers. You need to break the martial law imposed, and stop the scavenger's attacks on all the tribes and camps now dotting the landscape. They are crushing the isolated forces but, if united, could become powerful. Hope is contagious. It can start very small but spread like wildfire through the hearts of those desiring freedom."

"How are we to do this?" Max asked. "Where should we start?"

"You must destroy the Dark Society. Those who, by their secret works, overthrew the United States by infiltrating the courts, schools, and government, lying to the people, changing the laws and culture. They kept their plans in the dark and their members hidden from the general population."

"But, how do we find them?" Max questioned. "If they are a secret group, aren't they hidden?"

"They were in the shadows before the fall. Now, they are out in the open as the new leaders of the country. They hold all the positions of power, but there is still that spark – that love of freedom in most of the citizens. You just have to ignite it."

"How do we do that?" Cindy piped in.

"Up until now, you have been on the defensive. It's time to go on the offensive. Take back what has been stolen by the evil people who only desire power and control."

"But now they have Hudich's help," Sky remarked.

"Yes, but we can use Hudich against them. His intolerance for failure will work to our advantage. Hudich, himself, isn't the greatest threat at the moment either." The light continued to pulse with beams stretching and shrinking, some totally detaching from the main source and disappearing in a flash.

"That's brilliant. He could eliminate some of our enemy for us," Max said.

"Wait. What's a bigger threat than Hudich?" Sky jumped in.

"A zombie army is coming, and the conversion rate is one hundred percent."

"What zombie army?" Cindy's voice shook as she asked the question. "You're talking about my blood, aren't you?"

"Yes. Many that you infected, survived. Hudich is aware of all the dark society's efforts, and under his direction they have continued with their tests. They plan to unleash a virus that will literally change everyone. It is a virus that will end the war, but freedom will die as well. None, but three, will be able to resist. You must prevent this plan from going into effect."

"So, how do we do this while swarms of demons wipe out camps and tribes nightly?" Cindy questioned.

"You must topple the dark society." The voice continued and the light dimmed. "You have friends in danger. Go to them! NOW!"

"HOW?" Max, Cindy and Sky asked.

"Topple the dark society. Make that your priority. Start at the base."

"Who sent you?" Max pressed.

"The One." The light passed back through the windshield and rapidly zipped out of sight, leaving them in the dark once more.

A loud clunk brought them back to their senses, remembering where they were. Max instinctively reached out and attempted to start the engines, which sprang to life.

"Get us out of here," Sky ordered.

"What have I done?" Cindy moaned.

"It's not your fault. And we don't have time for a pity party. You're stronger than that," Sky encouraged her.

"And don't forget. I used my blood on Hudich. It may not be yours. I wonder who's in trouble. Grandpa? Our parents?" Max questioned.

Max steered the ship upward and it headed for the surface. "Once we're out of the water we can find out what's going on." The momentary relief Max had felt when the engines started turned to a sense of dread. His stomach jerked into a tight uncomfortable knot. *Who needs our help?*

"Are you going the right way? I thought…"

The ship broke the surface of the water and emerged into a clear night sky. Everyone's jaw dropped at the clear star-filled night.

"How long were we down there?" a prisoner questioned.

"I don't know." Sky shook her head while staring out the windshield.

"Make the call." Max broke out of his shock.

Cindy's fingers flew over her communicator. "Sam. They're under attack, trying to help a camp in Iowa. I'm contacting him now."

Max punched a few controls on the ship's console to bring up their location on a GPS map.

"There is a microphone," Max said, tapping the device hanging from the ceiling just above his head.

Max snagged the object. "Take us to Iowa."

The result was immediate as the bridge rotated west and the ship took off at an incredible rate of speed. The sudden increase in g-forces sent several of the former prisoners- flying into computers, chairs, and other cockpit items—while others skidded across the steel floor.

"Cindy, man the radar. We don't want to be caught off guard." Sky snapped her fingers and pointed to an empty chair next to Max.

Cindy dropped onto the chair while watching her communicator at the same time. "There's no answer. I have a feeling we need to hurry."

In a matter of seconds the ocean disappeared and land filled their view.

"Where in Iowa?" Max questioned. "It's a decent sized state."

"Between Waterloo and Dubuque," Cindy reported. "I got that from my mother."

Max spoke the new destination into the microphone and the ship adjusted course slightly. "I remember flying over the states at night when the entire eastern area was dotted with lights. Now." Max swallowed and a deep sadness darkened his thoughts. The view out of the windshield showed only fragments of lights. Most of these still issued from the major cities.

"Join them in the cities or die?" Sky added solemnly.

"Or go into hiding," a female from the group spoke up. "At least that's what we tried to do."

"Let's see what weapons this ship has." Cindy cracked her knuckles and started working the controls in front of her. "We've got laser cannons, missiles, you name it."

"What if we have to fight on the ground?" Max gave Sky a look before nodding to the rescued prisoners.

Sky took up another seat next to Max and started typing away. "The ship is almost impregnable."

Max shrugged his shoulders.

"Hey." Sky whirled around and spoke with more volume. "Anyone who doesn't want to fight is going to have to maintain control of the ship in case we don't return."

All the people they had freed moved as one, rising to their feet and standing erect.

"That messenger didn't just speak to you," one of them spoke.

"He said we would all have to take down this dark society," another added.

"We want to fight," a man volunteered, and the rest nodded their agreement.

"That's what I like to see." Sky returned her attention to the computer terminal. "There are weapons on board on the port side."

Several of the group raced through the doorway leading to the port side of the ship.

"Iowa is coming up in a hurry," Max commented, and the ship started to slow.

"There!" Cindy sprang from her seat to point at an area of lights in the distance. "That's not a city. And Sam knows to use light to keep the dark ones at bay."

Max tightened his grip on the controls and steered the ship in the direction of the light. "Everyone get ready. I'm only going to make a single pass before setting it down, so unload everything you've got." Max wiped the sweat from his palms on his jeans and took a deep calming breath.

"Why?" Sky demanded.

"Because I knocked a ship out of the sky with magic. If they know this, staying airborne could be extremely dangerous."

Several prisoners returned from the armory and proceeded to pass out weapons.

"HEY!" Cindy flipped a switch on her console and the windshield changed to an infrared view.

The lights from the compound turned a greenish color and thousands of enemy troops came into view, surrounding the camp. The massive hoard consisted of men and an array of monsters of various shapes and sizes from all around the universe. They swarmed the camp in a never ending attack. Weapons fired from both sides flashed across the screen.

"Are we...*izgini* ship," Max uttered.

Sky leaped out of her chair and pointed to an area crawling with the enemy just outside the walls of the camp. "There. Target that cluster."

Max adjusted the controls and Cindy opened fire with the laser cannons, holding down the trigger so that blasts of red laser fire incinerated the area. The ground beneath them began to boil, throwing debris in all directions.

Making a tight circle around the camp, Max allowed Cindy to cut a swath through the attacking army. The surprise assault confused and momentarily scattered the evil beings trying to crush the small camp.

"I'm going to risk another pass. See if we can drive them back farther." Max widened the ship's circle while Cindy cut another ring in the area around the camp.

Loud thuds and showers of sparks spread across the front of the ship as fleeing creatures flew into the path of the invisible ship, colliding with its shields. The ground fire followed shortly behind the midair collisions as the enemy targeted Max and the others.

"Put it down right there." Sky pointed back to the original mass she had Cindy target earlier.

"Right in the heart of the enemy? Are you *crazy*?" Max questioned.

"What better way to kill the host than putting some blockage in its heart." Sky winked.

"Who is that?" John pointed to the sky where laser blasts issued non-stop from out of the night. Sweat streaked down his face as he returned to defending the camp from the black mass of evil creatures and men attempting to crush them.

"I don't..." Sam struggled to retrieve his communicator from his pocket. Cindy's message immediately met his eye. "They're with us. They're my friends," he screamed.

Cheers immediately followed Sam's announcement as the ship's arrival gave them a much needed break in the assault. The enemy's confusion created a breakdown in their attack, giving the camp an opening to regroup and reload.

Sam's fingers tapped out a quick response to Cindy before he returned to the task at hand. "They're going to land. Don't shoot in their direction."

The pause lasted only a moment when a new wave of attackers launched themselves against the camp. It was as if Max's offensive only heightened the enemy's madness. They rushed the camp from the ground and air with reckless abandon. The enemy overwhelmed defenders of the camp all around the fence, dragging the individuals to their deaths, or to torment as a captive.

"Sam knows it's us!" Cindy read the message while continuing to fire the weapons.

"They're regrouping. Look at the sheer number of them. They mean business." Sky shot Max a worried look.

A moment after their second pass it was as if someone had doused the lights in the camp. They threw everything they could at the camp, their black twisted bodies created a dome over the structure.

"I have an idea. And you might not like it." Max shot a glance at Cindy. "Cindy, radio Sam have them clear out the center of the camp. If this ship comes down, I don't want to crush anyone."

"Do we know what the population of the camp is? Maybe we can fly them all out," a passenger suggested.

"Good question. Cindy?" Sky called.

"I'm asking what their population is as well. And they're moving out of the center, so whatever you're going to do, do it now."

Sky sprang to Max's side. "You're going to rotate the ship again, aren't you?" She pointed to a control on the right side of his seat.

"Yep!"

"Not again," Cindy groaned.

"Sorry, but when we start, give them everything we've got," Max barked to Cindy.

Max positioned the craft in the center of the camp and started to slowly rotate the cockpit around the axis of the ship. "I hope everyone has a strong stomach."

Cindy broke into the ship's other weapons while continuing to fire the laser cannons. Rockets and missiles zoomed into the enemy outside the site, depleting their numbers with each pass.

A massive explosion rocked the ship, knocking it out of position. Cindy waited for Max to right the ship and start them spinning before beginning her attack once more.

More and more explosions began to weaken the ship's shields. Max kept the ship circling quickly, while Cindy drove the enemy back with each new pass.

"The defenses are going to go," Sky screamed.

"We need to find out if the ramp is stationary like the hall." Max said.

"Hold on." Sky stepped up to the circling hall and waited for an opening without passengers. After finding her spot, she sprang out of the cockpit.

"The outer door is stationary," Sky's voice crackled through an intercom.

"Open the door and get everyone out," Max responded. "You need to go as well," Max told the few freed prisoners who had managed to remain in the cockpit.

"What about you?" one of them asked.

"Don't worry about us," Cindy said as another blast knocked them backwards, and Max quickly repositioned the vessel. "Get out, NOW!"

A few moments later only Max and Cindy remained in the cockpit. Nausea crept up Max's stomach and into his throat as the landscape continued to zoom by, messing with his head.

As the ship rotated around to the north, a missile exploded against the shields in a dazzling ball of fire and sparks that sent a large crack down the middle of the windshield. Max's heart raced and he struggled for air.

"Everyone's out. What's your next idea?" Sky's voiced crackled through the intercom once more.

"Get yourself out. We don't have much time," Max shouted back.

"What's your plan?" Cindy shrieked.

"We're going to cut the head off the beast. See that cluster of weapons and creatures that goes by to the north?"

Cindy continued to fire. "Yes."

"I'm going to crash the ship into it."

"WHAT? We will be trapped or worse—DEAD!"

"Trust me and don't stop shooting." Max winked at her as he stopped the ship from spinning so that the target was straight in front of them. "How are the shields?"

"They're at about twenty percent." Cindy targeted the enemy control area with blast after blast that exploded against an invisible armor, sending lightning-like strikes across the surface of the protective structure.

Max took out his laser rifle and blasted the cracked windshield several times before the dense clear metal exploded outward. "Get ready to jump!"

"What?"

Max punched the thrusters forward and then spun the deck so they were facing the camp. Snagging Cindy by the hand, Max led her over computer terminals and chairs before diving out the hole where the windshield had been.

They landed hard, tumbling and bouncing across the ground and on top of each other. Max immediately threw up a magical shield for protection as the ship crashed into the operations area of the enemy with a massive explosion that shot hundreds of feet into the air and outward in all directions. Hurricane force winds propelled heat, dust, and flying debris outward for several moments.

"Wow." Cindy staggered to her feet, covered in dirt, cuts, and bruises.

"Ah...I don't think we're out of this yet." Max nodded to a number of confused creatures all across the landscape and flying through the air. "We need to make it back to safety before they regroup."

7

Much Needed Help

Filling the entire tunnel, the rock forced Joe and Yelka out into the room. Yelka immediately cast a magical shield over them to deflect the hundreds of darts being fired from the spinning columns. Instead of the deadly projectiles ricocheting off Yelka's shield, they hovered inches away like angry hornets with their sharp tips pointing at Yelka and Joe.

After Joe destroyed the next pillar, the entire wall behind them with the blocked hallway began moving towards them, compacting the room.

"Stop destroying the pillars. I won't be able to hold this shield and run at the same time." Yelka nodded to the ever increasing number of darts hovering just outside the shield, blocking their vision. "Just start heading for the door on the other end."

"How are we going to get rid of these barbs?"

"I'm not sure, but I think you need to try destroying them before we can't see where we are going."

The small space inside Yelka's shield grew darker and darker as more darts blocked what little light filtered into the area.

"I have an idea but it depends on my compass working, and I don't know if this structure will interfere with it." Joe took out his compass.

Joe's stomach sank as the needle spun aimlessly for a moment or two. To his great relief, it seemed sluggish but worked.

"The door is that way. Just keep moving. I will keep us on track. When we reach the doorway, can you increase your shield to fill the entire exit so that the darts remain in the room?"

"I can try. Although, I better increase it now. If I can't see the hallway, I won't know when we are about to enter it."

"Good point."

Yelka's arms trembled as she pushed her hands outward, expanding the protection around them. Joe wrapped an arm around her shoulders while watching the compass to keep them on course. Eventually, the darkness created by the dome of projectiles forced him to use his magic to produce a miniature ball of fire to see the compass.

A couple of loud crashes echoed through the room and the wall behind them increased its speed.

"What was that?"

"I think the wall is knocking over the pillars and it is creating the same effect as if I'd destroyed them," Joe reported, while trying to help Yelka pick up her pace.

"I hope it's not much farther, I'm losing strength," Yelka commented as a drop of sweat rolled down her forehead. Her face tensed with concentration lines in the faint light.

The wall continued to gain speed behind them after destroying each column in its path, shrinking the room faster and faster. Loud pops followed right on their heels and their feet began crunching crushed remains of pillars that had been thrown in their path.

"I don't think my plan is going to work at this speed." Joe gulped air, his lungs burning from the exertion.

"Just get us into that hall."

They barreled ahead and hit the exit right when the back wall sealed off the entire room. The darts not covering a part of the shield on sides that made it into the hall were crushed by the closing partition.

"Okay, that got rid of the majority but how do we destroy the rest?" Joe questioned.

"Like this." Yelka closed her eyes and clapped her hands together over her head. A blue flame spread across the outer layer of her shield, increased in strength, and turned white hot.

Yelka held the fire as long as she could before dropping to a knee, gasping for breath. The flames and the shield disappeared, and Joe's ball of firelight revealed a pile of ash in front and behind them.

"Are you okay?" Joe questioned.

"I just need a moment. That took a lot of energy." Yelka remained on a knee.

"Hey…if the compass worked, we may be far enough away from the main structure to use our communicators."

"I hope so, I don't have the energy for another trap."

"We've *got* a signal. We will have an exit in a second." Joe took out a crystal which had been hanging around his neck. Every few seconds he waved it in front of them until it flashed with a white light.

They climbed up through the gateway and exited into the third floor of Joe's house.

"You need to notify Jax and his men to bring them back. When Hudich gets out of that temple he is going to go on a rampage," Joe stated the minute Rachel had turned off the force field.

"Did you get what you wanted?" questioned Rachel, a slender woman of medium height.

"Yes." Joe swung the backpack off his back and took out the book. "How are our other operations going? Did Max, Cindy, and Sky complete their mission? The others? How are evacuations going?"

"One second." Rachel worked the gateway's control panel, and a moment later Jax and a half dozen of his men stepped out of the gateway, looking haggard.

"What happened?" Joe questioned the moment the shield was down. The bright light that was the gateway disappeared, replaced by a twirling large ornate mirror which gradually slowed until it stopped.

"Well," Jax hunched over, resting on his knees and breathing hard, "we're happy you got out. Hudich blew the top of that temple clean off. We were worried about you. Then he sent his troops off in all directions, which gave us hope that they were after you. We gave chase and engaged them. Hudich joined the fight and had us pinned down. If it wasn't for the gateway, we wouldn't have made it."

"Yeah, we were trapped until we got away from the structure. It was blocking our signals," Yelka said.

"Maybe not." Joe rubbed his chin in thought. "Maybe Hudich freed us without knowing it. If he damaged the temple as you say, he might have destroyed the electromagnetic field it was creating. I mean, we were running for our lives down there. We might have missed any sign of Hudich's destruction."

"You might be right." Yelka wore a curious expression.

"Did you get it?" Jax asked.

Joe held the book up for Jax to see. Joe opened it and looked at a language he had never seen before. "And we kept it out of Hudich's hands. Now I think we need to get Linda and Lita to take a look at it. I'm not sure we know anyone who can read this."

"I hate to interrupt—but Max, Sam, and the others could use some help as well." Rachel checked her communicator.

"Who needs it the most?" Jax questioned.

"All of them. They're all in Iowa."

"WHAT?" Joe almost yanked Rachel's arm off to read her communicator. "Keep the book safe and fire up the gateway." Joe thrust the book into her arms, and then he and the others hurried inside the circle so the force field could be turned on.

The antique mirror started to spin bottom over top, gaining speed. A light appeared in the center and grew until it enveloped the entire mirror. Joe took a deep breath and then stepped into the light, followed by the others.

###

A detonation several yards behind the racing Max and Cindy sent them flying through the air and bouncing along the ground. Max struggled for breath while helping Cindy to her feet.

Laser blasts from the camp flashed just over their heads, while people within the camp tried to give them cover. Shrieks and cries from angry men and creatures rose above explosions and gun fire as the enemy pursued Max and Cindy.

Max cast a shield spell seconds before a massive black winged creature could snag them with its sharp talons. The force of its impact sent it spiraling dizzyingly out of control while knocking Max and Cindy flat. They impacted with the hard ground, bruising and scraping their bodies even more.

Before they had a chance to get back on their feet, they both launched spells to repel the attacking hoard. Max threw up a wall of fire while Cindy flung creatures and men left and right. It took all the cover fire from the camp and Max and Cindy casting endless spells to keep the enemy at bay.

Non-stop flashes of the lights from the camp and the battle reflected in a polished steel blade, indicating Sky had arrived to help them. She attacked the enemy with such fury that she beat back the surge by eliminating any who got within her range. Using a combination of magic and her sword, she was the perfect fighting machine.

Max and Cindy joined Sky in driving the enemy back far enough for them to make a break for the camp. The cover, which had been somewhat effective before Sky's help, seemed to increase as a regular Fourth of July show erupted just above their heads. Red and blue laser blasts mingled with spells sprayed the air.

To Max's great surprise, Grandpa and Yelka were there to greet them at the gate when they entered the city.

"It looks like you took a little detour from your main mission?" Grandpa raised his eyebrows while trying to disguise the pride in his expression.

"I take it you brought more than just yourself." Max threw a nod toward some of Jax's men working the wall above them.

"Yes, and it seems like we showed up just in time," Joe commented. "Their scouts said you took out the enemy's commanders. Now let's wipe out the rest."

Max and Cindy began to follow Grandpa further into the camp when Sky spoke up. "I thought you wanted to finish the job." Sky nodded towards the gate while pointing at it with her thumb. "We can't be very thorough locked behind these walls. I don't want to give any of them a chance to fight us someplace else."

"Running into the teeth of the enemy isn't a very smart move." Yelka shook her head disapprovingly.

"We're not going to run into their front..." Max cocked his head to the side while looking at Sky with understanding. "We're going to hit them from behind."

"Just be careful," Joe warned with a slightly worried expression.

"Are you in?" Max glanced at Cindy.

"I was going to ask you the same." Cindy nudged Max out of the way to join Sky at the gate and cocked her laser weapon.

"Just so you're aware, this is a take-no-prisoners mission. You see them, you wipe them out. The world and universe are splitting in two. There are not many fence-sitters left. You are either for good or you are for evil. We will not rejoice in their destruction but it is vital to win," Sky informed them.

Cindy nodded.

"Got it," Max responded. "How far out are we going?"

"A mile. That should allow us to sneak up on them." Sky opened the gate and disappeared as they stepped outside. "Straight out."

"Preselim se." Max's spell transported him a mile out and only a few feet away from Sky. Cindy joined them a second later.

They quickly ducked into the tall prairie grasses to safely check their surroundings. Only the wind blowing the grass, like the waves of the sea, stirred around them. In front of them, the battle raged in a show of explosions, magic, and weapons fire.

"I don't think they will be expecting this but let's not get sloppy. Check before you leap and watch each other's backs." Sky started back towards the camp, waving Max and Cindy to follow. She used the slopes of the rolling hills to keep them hidden from the enemy fighting ahead of them. When they were within forty yards of the enemy, Sky brought them to a stop. "Try to keep up," Sky whispered before attacking.

The three of them caught a large section of the enemy by surprise, cutting them down before they could counter. Max and Cindy fired their weapons at anything that moved, while Sky covered them with her sword, eliminating all attempts to end Max and Cindy's destruction. Their attack was so swift and thorough, it didn't allow word to spread that they were demolishing the rear ranks of the enemy.

Sky kept them moving, wiping out anything that moved around them. Sweat rolled down Max's forehead and soaked the back of his shirt, while his lungs started to burn from running and fighting. He tried to wet his dried lips but the heat and dust had left his mouth dry.

Within an hour they had destroyed enough of the enemy that Jax and his men, joined by others, had left the compound to deal the final blow to their foes. In the early morning hours all that remained of the opposition were either dead or too injured to flee.

Max dropped onto his bottom at the top of a hill, just outside the gates of the camp. He wiped the sweat from his brow while coughing several times from the smoky air. He slowly surveyed the damage. A bruised and battered Cindy and a dust covered Sky plopped down beside him.

"I'm beat. I need water but I'm too tired to go find any," Cindy moaned.

"I have to say. I feel…good. We've been moving these camps for months now, always running. It feels better to have fought and kept one. It's given me hope." Max smiled.

A smile spread across Cindy's dirty face. "Yeah!"

"I actually hate running and hiding. So this is much more up my alley," Sky added.

Grandpa exited the gate with Yelka, Sam, and a few others. They headed straight for Max's group. The closer they drew, the more the weariness of last night's battle showed in their sluggish movements and tired expressions. Grandpa carried a backpack over one of his shoulders, which he handed to Max when they reached the top of the hill.

"I figure you guys could use some food and water." Grandpa glanced around the blackened field, with smoke still rising out of the dirt.

"Thanks." Max opened the pack and passed its contents to Sky and Cindy. He couldn't remember ever feeling so famished in his life and, after downing an entire bottle of water, started in on some jerky.

"So, I hear you made a gruesome discovery and also had an unexpected visitor," Grandpa said and raised his eyebrows.

"From the stories of this visitor's message, I'm glad he showed up." Sam ran his fingers through his hair. "I don't think we would have made it without you."

"Yeah, he told us you were in danger," Cindy muttered with a full mouth.

"The prisoners also mentioned some dark society but didn't quite understand what it meant," Yelka said.

"Yes. Priority number one needs to be this virus and a zombie army," Max reported.

"Zombie army?" several of the town's people who had followed Grandpa, Yelka and Sam out of the camp questioned with concerned looks.

Max, Cindy, and Sky quickly explained what was going on at the secret base in Nevada where they had rescued Cindy and secured the book over a year ago. By the looks on everyone's faces, only Grandpa and Yelka comprehended what they were saying.

"Well, it seems we have lots of planning to do." Grandpa rubbed his chin in thought.

"I think one thing we should do is spread the news of this victory to all the camps in the area. Are there camps with which you have dealings?" Sky questioned.

"Yes." John stepped forward. "At least a half dozen. I'm John." He held out his hand.

Max, Cindy, and Sky exchanged greetings and introductions with John and others, shaking hands.

"Good terms or just business?" Grandpa asked.

"A combination of both. Some we have a good relationship while others are strictly business but necessary," John reported. "We will spread the word. I agree that all the sites could use some good news."

"I think there will be some serious consequences coming for this victory," Cindy said somberly.

"What do you mean?" one of the other camp members, Seth, asked with a worried look. "We won didn't we?"

"I think Cindy is referring to the punishments Hudich is going to hand out to his followers for their failure to destroy all of you." Sky nodded towards Cindy.

"Hold on. Hold on." Max slowly climbed to his feet and stretched. "I think Seth has a right to be worried."

"What do you mean?" Yelka questioned.

"While this victory is great news for everyone who wants to be free, it is bad news and a setback for Hudich." Max spun on his heels and scanned the area. "We need to *quadruple* this camp's fortifications, NOW!"

"What are you talking about?" many questioned.

"We dealt them a serious blow." Sam waved his arm towards the battlefield. "You think they want more?"

"I know they want more."

Sky sprang to her feet. "Max is right. How do you turn a negative for you into a positive? This place has now become a thorn in Hudich's side. He doesn't want hope to spread. He will want to crush it. The next attack will be worse and it will likely be soon."

"And it might not be with troops. We need to get anti-missile defense systems set up here immediately," Grandpa ordered.

"I'll get my men working on a whole arsenal of traps and fortifications around this place. We are going to need the best that Lita has," Jax added.

"I think you need to see if you can convince the majority of your closest neighbors to join you here. I fear Hudich's wrath is going to extend to them as well. He will want to crush the entire area," Yelka said.

"Max, Cindy, it sounds like you and Ell have a different job to do. Sky, I think we are going to need you here to help Sam and Jax prepare to make this place a fortress. I even think air cover is now a necessity. Actually, Sky, a change of plans. Maybe you should go with John and try to convince their neighbors to join them," Grandpa stated.

"I think I should go with Max and Cindy. You know what wimps they are. They need a lot of hand holding." Sky tried to lighten the mood.

"While I agree with you," Grandpa chuckled for a moment and then his face turned to stone, "we can't risk exposing you to whatever they are cooking in that lab. I'm not completely convinced Max, Cindy, and Ell are safe from some type of hybrid. This could very well be one of the most dangerous missions of their lives."

"What are they going to do?" asked a woman from the camp, appearing confused.

"They are going to prevent a virus that will convert the world. We would have no choice and nothing to stop ourselves from helping the enemy. We would become slaves to Hudich and lose everything, even our self-identity and very will to act."

8

An Unlikely Meeting

Max and Cindy stepped out of the gateway into the third floor of Grandpa's house. Both of their mothers greeted them with hugs and questions about their condition and recent events.

"So, everyone is okay?" Max's mother continued to ask, to which Max and Cindy kept confirming they were.

"What have you been up to?" Max finally asked after he and Cindy had relayed everything that had happened and what they were planning.

"We've had an endless line of traffic coming through," Rachel stated.

"I just showed up to relieve her when she said you were about to arrive," Cindy's mother reported while stretching her hands high above her head.

"We need to get busy. We need Ell as soon as you can get him here," Max urged.

"NO! What you need to do is go get some rest. You've been going for more than a day without sleep. We won't let you go anywhere until you get some sleep. I'm still your mother and Grandpa put us in charge of the gateway." Rachel signaled to herself and Cindy's mother.

"Yep. Rest, and then we'll think about letting you leave," Cindy's mother added.

"They're right. We will need to be fresh." Cindy took a stunned Max by the hand and led him down the spiral staircase.

###

Max awoke to complete darkness. It took him a moment to discern where he was. He checked his watch to see that it was around eight p.m. before swinging his legs out of the bed. The hum of the gateway drew his immediate attention. *Wow, I was tired. Is Cindy still sleeping?*

He took a quick shower and then headed to the kitchen to get something to eat. He paused halfway down the stairs as a lot of thumping rose above the constant hum of the gateway. The noises prompted him to turn, but before he could start back up the stairs a call from his mother grabbed his attention.

"Max, down here." His mother waved him toward the main floor of the house. "There's been a change of plans.

"What do you mean? I thought what Cindy and I were going to do was of top priority." Max followed his mother into the lighted kitchen where dinner had already been prepared.

Lita sat at the table, watching him with her large black eyes. A closed laptop computer rested on the table in front of her. "Hey, Max. I understand you have a specific mission. In fact, you are going back to where Cindy lost herself before."

"Yes, it sounds like we have to. We don't want an army like Cindy created, but bigger and under Hudich's control." Max took a seat at the table and started to dish up a casserole his mother had cooked.

"Oh, I agree. Remember, I saw firsthand what can happen." Lita smiled a thin smile across her pale alien face that reminded Max so much of her father, Olik that he couldn't help but return the gesture. "Anyway, if you remember, I had to use their systems to get a message out. It was this message that allowed you to rescue me…and Cindy."

"Yes…"

"So," Lita opened the laptop, "when Grandpa, told me where you were heading, he asked me to find out what I could about security. I decided to check my documents and plans of the facility."

Max put down the fork loaded with food that he was about to shovel into his mouth. "And…you have this information?" His heart rate accelerated with the excitement of additional unexpected help.

"I have some information but I can't verify it is accurate yet. Sadly, their network is closed off from the outside world now." Lita said. "But I'm sure the credentials I created still exist, as I used them for a time after we had all escaped to collect data on their work at your grandfather's request. Using information stolen from their systems back then, I think I could greatly assist you. Plus, if you can get me into their network with some devices of my own creation, I could use my credentials to access all of their systems. With all the destruction that went on there, Cindy's knowledge of the structure may not match the current state of things. If you can get me on, I will know everything."

"Do you have anything to go on?" Max took another quick bite of the casserole, while keeping his eyes on Lita.

"I might." Lita moved her chair closer to Max and rotated her laptop so that he could see the screen. "At the time my hacks worked, I had access to everything. One of the things I did was tie into their security system and access every camera. Well, pretty much anything I wanted. It might be prudent for me to monitor you on this mission."

"I won't argue. We may need you to locate the prime candidate or the source of the blood. We might have to take this individual hostage. Although, I have a suspicion who that person is and, believe me, we don't want him to be there," Max added.

"Once you have me in, I will start searching. My primary focus will be their security protocols and where to find the experiments," Lita reported.

Max sat up straight and glanced at his mother, washing dishes at the sink. "Where's Cindy? Shouldn't she be here?"

"Cindy's been awake for a couple of hours now. She's outside in the yard with Ell." Max's mother gave a nod in the direction of the backyard.

Max rose to his feet to get a better look out the window. He didn't have to stand erect before he caught sight of the massive creature Ell. The size of a medium elephant with thick, shaggy fur, razor sharp teeth, a hideous face, and a long bulbous nose, Ell looked like something right out of a nightmare.

A smile spread across Max's face as he watched Cindy with her arms wrapped around the strange creature. "When did you bring Ell through?"

"About four hours ago," Max's mother responded.

"Does Cindy know this stuff?" Max waved at Lita's computer.

"Yes, I went over everything with her. She still has detailed information about the layout of the place in her memories, but she is a little scared to dive into her mind," Lita said. "I think with what she can remember and my technology we can, hopefully, get you in and out safely."

"Do you think there is a danger of losing her again?" Max glanced at his mother, then back to Lita.

"I think she will be okay with you and Ell there. Plus, the stress of being a prisoner won't be there to drive her to desperate measures," Lita remarked.

Max's mother stared out the kitchen window at Cindy and Ell.

"Besides, from what Cindy said, it might not be her blood they are using."

"True."

"Are you saying they might have your blood?" Max's mother eyed them.

"There is that possibility," Max replied.

"WHAT? HOW?"

"Remember I injected Hudich with my blood. So, there is a very high chance they are using Hudich's blood, which means…"

"Well, you weren't able to control him like Cindy did the others," Max's mother pointed out.

"Nope." Max shook his head.

"Okay, now for the bad news. We probably aren't going to have use of the gateway to get us in or out any time soon. From what I've been told, it is being used nonstop for the fight going on in Iowa. This means we are going to have to find a different method of transportation," Lita said.

"That stinks but I understand. I suppose we could use magic." Max ran his hand through his hair, realizing for the first time since he awoke that the gateway had been stopping and starting every few minutes.

"I don't think that will work. We may be able to reach a certain point, but the last time I entered their system, their cameras and sensory equipment would detect anyone who got too close. They would know you are there the moment you entered their borders. We will have to find another way in," Lita informed Max.

"How close can we get, magically?"

"Not close enough. Without knowing a good arrival location and with all the equipment we are going to need, we would be spotted. We could use magic to get to a camp in the mountains of Utah, but then we would have to travel by car. Just getting there presents a whole array of dangers," Lita informed him.

Max's mother dropped a dish on the floor, shattering it.

"Mom, are you worrying again?" Max rushed to help her clean up the mess.

"Do you expect me not to worry? That would be like asking the sun not to shine. I just wish…" She started to sob. "This whole thing was over. That none of this would have happened."

"Me too." Max hugged his mother.

"Me three," Lita added.

Max's mother reached out and pulled Lita into a little group hug.

"What's happened? Who's been killed?" Cindy asked fearfully, coming in through the back door.

"No one. Mom's just having a 'mom' moment," Max replied, motioning with his fingers.

Cindy plopped down in a chair and exhaled. "Whew! You scared me to death."

"I'm sorry." Max's mother sobbed and wiped her eyes on her apron. "It just seems to me that each new mission gets more dangerous for you kids. I just wish someone else could do it."

"So do I," Cindy concurred. "But…unfortunately."

"I know. I know." Max's mother replied.

"Just do me a favor. Try to keep the details away from my mother as long as possible." Cindy shot a glance at the ceiling as if she could see her mother three floors up, running the gateway.

"Maybe you should go and help her. That way you don't have to hear everything." Max chuckled but quickly changed his expression after his mother shot him a serious glance. "I'm just saying it might be easier for you."

"Not knowing is worse." Rachel got out a broom to sweep up the broken fragments of the dish.

"So, does this camp in Utah have all the equipment we need or are we going to have to transport it with us?" Max asked.

"No, they don't have everything we need. We are going to have to take a lot with us," Lita commented.

"I haven't really ever transported much using magic. I'm not sure how that is going to work out," Max said.

"You've at least taken me. I haven't *ever* transported anything but myself," Cindy added.

"I'm going to suggest something that might seem completely crazy at first, but I think it might be the safest choice. I say we drive all the way there," Lita suggested hesitantly.

"What?" Rachel spilled everything she had swept into the dust pan back onto the floor.

"I don't think that…will work," Cindy wore a doubtful expression on her face.

"That would be a lot of time out in the open. You know what's out there." Max waved his hand to indicate the outside world. "It's not the same as it *used* to be with freedom to move about when you only had to worry about gas mileage and traffic. Evil things and people now wait to prey upon the weak."

"Yes, but it is the unexpected. Sometimes, that is the best choice." Lita smiled. "Plus, I would be willing to bet the enemy is watching this location for any use of magic. They know we are their biggest threat. They would be fools not to spy on us for any spike in magical activity."

"That's true. They definitely wouldn't be expecting us to just drive out of here," Max agreed.

"And, with a vehicle we could definitely pack all the necessary equipment, plus weapons," Cindy said.

"BUT YOU'RE STILL TALKING ABOUT EXPOSING YOURSELVES TO OPEN ATTACKS," Rachel shrieked. "THAT'S NOT SMART."

"There isn't anything safe about what we are going to do. But we do need to get there, and Lita needs equipment to help us stay safe. Without the gateway, this is probably going to be the best bet." Max took his mother's hand and patted it.

"I think we have been in worse situations. That spider's lair for instance." Cindy raised her eyebrows.

"Need I remind you, you almost died there? So that isn't comforting."

It took them several minutes to calm Max's mother down and convince her to give them the keys to the car. Then they quickly ushered her upstairs to help Cindy's mother on the third floor. Her constant outbursts and constant worrying wasn't getting them anywhere. Once they were finally alone, they began mapping out the route to drive to the Nevada desert where they would attempt to enter the top secret facility for the second time.

"I don't think we should tell our mothers when we are leaving. We should just go," Cindy added while glancing at the ceiling.

"Excellent idea. Hopefully, with how often the gateway is stopping and starting, they will be too busy to pay close attention to us," Max said.

"Uh oh, do you know how to drive a large truck? How are we going to get Ell there?" Cindy pointed to the large beast in the back yard.

"I forgot. That's a good point. That will make things a little more complicated. A large truck will be harder to hide," Max mused.

"I don't think the size of the truck will matter, if they are watching the road, a motorcycle would be spotted. Travel is limited to routes between camps that are friendly with one another and trade to survive," Cindy said. "The more important question is—do we have a truck big enough to transport Ell and, if we do, can you drive it?"

"How about Cindy and I get everything we need ready and you take Ell and go find a truck," Lita suggested.

It took Max, with the help of Ell, the better part of an hour to find a suitable vehicle. An old farmer who had moved into town when the order fell and brought a lot of his farm equipment to keep it safe for the future, loaned him a dump truck. The man spent a half hour making sure Max knew how to operate the thing. He also gave him several barrels of fuel, which they loaded into the back before rigging a make-shift covering to give Ell a little shelter from the sun before Max headed back to Grandpa's house.

"What the heck is that?" Cindy rolled her eyes at the sight of the old large truck. "That thing won't make it eight hundred miles."

"I wish we had use of the gateway. I'd like some of my people to have a go at it," Lita added.

"Is there anything you can do?" Cindy asked her.

"I'll take a look at it. But we don't have a lot of time. I think we should leave at dusk when visibility is the poorest." Lita approached the vehicle and proceeded to give it a once over.

"We should probably load the food, water, weapons, and other supplies for the trip." Max said to Cindy, while Lita went to work.

They spent the next couple hours preparing the truck for their journey. They rigged weapons from several vantage points around the vehicle while Lita fine-tuned the engine and made other adjustments to enhance the performance of the old truck.

Even though Max worried about his grandfather and his friends back in Iowa, he was grateful for the constant stopping and starting of the gateway, which kept his and Cindy's mothers occupied. The knot in his stomach was already tight enough from thoughts of what they were about to do. He didn't need her adding more pressure with her constant worrying. He would have preferred to slip out of town without speaking to his mother, but he knew that wouldn't be a good idea.

As the sun reached the top of the western mountains, Max grabbed Cindy's hand and they headed upstairs.

"Make it quick," Lita called after them.

"I really don't want a lecture," Cindy moaned as they made their way inside the house.

"Me either."

When they entered the top floor, Cindy's mom was sleeping on a blanket near the wall while Rachel worked the control panel. The force field was up as several of Jax's men, along with others Max didn't recognize, moved equipment through the gateway.

Max tapped his mother's shoulder, and she jumped, letting out a sharp gasp.

She whirled around, patting her chest and breathing heavily. Strands of hair hung across her worried face. She looked exhausted, with dark circles under her eyes. "You scared me."

"Sorry, I didn't think we should leave without saying goodbye." Max tried to avoid her gaze in order to not see the worry he knew he would find there. He needed to focus, and feeling guilty about stressing his mother out would not help the situation.

Rachel threw her arms around her son and squeezed him tight. "Don't do anything stupid. If you need help message me, I will open the gateway."

"We'll be careful. I will send you updates." Max struggled with his emotions for a moment. "We have to go."

"I know." Rachel pushed him away.

"Go back to work." Max motioned to the men watching them from the other side of the force field.

A twinge of regret tugged at Max when he noticed his mother's body trembling. He looked over at Cindy to see her pulling herself away from her mom. They hustled down the stairs and out the front door without saying a word. Lita and Ell waited for them on the dirt road to the right of Grandpa's house.

Cindy immediately put a hand on Ell and started to communicate with the massive creature.

"Do you want to go now or wait a bit?" Max shielded his eyes while checking the sun as it started sinking behind the mountain.

"Are all these houses empty?" Lita nodded toward the street leading up to Grandpa's house.

Gone were the well-kept yards that greeted Max when he'd first arrived. Only Cindy's house looked occupied. The others had broken windows and damaged property. Weeds and grass grew up to Max's waist.

"It's kind of sad. It looked better when the enemy occupied these places. Now they are all on the other side of town. If there is anyone remaining, they are here to spy," Max said.

"Maybe we should send Ell on a quick jog. He can scare any unwanted eyes out." Cindy scratched behind Ell's ear.

"What if there are booby-traps? I'd hate for him to step into one," Max warned. "I say we chance it. We haven't seen anyone in months. Ever since the country fell."

"Maybe just send him down the street to see if he smells anything out of the ordinary."

Ell nodded his head and took off at a trot down the street. Max, Cindy, and Lita watched the monster working the neighborhood. They waited anxiously as Ell entered yards and a couple of the houses. He returned and they each put a hand on his side.

The houses are empty...of everything, even magic.

Good job, Cindy replied and the others agreed.

Max lowered a ramp and Ell climbed into the back of the truck. After making sure Ell was secure, the others got into the cab and Max started the engine. Max put the vehicle in gear and started slowly down the street he had walked in the storm all those years ago. The sun had dipped behind the mountains and the town was covered in twilight. Max kept the lights off to avoid drawing any unwanted attention.

At the end of the road the bus terminal came into view, reminding Max of that first day when everyone in town turned up to mark him with a curse. He glanced at the scar across his right palm where Marko, the traitor, had destroyed the curse.

This area of town appeared deserted. The buildings stood badly in need of repair, and garbage littered the street. Max turned onto the road leading to the main highway and made his way out of town. He shifted gears and accelerated.

"LOOK!" Cindy pointed to a trail of dust rising into the air behind a small hill to their right.

"Whoever it is, they're heading right for us. Better get ready," Max said, his heart racing. "I was hoping we'd get out of here without being noticed. Put your heads down. Let them think I'm alone."

"We might have to…you know…kill them, so we can get away before word spreads," Cindy added as she and Lita got as low in the seat as possible.

As they crested a hill, a car entered the main road from a dirt one and skidded to a halt. Bright lights issued from the head lamps and lights mounted along the roof of the car. A large plump man flew out of the car and leveled an automatic weapon towards Max and the others.

Max hit the brakes and the heavy truck's tires squealed, leaving a trail of black marks.

"Get out of the car with your hands up. You are not authorized in this area," a familiar voice barked.

Max exchanged a quick look with Cindy before opening the door. He stepped out onto the pavement while raising his hands above his head. He squinted his eyes into the blinding lights. The man next to the car was only a shadow in the intense beams.

"Are you alone?"

"Yes." Max responded taking a tentative step forward. "Well, except for him." He nodded towards Ell, who was standing in the back of the truck.

"Max?" the familiar voice asked. "I never thought I would get this opportunity. It must be fate or luck."

"Larry?" Max felt like he'd been punched in the gut.

9

Going on the Offensive

Alan, a tall gray-haired man wearing an expensive business suit walked the hall with authority. He held his head high, carried himself with pride, and marched with a purpose. He headed straight for the double doors at the end of the hall, where two fully armed guards stood. The moment before he reached the door, one of the guards reached out and opened it for him.

He stepped into a dimly lit room where a group of twenty people sat around a long, expensive, mahogany conference table. Most eyed Alan with a great amount of disdain as he walked up and took a seat at the head of the table.

"You know why I'm here, ladies and gentlemen. We've had some…failures. I'm here to make sure we are on schedule and that there will be no delays," Alan said, disappointment evident in his voice. His tone added to the thick tension which was already present in the room. He could feel their dislike for him, and he relished the fact they wanted nothing more than to have him gone, but their fear of his powers kept them in line.

"We sent a sizable army. They had some help," a woman at the table proceeded.

"We aren't interested in excuses. Weakness and failure will not be tolerated."

"How can we anticipate every scenario? We have given in to all of your demands. I don't think threats are all that necessary," said a balding man on the other side of the table, leaning in so Alan would know who was speaking.

"We don't make threats. We make promises. When someone fails to live up to our expectations, they are replaced or dispatched." Alan smirked. "Lucky, for you, Hudich is feeling charitable and is willing to give you all another chance."

Everyone at the table flinched at the mention of Hudich by name, and the color visibly drained out of their faces.

"I hope…he has found us to be of good service," a short man with thick glasses squeaked.

"I will admit that the connections you made with ISIS and some of your other cohorts, along with our alignment with the communists and additional malevolent forces, have proven valuable in our taking over the majority of the worlds. Clever, using the devil to do your dirty work to push your socialist agenda and goal for a one world government. But without us you would have never been able to control them. You can't wake up the devil and expect him to behave. If we hadn't stepped in to help, they would have beheaded you, or worse, long ago." Alan shook his head with disgust.

"We had control," a large, fat man with a red face blustered in defiance.

"You only had the illusion of control. If your *allies* hadn't turned on you, *our* enemies would have taken you out. So, we have protected you from two different factions you couldn't have defeated. You owe us your loyalty," Alan stormed. "Now, what are your plans for the camp in Iowa?"

"We are going to hit them again, *tonight*."

"I hope this time tomorrow, I won't be sitting here asking these same questions. That wouldn't be good…for you. What about England?"

"Only a few pockets of resistance remain. After those remaining fighters are defeated, England will be in our control. People are learning to fall in line or be destroyed," a different man answered.

"And, our project in Nevada? How is it coming along?"

"We…have some concerns with that," another brought up with a quivering voice.

"Oh?" Alan raised his eyebrows in a mocking sort of way.

"Wh—while we're working on the…" the man swallowed, "virus. We noticed we haven't yet discovered a cure."

"And?" Alan eyed the man.

"W—won't all of us be infected?" he asked.

"That would include you. That doesn't bother you," a woman added.

"S—so we think we should wait until we have a suitable antidote before we begin releasing the agent," the man quickly added.

"We think it wise to delay until…" another started.

"DELAY?" Alan shot the speaker a deadly look that silenced him immediately.

"J—just until we've had time to develop, to make sure…we're safe," another said.

"There will be no delays. That virus will end the war. It will be delivered on schedule or there will be severe consequences." Alan's face twisted with rage. "You think because you were going to be the one world government that you have a say. You are no longer on the top of the food chain. We give you privileges because you have proven useful. If I were you, I wouldn't give Hudich a reason to think you aren't beneficial to his plans."

"Don't forget, Hudich could choose to put you on the front lines. I know you don't like us and you long for the days when you had the illusion you were in power. But you see, we have been in control all along and were waiting for the right time to strike. So I suggest you do as you're told or lose the few comforts you have. Now." Alan took a deep breath. "How is our little trap coming along?"

"We should be ready within the week. We are still confused by…" The woman shot a tentative glance at the others as if she feared she was crossing some line. "I mean, with…all your power, how do two teenagers pose that big of a threat?"

The others at the table nodded their agreement.

"They are crucial to the plan. They could present, let's say, a complication to our progress. That is all you need to know." Alan sat back in his chair and tapped his fingers on the table.

"How could two teenagers pose a threat to a virus? And you have more powers than we do. Why haven't you already gotten rid of them?" a shifty eyed man asked.

"They…the only thing you need to know is they are to be eliminated and they have special abilities that help them detect magic. Hudich has given you a great opportunity to prove your worth. Plus, your Muslim friends and Special Forces do not know magic, which will help them to get close without being detected."

Alan rose to his feet. "I suggest you handle the camp that gave us trouble and you keep your other tasks on schedule. I hope I don't have to visit you anytime in the near future. That will not bode well for you." Alan arose, spun on his heels, and marched out of the room.

###

Everyone in the conference room watched Alan leave. They sat in silence for almost fifteen minutes, staring at the door as if waiting to see if he would return. After the pause, there was a collective exhale which filled the room.

"What do you make of that?" a woman asked.

"Of him letting us off the hook for failing to destroy that camp in Iowa?" asked the youngest male seated at the table.

"No, you idiot. The fact we have to take out two teenagers before we release the virus. Don't you see what this could mean?" the woman raised her voice.

"I was wondering the same thing? What do these teenagers have to do with the virus?" the shifty-eyed man asked.

"Maybe they are the source of the virus," the large red-faced man commented.

"Yes, but they might also hold the cure, if they have been infected and still survived," the woman added.

"I agree. To want two specific targets removed before the release of the virus would indicate they have something to do with it," a black man sitting opposite where Alan had sat finally spoke. "Maybe this could be the key to ridding ourselves of Hudich and his stooge Alan. Up until now, we have gone along because of their superior powers. Stock piling arms and learning magic while we bought time. Well, time is running short. These kids may be the key to leveling the playing field. I say we work on a plan to take them alive."

"It's going to need to be a monumental plan. I did some research like you asked after we received the order. The girl, at least, is the same one we took captive and placed in that facility shortly before it was almost destroyed. We didn't know what had happened to her until now," reported a small man with thick glasses that made his eyes look huge.

"What did our security tapes show?" the woman asked.

"Nothing, and all the survivors seemed to suffer from some sort of memory loss," the man added.

"So, these kids have some skills," the man at the end of the table mused.

"Yes. We would have to account for the fact they could be as powerful as this Hudich, or more so. Otherwise, why wouldn't he have taken them out already himself?" the small man questioned.

"Hudich has multitudes of all kinds of nightmares at his disposal. Certainly, these kids aren't alone?" the woman interjected.

"I dug there too. They are part of a group of people which includes an elderly man who, until we overthrew everything, was under FBI surveillance."

"We need to get eyes out there again. See what's going on. This could help us formulate a plan." The man at the end of the table held his hands out in front of him, tapping his fingertips together.

"We will have to be very cautious. Hudich has a base there as well. If he finds us spying, we won't be able to execute any plan," the small man reported.

"We could always say it is all necessary to execute his orders."

Joe stood a few feet behind Yelka atop the battlefield trampled down from the previous night's fight. Smoke still rose all around the battlefield, and scavenger birds fought for scraps of the victims. Joe watched Yelka out of the corner of his eye while keeping guard against any hidden dangers.

Yelka muttered spells under her breath while weaving her hands in the air like she was painting on a canvas with her hands. Occasionally, she would pause and lower her hands and head before starting again.

Joe followed her as she worked her way around the camp, performing the same rituals at several different locations. Every now and then he paused to see what Jax's men were doing to fortify the battered camp. They had reinforced the walls with high durable shielding built by Olik's people which, with electricity added, also generated a powerful force field. Others worked on setting up traps and different surprises around the combat zone. With all the work going on it was difficult to hear anything above the construction pounding and squawking birds preying on scraps.

Joe checked the position of the sun and figured they only had another four hours until dusk. *We need to be ready.*

Yelka lowered her hands and turned to Joe. Her face looked worn and tired, while strands of her loose grayish-blond hair whipped around her face. "That's all I can do. It's not what protects your house, but it will cause the enemy a lot of trouble to try to break through."

"Let's hope they aren't expecting it. That may lower the odds."

"Yes, I made it as deadly as I could," Yelka said and gave a faint smile.

"INCOMING!" a voice called over the battlefield, drawing everyone's attention.

All eyes turned to the northwest section of the battlefield. For several minutes, everyone waited for any sign of who was advancing towards the camp. Finally, the sound of engines broke the cries of the birds and the work going on around the camp. The approaching vehicles prompted the workers to stop and look up. Over the tops of the hills, a convoy of about thirty trucks, cars, and semis made their way down an old road leading to the camp.

All of the vehicles had been rigged with weapons and had people riding in and outside the transportation. Most of the windows had been replaced with bars and spikes and other crude shields that kept anyone from getting too close when they were moving.

Sky stood in the back of the first truck like a roman soldier riding a chariot. A tall muscular man, with tattoos and a scowl on his slightly battered face, wearing bands of bullets crisscrossing his chest rode next to her. All the people riding on the cars and trucks wore make-shift body armor and manned high caliber weapons.

Several motorcycles and an armed jeep raced out of the camp to intercept the oncoming vehicles. They made a quick circle around the entire motorcade before taking position as the lead escorts.

Joe and Yelka made their way around the camp toward the main gate. John and Sam waited and watched the convoy as it rolled slowly in their direction. The vehicles all came to a stop about thirty yards in front of the gate. The man with Sky waved his arm in the air and all the vehicles in the convoy turned off their engines, bringing a tense silence over the battlefield. Even the birds seemed to sense the strain of the situation and waited for a release.

"Victor, how are you?" John called to the man standing next to Sky.

"I've been better," Victor grumbled, shooting a sideways look at Sky.

Joe turned his back to the group gathered in front of the gate, and began to chuckle. He tried, unsuccessfully, to avoid drawing attention. A slight cough from Yelka drew his attention. He met her gaze and she nodded to the gate. He turned to see everyone staring at him.

"You find something amusing do you?" Victor growled with a glare.

"Uh." Joe felt his blood rush to his face.

"He's laughing because he knows what happened." Sky flashed a mischievous smile before hopping out of the back of the truck.

John stood with his mouth open, glancing back and forth between Sky, Joe, and Victor. "Does anyone care to explain?"

Sam leaned in and whispered in John's ear. A smile slowly spread across John's face. "Well." He cleared his throat. "You're here so let's get to work."

"She's a nasty one, that one." The battered Victor climbed out of the truck. He marched towards John where they exchanged handshakes. "I'll be honest. I'm not happy to be here but I lost a bet."

"You and your people are more than welcome. After what we faced last night, I'd hate for your people to have to face that alone." John nodded to the still smoldering battle field.

The rest of the day was spent making battle plans and preparing the camp. Traps were laid all around the area, and groups of fighters were positioned outside the camp to prepare for guerilla tactics.

"I've got some air support coming in as well," Joe announced to a group huddled around a map of the area. "I figure they aren't going to mess around. We need to be ready for incoming ships and missiles."

"There is something else I think we should plan for," Sky spoke up, drawing everyone's attention. "If it happens like we think, that is if they unleash hell on this place, there is the very real chance that higher ups will be here to make sure the job is done. What if we were able to take one or more of them captive? They might be a source of valuable information."

"That might take a small army. If it's worse than last night, I don't know that we have enough man power." John shot a nervous glace at the others around the table.

"I don't need an army, maybe just two or three people who know what they're doing," Sky replied. "With smaller numbers, and if we are dressed all in black, we may be able to move about the enemy undetected in the middle of a battle."

"That could be a suicide mission." Sam flashed a concerned look.

"Not if we do it right." Sky smiled and her eyes flashed with an inner fire. "Are we in this war to win or just survive? Just surviving isn't winning in my book."

"Nor mine. I'll go with you. And after this morning, I have something to prove to you," Victor piped up, rubbing his temples.

"Well, let's hope you fight people better than one on one with me." Sky winked.

"I guess you'll find out." Victor smiled for the first time all day.

"Anyone else?" Sky questioned.

"I'll go," Sam volunteered. "I'm not great at hand to hand combat, but I'm probably the next best fighter with magical abilities."

"I appreciate it, Sam, but I think we need someone without your skills. I'm betting there will be some powerful creatures who would be able to detect good magic. I can hide mine from anyone, but your magic wouldn't be much use to us if it gives us away."

"I think I can find someone from my camp, then all interested parties will have a representative," John offered.

"Where do you want to set up? You better be in place well before dark." Joe motioned to the map.

"Do we have an indication where any of them are massing yet?" Sky questioned. "I would like to join them before dark. They won't expect that, which means we should be able to slip in undetected."

"We haven't received word about their location or that there will even be an attack," Joe responded. "But I feel it. What do you think Yelka?" Joe glanced at Yelka, who was quietly studying the map.

"It has to be in a major city, if they are trying to stay out of the sunlight. The question is, are there any structures big enough to hold an army?" Yelka replied in a quiet voice."

"There's a dome at the University of Northern Iowa. It could hold a sizeable army," Victor said.

"There are also shelled out buildings with underground parking which would make a good hiding place. If they intend to crush us, as you say, I'm betting they aren't all in one bunch, but scattered throughout the surrounding areas. I would guess we are going to get it from all sides," John added.

Joe snapped his fingers and stood up straight. "How would you like to just check out that dome for us?" He glanced at Sky.

"What are you thinking?" Sky asked.

"We have missiles of our own. If there is a sizeable force hiding in it, let's take it out before nightfall. I just don't want to bomb it if there are regular folks hiding in it."

"Why haven't we been doing that all day? We could have checked out several locations by now. Go on the offensive," Victor urged.

"I don't know that we have the men or vehicles to spare and it is still a high risk job," John added.

"How fast can we get there?" Sky questioned.

"I can get us there in an hour," Victor answered. "Faster on a motorcycle, but if we are heading into an enemy camp, a bike would be too noisy. They would hear us coming from miles away. We have a vehicle that we altered to be super quiet for raids and stuff. I think it will work in this case."

"John, bring your man and we'll get going. An offensive could definitely throw off their game plan and bring hope to others," Sky said.

Joe and Yelka were helping Sky and Victor pack the designated vehicle with supplies, when John showed up with a tall slender man sporting a crew cut.

"This is Kip." John introduced him to Sky and Victor.

"Do you know what you've signed up for? This isn't going to be a picnic in the park." Sky eyed the man.

"Yes. Plus, I have experience with these kinds of operations. I'm an ex-Navy seal. I actually miss this sort of thing. It's a lot more satisfying to deal out punishment than to sit back and try to avoid it." Kip smiled.

Kip went to work helping Victor, while Joe and Yelka pulled Sky to the side.

"Be careful. This isn't a game and your new companions don't have your skills. You will have to keep an eye on them," Joe said softly. "But, I do feel better that you aren't trying it alone. We need more help. Trust your companions."

Sky patted Joe on the shoulder. "I will do all of those things. I want to win, but winning without your friends doesn't result in the proper celebration."

"Yes, but this is war and in war there are casualties. Sometimes that includes friends and family." Joe frowned.

"I'll be careful…I *promise*."

"Plus, keep a tight control on your magic. Don't let it give you away," Yelka warned.

"I will."

"I have a present for you." Sam approached and tossed a bundle of clothes to Sky. "If you're going to mingle with the enemy, you better dress like them."

"Where did you get these?" Sky peered at the black clothing.

"You don't want to know," Sam smiled grimly.

They quickly finished packing their supplies and said their goodbyes before heading out on the road.

With Kip riding shotgun, Victor drove, while Sky rode in the back seat. They traversed the main highways but the difficult road conditions forced them to frequently weave and swerve. Sometimes they traveled dirt roads to avoid other camps or piles of deserted cars and trucks.

The sky, which had been sunny all morning, started to show signs of an approaching storm. Dark clouds massed along the horizon and a haze moved over the land.

"There's no wind," Kip muttered.

"What?" Sky questioned from the backseat, still staring at the countryside through the window.

"There's no wind. The air isn't moving."

"Which is usual for a storm coming in," Victor added while leaning forward to look up at the clouds.

"It isn't a normal storm," Sky commented. "It is coming to hide the sun. We need to hurry. Without the sun, Hudich's troops will be able to attack earlier than nightfall."

At Sky's warning, Victor pressed the pedal down, spurring the vehicle forward rapidly. "We should be there in about twenty minutes."

"We need to approach with caution. We may want to take a peek from a distance," Kip suggested.

"I know a good spot. The airport is north of town. We could use the tower as a vantage point," Victor responded. "I can take Highway 218 to swing around to the airport and not get too close to the dome."

Before the city appeared on the horizon, clouds drifted across the sun, casting shadows over the countryside. A strange, random thumping came and went and grew in volume with each passing moment.

"Drums. They *are* here, and they're awake," Sky reported.

Sky and Kip kept their eyes to the west where the top of the dome rose above the city, while Victor took them around towards the airport. Victor slowed and drove more cautiously to avoid any unseen dangers.

"This city is only a shell of its former self," Victor commented.

This comment drew Sky's attention away from the dome, to the crumbling city around them. Broken windows were the norm in almost every building. Very few structures remained intact and garbage was strewn everywhere. Stray dogs scurried about, scavenging for any kind of meal.

"Do you think there are any 'decent' people left here?" Sky questioned.

"If there are, they won't show themselves. Cities are basically preying grounds. No one is safe. There is always someone meaner or nastier around the corner," Victor said.

As they headed towards the airport, the clouds stretched and grew until they fully obscured the sun. Rain drops splattered the windshield. Victor drove the car down the airport exit, when a black-winged beast sprang into the air and began circling the dome.

"STOP! STOP! STOP!" Sky shouted.

Victor applied the brakes and the vehicle came to a shuddering halt.

"Take us under the overpass and stop the car. They're not only up but they're out. Let's hope we weren't spotted," Sky continued to scan the open air above the dome, which was partially obscured by the downward sloping ramp.

"You saw it too?" Kip met Sky's eyes.

"Yes."

Victor turned left on Broadway Street and drove under the freeway where he parked the car. "Should we call in the strike?" Victor turned off the vehicle and the three of them climbed out and slowly made their way up the slope.

A high shrill shriek filled the decaying city, raising the hair on everyone's necks.

Sky and the others poked their heads above the edge of the freeway to see the beast perched atop the dome. He stood upright like a man, but with a height of over seven feet. Black robes covered his body except for large bat-like wings protruding from his back. There were no visible facial features except for two bluish glowing eyes that floated in the middle of his blank, dark face. His mouth opened like a tear in a fabric and the hair-raising scream issued from it.

The light rain turned into a downpour, soaking them to the skin. Drum beats began to echo across the town with three steady beats every five minutes.

"Should we call in the strike?" Victor questioned again.

"Do you think there is any chance there are innocent people hiding somewhere inside the dome?" Kip asked.

"Yes—we should call in the strike, and no—they would have used magic to ferret out any possible life forms. No one inside that dome who wanted to stay hidden would have been able to do so," Sky replied. "I'll call it in." Sky took out her communicator and typed out a message.

A moment later Sky read the response. "Don't look at the blast."

They all turned their faces away from the dome as the roar of a rocket filled the air. A ground-shaking explosion rocked the entire area. A wave of heat and dust rushed over them, momentarily stopping the rain from reaching them, ripping trees out of the ground and destroying unstable buildings.

Sky buried her face in the sleeve of her jacket to avoid breathing in the dust particles already stinging her eyes. A sharp ringing filled her ears, muffling all other sounds. She called out to her companions in an effort to make sure they were okay.

Two shadows moved next to her, coughing and rubbing their eyes. The rain returned, forcing the dust out of the air.

"That was more powerful than I expected," Victor said in a hoarse voice, when strange calls started to rise all over the city.

"I think the army stationed here was bigger than we thought," Kip added.

The recognizable hair-raising scream of the black beast from the dome rose to a new decibel. A hint of madness was in its tone as it spread across the city, followed by responses all around Sky and her companions' location.

"I think we're in trouble." Sky shot them a worried look.

10

A Surprise Ally

They were waiting for us. No one has left the town except by the gateway and Larry is waiting for us. Max gritted his teeth as his anger boiled at this turn of rotten luck.

"We may have to eliminate him," Lita whispered. "If he alerts them now, we will have to fight all the way there. If we can delay them from knowing someone left this way, they will still have to find us."

"As much as I can't stand Larry, I don't want to kill him. Maybe we could bind him and take him back to town as a prisoner," Cindy suggested.

"Don't try anything stupid." Larry snapped his fingers and more lights from both sides of the road sprang to life, blinding them further.

"Oh…crap!" Max muttered, envisioning Larry's large face with a smug grin spread across it.

"Get out of the truck slowly with your hands in the air and move away from the vehicle," Larry ordered.

Max stepped out of the vehicle, followed by Cindy and Lita. He shot a quick glance towards Ell, who had hunkered down in the back. *I don't think they know he is there.*

"Well, well, well. I never thought this day would come and I'd get this opportunity." Speaking in a pleased voice, Larry rubbed his hands together.

"What do we do?" Lita whispered.

"We need to draw them all out so we can account for everyone," Cindy replied under her breath. "If we miss one, it could prove fatal. This is no longer a game of baseball on a sandlot."

"Where's your pink-headed bimbo of a girlfriend?" Max shouted.

This remark brought Larry to a halt. The image of Larry's smug face turning to a twisted-up bright red knot flashed in Max's mind, giving him a smidgen of joy.

"Not a smart comment from someone about to eat a lot of lead," Larry spat. He started forward once more. "Turn around and put your hands on the vehicle before I light you up."

"What makes you think we won't light you up?" Max taunted, while turning and placing his hands on the truck.

"That's the risk to you, not me. You don't know how many of us there are." Larry drew nearer and nearer. Suddenly there was a different, more desperate tone, to Larry's voice. "I've wanted to catch you and talk to you for over a year now."

"Long time to wait on the edge of town. How did you and your friends draw this great assignment? I thought you were moving up in the world?" Max hissed through his teeth. *We need to get out of here. We don't have time to waste.*

"I imagine his gang screwed up royally to get themselves sent out here to wait," Cindy sneered.

Larry's footsteps drew up behind them. "I want to help you," Larry whispered.

"WHAT?" Max blurted out.

"YEAH RIGHT!" Cindy added.

"*Keep* your voice down!" Larry cautioned in a hushed voice.

"*You're* serious?" Max questioned. *What's he trying to pull? This has got to be some sort of a trap.*

"Yes. I *really* want to help you," Larry whispered. "There are only four others out there. Two in each car, but I suspect one is holding on to the radio right now. PUT YOUR HANDS BEHIND YOUR BACK. I'm only going to pretend to bind your hands to lure them out."

Max shook his head. "Why?"

"My question exactly," Cindy added, shooting Max a sideways glance.

"Who is he?" Lita questioned.

"I'm not sure. I thought he was Larry," Max whispered. "I don't know who this is."

"SHUT UP!" Larry barked and pretended to use a great deal of force securing their hands behind their backs. "Hold the tie with your fingers to keep it from falling," Larry muttered in their ears as he acted out the scenario of tying them up. After fixing their hands, he spun them around forcefully.

"Do we attack you too?" Max questioned, his face twisting in confusion.

"Nope, if I make this move there is no going back."

"And you want *that*?" Cindy eyed him suspiciously. "*Why*? What are you playing at?"

"THEY'RE SECURE," Larry hollered.

"Do you want me to call it in?" a voice responded from the car.

"NOPE. It will be a much better prize if we just show up with this group. They are two of the most sought after."

Gunfire erupted all around them. Two missiles targeted the cars, which went up in two huge explosions. A shocked Larry looked down to see blood spreading across his stomach. His terrified eyes met Max's as he fell forward.

Max caught Larry before he could fall to the ground. His weight forced Max to rotate around to rest him on the ground in front of the truck.

"Hold on. Hold on. Lita," Max called and Lita jumped into action, working on the wounded Larry.

Max whipped around and threw up a shield, while dust clouds from vehicles zoomed in from all directions. The roar of engines filled the air.

"Stay where you are. We have you surrounded," a voice spoke through a loud speaker.

"Get the guns," Max ordered Cindy, who flew to the front of the truck.

Two black helicopters rose into the darkening sky several hills over. A dozen military transports stopped and a wall of soldiers poured out to form a large circle around them.

"Max!" Cindy tossed Max a laser gun.

"Throw up a shield. I'll be right back." Max released his spell. "*Preselim se* hills." Max transported himself to a hill behind the closing troops.

One of the copters circled over the truck, shining bright spotlights down on Cindy and the others. Ell sprang from the back of the vehicle and let out a roar that halted the advancing enemy in their tracks. Several soldiers tried to fire at him, but Cindy's shield deflected their shots.

Max adjusted the power level to his weapon and dropped onto his stomach. He sighted in one of the helicopters, targeting the back rotor, and then opened fire. He misjudged the speed of its flight, sending his blast wildly into the night, but his second hit the mark, destroying the rotor. The helicopter spun wildly in the air, drawing everyone's attention to the sudden attack.

Cindy momentarily released her shield and dropped several of the surprised troops before throwing her protection up again. Ell raced forward, scattering the combatants in all directions.

Max turned his attention to the second helicopter racing in his direction. He held down the trigger melting away the front metal to the ship. The copter nosedived into the hill in front of him and exploded into a huge ball of flames. Max looked away to avoid the searing heat which rushed over him.

It took several seconds for the scorching air to subside, allowing Max to race to the aid of his friends. "*Premakni! Premakni!*" Max blasted several of the enemy off their feet, who had been targeting Ell from behind.

Ell closed the gap between himself and three fleeing soldiers who were racing towards a hill. Max spotted two men behind the hill, ready to open fire once Ell drew into range.

Moving his arms and hands to the side, Max cast a spell which threw the soldiers waiting for Ell right towards him. Ell snagged them out of the air with his massive jaws.

Cindy followed in Ell's wake, shooting and casting spells at anything that came in sight.

"*Preselim se.*" Max zoomed over the battlefield and behind a line of parked military vehicles. He spun around from the direction he'd landed and opened fire on a dozen soldiers taking cover behind the vehicles. Max's attack was so swift that the troops didn't have time to respond before he had cut them down.

Max sprang forward and climbed on top of a Humvee to get a better view. Cindy and Ell were heading back towards the truck, while a single military vehicle raced across the hills. Max fired off several shots, but the hummer was already too far out of range.

He hustled to where Lita worked on Larry, with Cindy and Ell watching the scene.

"Is he going to be okay?" Max questioned. Confusion flooded through Max at the sight of Larry wounded. For years he had hated Larry and, with the escalation of the war, he would normally have felt a measure of satisfaction at seeing another of their ranks gone from the battlefield, but this time he actually felt sorry for Larry.

"Yes. He has lost a lot of blood so he's going to be weak," Lita reported.

"What are we going to do with him?" Cindy glanced at Max after wiping some loose strands of hair out of her eyes.

"I don't know but we need to get out of here and in a hurry. No doubt, these explosions and the smoke are going to draw attention. They are definitely going to know someone came this way," Max said.

A pale, weak Larry clinched his facial muscles. "Take me with you. It's better if they think I'm dead."

"Why the sudden change of heart? I mean, you've always shown us so much kindness and affection," Cindy asked with sarcasm. "Remember, like when you tried to beat us up on the baseball field?"

"I know. I'm sorry. I didn't see." Larry kept his eyes shut against the pain while Lita continued to work on him.

"But you see now?" Cindy's voice rose in agitation as she leaned in closer to make her point. "And who were those troops?" Cindy waved at the military vehicles.

"I'm not sure. They weren't supposed to be here. I don't think they were here on Hudich's orders. That was my job," Larry answered.

"He's good enough to move," Lita reported. I don't want to give him any pain killers yet, or we'd have to carry him."

"Where are we going to put him?" Cindy huffed.

"Can you drive for a bit?" Max asked.

"Yes."

"Let's put him in the back with Ell." Max winked. "I can question him with Ell. Give me the pain medicine." Max held out his hand and Lita dropped a small gun-like device with a covered needle on the end in Max's palm.

"You're going to put me with that?" Larry asked after finally opening his eyes and focusing on Ell.

"I'll be with you. He's only dangerous when we want him to be." Max smiled.

"I'll explain it to Ell." A huge grin painted itself across Cindy's face before she walked over to Ell, who had been watching from a few feet away.

Max waited for Cindy to get Ell in the back of the truck before Max helped Larry climb in. Max set Larry against the side of the truck near the tailgate before going through their supplies and retrieving a couple of sleeping bags to make their ride less bumpy.

"I'll send you a message if we need anything. Plus, I'll communicate with our mothers to let them know we're okay. I'm sure they heard the explosions and are worried." Max waved his communicator in the air for Cindy to see. "And don't worry about our comfort. Put as much distance as you can between us and this spot."

Cindy shut the tailgate and she and Lita disappeared to the front of the truck. A moment later the engine roared to life and they started forward once more.

Max sent a quick message to his mother before turning his attention to Larry. "So, you've decided you want to join our side?" Max questioned. "Why should I believe you and why didn't you contact us before?"

Larry had opened his mouth to respond when Max held up a finger.

"Before we begin. I need to tell you more about my friend Ell here. He can't speak but he can communicate. He does it through touch and with thoughts. He will be able to tell if you're lying. Now, you can certainly understand my skepticism and our need for caution, can't you?" Max stared into Larry's eyes.

"Yes." Larry shot a nervous glace at Ell, who was eyeing Larry from only a couple feet away. "What do you need me to do?"

"We're both going to put our hands on Ell's leg and then were going to have a conversation. More of a question and answer session. I'll ask the questions and you'll give the answers."

"Okay…" Larry continued to eye Ell nervously.

Max waved Ell to move closer and then Ell lay down in a comfortable position only a few inches from Larry. Max reached out and put his hand on Ell's front leg. "Now you."

Larry's hand trembled as he slowly stretched it out and put it next to Max's hand.

Larry, can you hear me? Max thought.

Yes.

Larry, this is Ell. He's going to be our lie detector.

Larry. Ell thought.

Ell. Larry's eyes were the widest Max had ever seen them.

Trying to conceal a smile at the pleasure of seeing Larry so bewildered, Max continued. *So, Larry, why would you want to join us?* Max questioned. *What proof do you have that you're sincere?*

I've seen the possible endings to this war. Larry swallowed, meeting Max's gaze. *I've seen what happens at the end. I've seen The One.*

You've seen... The One? How? When? Max pressed.

The One who sent us on this journey? Ell questioned.

Yes. Max answered Ell.

You're on a mission for The One? Larry wore a confused expression. *So, he is real?*

Yes, he is real. How and when did you see him? Max asked.

I saw a vision of him. When Brian and I captured an alien and his spacecraft over a year ago. He had some sort of power like Ell. He touched me! Put images into my head. He showed me the future.

How do we know you aren't making this up? Max questioned. *You could be on a mission from Hudich, sent to infiltrate and destroy us.*

The only proof I have that I'm trying to help you is this. When Hudich left Pekel the last time, a rock was thrown through your window, giving you this information.

How do you know that?

I delivered the message. I threw the rock. I let you know Hudich had left. Anyway, I tried to convince others of what I saw and how it would end. Eventually, I was laughed at and pretty much disowned by my father. They put me on this lowly post. A post we never expected to use. We knew you had the gateway. The odds of anyone leaving by vehicle were almost zero. So, this meeting must be fate.

Max reached out with his free hand and removed Larry's hand from Ell's leg.

What do you think? Max asked Ell.

I think he's telling the truth. If he's willing, I might be able to show us what he saw. He would have to allow me to have access to his mind. I cannot force my way into his memories.

"So, Ell feels you're telling the truth," Max reported.

"I *am* telling the truth," Larry responded.

"We do, however, want to try something else. We want to see what you saw. Ell can do that but you have to allow him access into that memory. He can't force it out of you. What do you say?"

Larry took a deep breath. "Let's do it." He put his hand back on Ell's leg.

By the time Max and Ell had shared in Larry's vision, night had fully settled in. An almost full moon gave them enough light to see by. After being given the pain medicine, Larry rested on the bed of the truck, while Max and Ell stood watch for any sign of danger. They traveled out in the open, the sagebrush covered landscape offered little in the way of cover.

Max put a hand on Ell's side. *I'm going to have Cindy stop at the first place we can find cover. Our headlights are going to attract attention.* He took out his communicator and sent Cindy a message.

About an hour after Max had requested the break, they started climbing a small mountain range where cedar trees began dotting the hills, and larger pine trees appeared farther up the range. No other lights existed in any direction. Just before the summit, Cindy turned off into a rest area. Instead of heading toward the open parking lot, Cindy pulled the truck under the freeway. She stopped where they had some cover from the interstate above.

"How are you feeling?" Max asked Larry, while waiting for Cindy to open the tailgate.

"Physically, I've been better, but I *am* actually happy for the first time in years."

Max flashed a weak smile. He continued to struggle with his emotions toward Larry. He had hated him so long and, even though he had seen what caused Larry's transformation, he had a hard time showing compassion for the injured rival.

"How's the ride back here?" Cindy asked while letting them out.

"Bumpy but I think we should stop for the night. Our headlights are giving away our location." Max climbed down.

"Let me check his wounds," Lita said, and Max helped her into the back of the truck.

Max met Cindy's gaze and she nodded away from the truck. Max followed her to a spot under the next lane of the freeway.

"What do you think?" Cindy whispered.

"He's telling the truth. He showed me and Ell a vision an alien put into his mind."

"How do we know he isn't under some spell? That Hudich didn't plant those memories inside his head? This could be all some sort of trap."

"I agree. I'm not comfortable, but I think that's just because he's Larry. I think you need to talk to Ell. Let him tell you his impressions. I also think we should drive up into the trees here and get some sleep. I don't like that we are the only lights out here at night. It makes us an easy target. Plus, if those troops were government men not working under Hudich's orders, they will have access to the technology to track us."

"I'll take Ell for a little walk, see if I can find us a good spot." Cindy spun back towards the truck and a moment later Max watched her and Ell climb the hill into the trees.

"He's doing a lot better. Maybe another eight hours and he should be ready for about anything," Lita reported when Max joined her at the vehicle.

"Well, we're going to stop for the rest of the night. We feel the lights are like a homing beacon. Cindy and Ell are looking for a spot now."

"Let me get my equipment and I'll do a sweep of the area, check for any non-magical surveillance devices watching this area," Lita said.

"Good thinking. So, Larry, are you ready for a break?" Max stepped up to the back of the truck.

"Yeah, it'll be better to not to have to deal with all that bouncing around."

Max barely located Larry's eyes in the darkness under the bridge, which blocked the moon and starlight. His eyes seemed sharper than they had a few hours ago and his expression was more relaxed.

"Thank you for not leaving me back there in the road." Larry held out his hand.

"You're welcome." Max accepted Larry's gesture and gave his hand a shake. "We didn't have much choice. We don't want anyone knowing we were out on the road."

"May I ask, *why* are you traveling this way and not using the gateway?" Larry questioned.

"Well…"

A roar from Ell off into the trees snatched everyone's attention. Cindy's voice rang out and sparks flashed into the sky.

"Max, they're coming!!!" Cindy screamed.

11

The Dam

Max's blood froze as he whirled around in the direction of Ell's roars and Cindy's warning. His heart threw itself against his chest and pounded in his ears. A soft hum pushed its way down the hill and a smell similar to an electrical fire filled the air.

"I don't detect any advance technology or weapons, but there are multiple life forms moving down the hill towards us. And..." Lita smacked the device she was holding in her hands with one of her palms. "There seems to be some kind of interference. Like...electromagnetic."

Max held his arm out in front of him but could just make it out in the darkness. "There is a lot of electricity in the air. The hair on my arms is standing on end."

"I can feel it on my head," Larry commented.

"Get us some night vision goggles and weapons," Max ordered Lita, who disappeared to the side of the truck.

"Get me up?" Larry adjusted his weight and stretched out his hand.

"Are you sure?" Max questioned.

"Yes. I want this."

Max pulled Larry to a sitting position and then handed him a set of night vision googles, before putting a set on his own head. He glanced around the hill but spotted no signs of life.

"I don't see anything," Larry commented before Max could say anything.

"Switch to thermal imaging," Lita ordered.

Max changed the setting on his goggles and the heat signatures of a dozen individuals appeared a little ways back up into the trees. "I make out twelve but there are probably more, blocked by the trees."

"I still don't see them." Larry fiddled with the settings before Lita made the proper adjustment for him.

"So, how do we want to handle this? We haven't heard anything from Cindy or that thing, Ell, for a minute or more," Larry questioned.

"That means whoever they are, they must have something up their sleeve, to take them both down." An uneasy feeling spread across Max as if the temperature had dropped several degrees.

"I still don't pick up anything special in the way of technology. But…there is an awful lot of electricity in the air. So, they have something going on up there," Lita confirmed.

"I'll agree with that. It looks like they're just waiting for us to come to them. They appear to have taken up defensive positions and aren't advancing," Max added. "So there must be some sort of trap somewhere."

They sat in silence, staring up the hill through their high-tech goggles, trying to decide their next move.

"Do you think they know we're here, or did they just set up a perimeter and we are only seeing the people on our side?" Lita questioned.

Max changed his position to the other side of the underpass to see if he could spot more heat signatures. On the opposite side of the road he detected a couple more heat signatures, which appeared to be facing a different direction. Max paused and took a deep breath. He sent out sensory spells he had inherited from the spider poison, in an effort to feel other sources of magic.

"Hmmmm." *Nothing!*

"What do you think?" Lita asked when Max rejoined her and Larry by the truck.

"There are people, at least on that side, watching that direction." Max pointed to his right. "But I don't sense any magic *at all*."

"I could send out a drone and do a quick flyover," Lita suggested.

"Excellent idea. Just be aware that if you hover in any spot too long, it's bound to draw fire," Max said.

"I don't know," Larry piped in. "It's dark and that hum seems to be coming from their direction. If it is louder up there, they may not notice."

"That's true," Max agreed, wiping his arms with his hands in an effort to get the hair to lay back down.

"Ha!" Lita blurted. "My drones operate soundlessly."

Lita went to the side of the truck once more and returned with a flying saucer-like drone about the size of a Frisbee. She placed a twenty by twenty-inch flat screen on the tailgate and then, taking a small remote in hand, she sent the drone silently into the night.

Max and Larry leaned into the monitor from opposite sides to watch the split display, which was divided into infrared and thermal imaging. For almost a half hour, Lita maneuvered the drone over an area about three miles in diameter. The images on the monitors revealed a camp with several hundred occupants and some small buildings. It also revealed that armed men had created a perimeter around the camp, with the majority watching the path Cindy and Ell had taken.

"I didn't see Cindy or Ell, did you?" Lita questioned.

"They could be in one of those structures," Max said.

"Go back over the southeast corner," Larry suggested, drawing looks from Lita and Max.

"Hey, there were some strange heat signatures in a section of trees."

Max glanced at Lita and nodded.

Lita flew the drone over the area Larry had requested.

"THERE!" Larry pointed at the thermal imaging screen where several small heat signatures appeared on the screen.

"Those are too small to be *Ell* or *Cindy*," Max observed.

"Yes, but look how there is almost a pattern to them like, whatever it is, is behind something." Larry motioned to the distinct layout of the white hot images.

"I think he's right." Lita drew closer to the screen. "It looks like..."

"They're in a pit," Larry finished.

"With a grate or some other covering keeping them in the hole," Lita added.

"They aren't moving. I hope they're okay," Max said.

"It appears there is something else going on there. Look at these strange poles around the pit." Lita indicated the structures. "I think I saw something similar around the entire camp."

"Maybe that's what's giving off the electricity?" Max shrugged his shoulders while glancing at the others.

"I didn't see anything big enough to give off the electrical charge we are feeling, did you?" Larry held his arm up to show the hair still standing on end.

"Ah…No!" Max agreed.

Lita circled the camp several more times in search of anything that could generate a great amount of energy, without success. "So, where are they getting their power from?"

"They have to be bringing it in from somewhere," Larry said.

"I don't remember seeing anything on the road coming here. This land is pretty empty," Lita commented.

"Take the drone up. Let's get a high level view of the area," Max suggested.

"There are power lines." Larry pointed to the infrared screen.

"Follow those," Max ordered.

"Why don't we just blow the lines?" Larry questioned, while Lita followed them with the drone.

"I'm not sure I want to destroy their power source. They may not be evil, but just protecting their territory. If we cut off their power, they may fall victim to Hudich's armies. Besides, I'm sure Lita here has some sort of EMP that would disable all the electricity in the area. Whatever they *do* have was able to subdue Cindy and Ell, which isn't an easy task. Although, they must not have any magic, or I think both Cindy and Ell would have picked up on it."

"How do you do that? Is it something you can teach me?" Larry questioned.

"Sorry, no. It is a side effect of something terrible that happened to the three of us."

"There appears to be a hydro-electric dam about thirty miles to the south," Lita reported. "How do you want to do this?"

"I will transport myself there and shut down their power. You two stay here and watch the truck," Max ordered.

"Hold it. Lita here has enough firepower to keep them at bay, especially if they only have conventional weapons. I think I should go with you. If they snared Cindy and that thing in a trap, you can bet they have set some up around their main source of energy. You *will* need someone to watch your back," Larry said.

"He has a point." Lita tilted her head to the side. "I think I should get the EMP ready, just in case. If you get in trouble, send me a message and I will set it off."

Max opened his mouth to object.

"Hey, I don't think you have time to argue if your mission is very important. We are burning daylight or, in this case, moonlight," Larry said.

"Are you strong enough to transport yourself there?" Max handed Larry a laser weapon.

"Yes. I'm sure I can make it. As fast as whatever she did to help me has worked, I'm starting to see how your technology has given you an advantage over the years."

"Yep." Max smiled. "I'm going to the road, here." Max pointed on the screen. *"Preselim se road."*

Max landed on the pavement, taking a couple of quick steps to keep his balance. A moment later, a weakened Larry appeared and stumbled forward, then fell. Max reached out and snagged Larry before he hit the ground. Max managed to keep Larry from landing hard on the asphalt, but Larry's weight pulled Max to his knees.

"Thanks. I guess I'm not at full strength yet. You never realize how much energy magic uses until you're injured." Larry got up on his hands and knees, taking several deep breaths.

"Are you going to be okay?" Max questioned, eyeing Larry worriedly. Larry had been right about needing someone to watch his back, but if he wasn't up to the task, he could make things worse. Plus, they still needed to get back to the truck.

"Yes, don't worry about me." Larry rose to his feet.

"Okay." Max turned his attention to the dam and hurried to a spot where he could see the entire structure.

"Have you ever visited one of these things before?" Larry questioned as he joined Max.

"Nope, you?"

"Yes, and they are usually well lit. This place is definitely being protected because there are no lights. Plus," Larry held out his arm. "I don't remember there being this much electricity in the air. Whatever they've got going on at their camp is going on here too."

"I'm still not picking up any magic either," Max reported. "Do you see any guards?" Max scanned the surface of the dam with his night vision goggles.

"How far away are we?"

"I'd guess eighty or a hundred yards."

"Do you think you can hit it...without magic?" Larry snatched up a rock and tossed it a few feet in the air before catching it again.

"I can out throw your weak arm." Max picked up a nearby stone.

"Prove it." Larry rose up and threw a rock. It flew through the air with a slight arch before landing on the surface of the structure and bouncing several times. The impact broke the electrical hum with several loud thuds on concrete knocks.

Max followed Larry's example and heaved his rock as hard as his could. The improvised baseball landing the same distance away as Larry's. "Okay, we'll call it a tie."

A few moments after their rocks had impacted on top of the dam, two armed men with flashlights exited a door from what looked like a small guard house. They walked slowly across the top of the dam, shining their lights all around.

Max and Larry jumped behind some trees in order to avoid being spotted.

The crackle of a radio broke through the hum of the electricity in the air.

"We don't know what it was but we definitely heard something." One of the men held a walkie-talkie to his lips.

"We've got a situation up here, so keep your eyes open. These are magical devils, so who knows what they will try." A voice crackled back through the radio.

"What if we need help?" the man with the radio asked, still scanning the surface of the bridge.

"Over here," the other called while picking up one of the rocks and waving to the other.

"We found something," the man spoke into the receiver as he hurried to the other.

"What?"

"A stone," the man reported after reaching the other man.

"A STONE!"

Both men began shining their flashlights on the hills on both sides of the dam, while slowly backing towards the guard house.

"Yes, some rocks. And they weren't there during the daylight hours. And there is no way they could just fall onto the top of the dam. I think you better send reinforcements."

Max yanked out his communicator and his fingers flew over the keys.

"What are you doing?" Larry whispered.

"Telling Lita to start a diversion."

Max had barely finished his statement when a large flash of light illuminated the sky and a huge explosion to the north vibrated the ground. A soft rumble like thunder broke the electrical hum around the dam.

"Sorry, you two are on your own. We've got trouble."

Max and Larry exchanged a quick look. They rose to their feet and shouted their spells, without result. The men's flashlights zoomed in on them and gunfire sent Max and Larry dropping to the ground.

"Set your gun to stun." Max showed Larry while adjusting his own weapon.

Max and Larry opened fire at the retreating men.

"We're under..." Max hit the man holding the radio while Larry took the other down.

"Come again." The radio crackled and after a short pause, "What's happening down there?"

"I better tell Lita to keep it up." Max sent another message, which was followed by another explosion a few seconds later.

"Why didn't our magic work?" Larry eyed the dam curiously.

"That's a good question. Is it possible someone figured out how to neutralize magic? I mean, Lita is pretty darn smart and so was her father, but they never talked of ways to stop magic."

"Maybe no one ever asked the right question?" Larry suggested.

"Let's hope his comment about them being the only two on guard was correct." Max started toward the dam with his weapon at the ready. "And what question?"

"Well, everyone I know only ever thought about combating magic with magic. Maybe your side was the same. No one ever thought of an issue like, I wonder if there is a way to stop magic from happening."

"Great point."

Halfway down the road, Max stopped. "Wait!"

"What?"

Max spied a small stone on the edge of the road. "*Pridi!*" The rock zipped through the air into his open hand. "Okay, so our magic doesn't appear to work towards the dam but is still good here."

"So, there is a limit to how they are blocking it. I'm willing to bet it has something to do with this electrical charge in the air." Larry stretched out his hand and cast a spell towards the structure, without any result.

"I won't take that bet." Max started forward once more. "Still, even if it's limited by some electrical charge, this could be a huge discovery."

"I agree."

They hurried the rest of the way down onto the dam and secured the men with plastic ties. Lita continued to set off explosions in the distance, which Max accounted for the guard's radio staying silent. While on the surface of the dam, both Max and Larry tried to use their magic, without success. The charge in the air was so strong the hair on their heads stood on end.

"I know we have night vision but these may come in handy." Larry handed one of the guard's flashlights to Max. "Okay, how do we shut this baby down without destroying it?" "I'm not sure but there has to be some sort of control panel and we need to hurry." Max took the flashlight and then waved Larry towards the guard shack.

They entered the tiny building, which consisted of one small room with a table and two chairs at the entrance to the dam. A few supplies and a television playing an old movie from a blue ray, flickered in the corner. The lights on the inside of the dam burned brightly, allowing Max and Larry to remove their head gear.

"There's some stairs." Larry pointed to the back corner of the room.

Max joined Larry at the stairwell where a set of steep steps spiraled downward. "Maybe you should go first. That way if your strength gives out, you won't take me with you."

"I'm just here to watch your back. Not land on it." Larry flashed a quick grin.

Max started down the stairs, shuffling his feet in an effort to hurry. Larry's heavy breathing and their shoes on the stairs echoed off the cement walls, as he struggled to keep up with Max's pace. Max kept one hand on the rail because of the steepness of the staircase, and his other hand held on to his weapon, in case any unknown workers or guards were in the lower levels. The intermittent lighting in the stairwell left parts of the staircase in shadows.

Sweat formed along Max's back and forehead and his breathing increased. A brighter glow twenty yards down the steps indicated the opening of a side room. Max came to a stop upon noticing the light. He allowed Larry to catch up to him before motioning to the light. Max then held up a hand and then pointed to his chest while mimicking heavy breathing in order to signal for Larry to catch his breath.

They paused for a minute to control their panting. The hum of electrical equipment floated up the stairs to their position. Max watched the beam intently for any shadows or changes in brightness, but nothing seemed to be moving.

"Are you ready?" Max mouthed to Larry, who gave a quick nod.

They proceeded down the steps at a much slower pace, placing their feet carefully in an effort to make as little noise as possible. The light issuing up from the room remained constant, while the hum of machinery grew more intense.

Max stopped on the step above the landing that would give him access to the room. He slid down along the wall to the platform level, where he would be hidden from anyone inside the room. Slowly, he took a peek inside to see computers and various other machines used to control the operations of the dam, but there was no sign of life. After a short pause, he waved Larry to follow him and they stepped out into the room with their weapons ready.

The room was a lot larger than Max had realized from the stairwell. A wall in front of them, with computers and control components, partially blocked a room with condensers and other machinery.

After a brief sweep of the room, Max slung his gun over his shoulder and approached the main desk. "This looks like the right spot."

"I'm just going to poke around a bit, make sure we haven't missed something," Larry reported, and then made his way around the wall.

Max scanned the desk for anything that would shut down the power, when his eyes locked on an emergency shutdown switch. Max's hand shot out like a striking snake and pulled the lever. The white lights in the room went out, replaced by the soft glow of red emergency lights.

"I found it," Max shouted. He swung his head around the corner of the wall to find Larry, when his face collided with the barrel of a 44 magnum handgun. White lights popped in front of his eyes as pain spread across his face. He staggered backwards, trying to gain his balance while clamping his hand over his forehead.

"Who are you!" a rough voice demanded before a strange streak of light flashed, and another blow caught Max on the side of the head, sending him to the ground.

12

Stopping Magic

Max's head spun dizzily from the blow to the side of his head, and he tried to regain his balance. He quickly threw up a shield spell, and a second later another arc of light zipped through the air and a fist collided with his face again, toppling him backwards.

"Your magic won't work on me, you devil," the rough voice said and laughed.

Blood gushed out of Max's nostrils, and streamed down his lip and the back of his throat. He quickly blinked the water out of his eyes, spotted the wink of the strange light, and dodged the next incoming fist. Dropping to his stomach, Max rolled hard in the direction of the light, when he collided hard with the legs of his attacker. He arched his back away from the attacker and kicked the man's legs out from under him.

There was a crash like the sound of a rolled up chain link fence hitting the ground, and sparks and streaks of light flashed in the air. The man gasped as his weight hit the floor hard.

Max, a little dazed, jumped to his feet and located the fallen man.

"Freeze!" the man ordered while leveling his 44 at Max. The man wore a strange suit, which appeared to be wrapped with sparse loose wire. Sparks and flashes of light arched across the suit with each movement the man made. Black cables ran from different areas all over the suit to a backpack.

"PRIDI!" Max stretched his hand towards the man's weapon, with no result.

"I told you, freak, your magic won't work on me."

"How about a gun?" Larry threatened with venom as he appeared, jabbing the barrel of his laser gun into the man's temple. "Your suit might stop magic, but will it stop gunfire?"

The man slowly raised his hands in the air. Larry snatched the 44 out of the man's hand and tossed it across the floor. "Now get up!"

"Thanks." Max gently massaged the lumps forming on his head, while catching his breath. "How did you know?"

"Know what?" Larry questioned.

"That it's his suit that's blocking our use of magic?"

"Just a second." Larry spun the man around, and grabbed what looked like a black plug, where all the cables running around the man's suit entered, and yanked hard, separating it from his backpack.

The arcs of blue light and sparks stopped and the room was, once again, bathed in only the red emergency lights.

"Watch him." Larry released the man and stepped backwards away from the prisoner while keeping his gun on him.

Max shook the circling pinpricks of lights out of his head and leveled his weapon at the man. His pulse pounded in his head, adding to the pain where the man had struck him.

Larry momentarily disappeared behind the wall, and when he returned he held a small metal trashcan. "I figured it out like this." Larry used a spell to send the trashcan across the room. "I saw him and you from the other room. I reckoned he didn't know I was there or he would have waited to attack. Anyway, I sent a couple of spells directly on him and they didn't work. The last thing I tried was to send that trashcan at him. Funny thing, it flew across the room just like it normally would, until right before it reached this side of the wall and dropped to the ground. That told me something had to be blocking my magic. The suit was the logical choice."

Max lowered his weapon and approached the man. "Who are you? We're not going to hurt you, even though I owe you one." Max touched the lump forming in the middle of his forehead.

Larry flicked on his flashlight and pointed it at the man's face. The beam of light revealed an elderly gentleman with long gray hair, about the same age as Grandpa Joe except instead of Grandpa's slender frame, the man had a husky build with a little bit of a gut showing.

"Who are YOU?" the man barked in a gruff voice.

"We're the ones asking the questions," Larry said, jamming his gun into the man's midsection.

"Larry." Max waved Larry away from the man with his hand. "Lesson one, if you're going to be working with us, play nice."

"Well, if you need anyone to get rough, I'm available." Larry smiled before backing away.

"I'm Max. This is Larry. So, who are you?" After a moment of silence, Max added, "I promise no harm will come to you."

"What about the guards?" the man threw a nod towards the top of the dam.

"They are alive and well. They are bound but otherwise unhurt," Max said. "If we show you, will you trust us?"

The man stared at them for a few seconds. "No, but I might be more cooperative."

"Fair enough." Max nodded towards the stairwell.

The trip up was a lot slower than the climb down. Not only did it take more energy to climb the stairs, but Max and Larry's elderly prisoner had to stop frequently to catch his breath. Larry didn't complain about the lack of speed, unlike the impatient person Max had always known him to be. Max figured Larry needed the breaks as much as the old man because of his recent injuries.

"You may remove their gags," Max informed the old man while fishing his communicator out of his pocket, after they had reached the surface.

"Any news?" Larry noticed Max eyeing his communicator.

"Ah…yeah. Apparently, when the electricity went off, Lita told Cindy that she and Ell could now use their magic. Let's just say they weren't too happy about being taken prisoners. They've captured the camp," Max answered.

"What did they do? How many did they kill?" the man in the strange suit spun around from ungagging the two guards, rising to his feet with a look of panic stretched across his face.

A slight twinge of dread spread through Max. He knew Cindy and Ell would never intentionally kill anyone who wasn't part of the enemy, but accidents can happen in a magical battle. The need to know how this man was able to block spells could very well hang on the answer to his question. *I hope no one was accidentally killed.*

Max slowly typed the question into his communicator and waited nervously for the response. *Please be good news. Please be good news.*

After reading the message, he exhaled a sigh of relief. "No casualties. A few injuries, but they're being taken care of right now."

"Who are you people?" the old man asked, his voice filled with wonder.

"Believe it or not, we're the good guys and we're here to help," Max replied. "With what you've discovered here and our help, we can move you to a much safer location with greater numbers, for protection."

"What makes you think we need your help?" the old man argued.

"Because you don't have the numbers to fight a force with conventional weapons. Evil is sweeping across the country, taking down camp after camp. If we stand together, we have a chance. Alone, we will be eliminated one at a time," Max said.

"Listen to him, he knows what he's talking about. I used to play for the opposing team until just very recently. Those dark, magical forces have joined with the Islamic state and other terrorists from our world. They will hit you with greater numbers and superior firepower. Your magical defenses will not hold them for more than fifteen minutes. Only total domination will satisfy them," Larry added.

"Oh, you might make it awhile because you are well hidden, it was just blind luck we stumbled upon you, but really, how long will that last? They are now using satellites and technology to track all the remaining opposition groups on the planet. Eventually, they will find you," Max warned.

"Where would you suggest we go?" the old man questioned.

"There is a bigger camp about eight hours from here, where those of us on the same side are gathering. We can take you most of the way there, or you can go..." Max started to motion back towards Grandpa's small town before Larry interrupted him.

"They can't go back to town. Remember the border is being watched. I'll bet even more so since our little incident there," Larry interjected.

"Yeah." Max turned back to the man. "So, you can stay here and take your chances, which I don't recommend, or you can come with us and possibly take the fight to them." Max reached in his pocket and took out a knife, which he offered to the man. "Cut them loose."

The man eyed the knife for a moment and then accepted it. "I'm Walter."

"Nice to meet you, Walter."

After Walter had cut the guards free, Max convinced them to leave the electricity off because they were probably being tracked. They rode in a jeep, which Walter and the guards used to travel back and forth between the camp and the dam.

"We chose that location because of the trees," Walter informed loud enough to be heard over the wind generated by the speed of the vehicle as they sped along in the dark, with only the moon to light the way.

"Don't you worry about deer?" Larry questioned nervously.

"We're more worried about being spotted," the driver answered.

"So, how did you figure out how to block magic?" Max questioned, after watching the driver fly down the road in the dark. "I haven't told you about our mission. I mean, why we are out here, but it has to do with an evil magical virus. I'm wondering if what you've discovered here would protect people or not."

"Well, you see, I know a little bit about magic." Walter made a small flame of fire appear above the palm of his hand before closing his hand to extinguish the fire. "I also know that magic isn't really magic. What I mean is, it just doesn't happen. It's a way of communicating with the environment around you. Either through the ground, water, or air, you have to control certain elements to send your message and carry it out. I just figured out a way to block the messages from connecting."

Both Max's and Larry's jaws fell open and they exchanged a quick glance.

"I was involved in an experiment a long time ago while working for the government. I know about these other worlds and what our government did that exposed us to greater threats."

Max's head started to spin and he glanced at Larry, who didn't seem to have put the pieces together.

"Then…you may know my grandfather." Max eyed the man, thinking he looked roughly the same age as Grandpa.

"I might, huh. I highly doubt it. The government tried to silence all of us. I've been in hiding for decades. I'm pretty sure everyone…"

"Joseph Rigdon." Max interrupted.

Even in the moon and starlight, the shock that spread across Walter's face was easily visible. "J—Joseph is…still alive?"

"Yes. He's my grandfather." Max gave the three a brief history of who he was and what his grandfather had been doing. He explained how his grandfather had created his own gateway, and that strange inhabitants from other worlds were now fighting on earth and throughout the universe. Larry added in a small bit of information about the enemy and his reasons for changing sides.

"SHH! Stop! Stop! Stop!" Larry barked with his head cocked to the side after finishing his tale.

The driver responded to the urgency in Larry's voice and put on the brakes. "What?"

"Turn off the engine and *listen*," Larry ordered.

Without the noise from the vehicle's engine, there was a faint chopping sound in the distance.

"Helicopters?" Max looked at Larry.

"More than one," Larry responded.

"Look!" The guard in the passenger seat stood and pointed to the south where spotlights shone down on the highway heading away from their location.

"It's a good thing you didn't have your headlights on," Larry commented.

"Yeah..." the driver exhaled.

"Let's get back to the camp...*now*!" Walter commanded and the driver fired up the engine and sped away.

"What are you doing out here?" Walter eyed Max. "You weren't just traveling through here by chance, right? If you're Joseph Rigdon's grandson, and he's alive, he knows what's out there, which means you know what's out there. Joseph was always a man of action, planning, and preparing. By the look of your weapons, he's been busy. What kind of mission are you here for?"

"I told you. We are on an urgent mission. The enemy is developing an evil magical virus that, if released, would mean the end. A very quick end. It would mean the mass conversion of everyone to their side. Loss of freedom and self," Max informed them.

"I hoped to live out my last few years in peace, but a virus isn't something I thought would happen. Or, at least a magically engineered one." Walter leaned back in his chair in thought.

"How many are there in your camp?" Max questioned.

"Almost three hundred."

Larry leaned into Max's ear. "I was with you about getting these people out of here, but if they are patrolling the road, it will be hard to hide a convoy of vehicles."

"I agree, but we can't leave them out here."

"Give them directions or send someone to guide them out of here in a couple of days," Larry suggested.

Larry continued to surprise Max. This wasn't the same bully he had known. Max always thought of Larry as a dumb brute, but he actually showed signs of logical thinking. "Good plan."

The rest of the way back to the camp, Max caught Walter up on what Grandpa had been doing over the years. Walter nodded quietly without interrupting.

"So, Yelka is still helping you?" Walter asked. "She's the one who taught me how to perform enchantments all those years ago. If not for her explanation, I wouldn't have ever figured out how to block the magical messages that manipulate the environment."

They arrived back at what appeared to be an empty camp, as the sound of a helicopter's blades chopping the air rumbled in the distance and continued to grow in volume. To the north, spotlights shone unrelentingly down on the freeway, giving them a visual on three helicopters patrolling the area.

The driver didn't slow the vehicle, but dove deep into the trees. He took out a radio. "Open the door, we're coming in." He drove the jeep right into an underground bunker and parked it next to several other vehicles, including Max's, as well as additional trucks.

Max found the sight that greeted them to be rather comical. They stopped in a room about half the size of a football field. On one side, all huddled together like frightened children, were the inhabitants of the camp, while Ell and Cindy waited on the other side.

Where's Lita?

Walter sprang from the back of the jeep with the same energy which Grandpa possessed. Waving his hands above his head he spoke in a loud voice. "These people are not here to harm us. In fact," he wrapped an arm around Max's shoulder, "This is Max, the grandson to an old friend of mine."

A soft murmur rolled through the crowd grouped together, opposite Cindy and Ell.

"Why are they here?" someone from the crowd questioned.

"Well, they just happened upon us by chance, but Max has convinced me we need to leave." Walter gave Max a wink.

"Where will we go?"

"Are you sure?"

"I don't want to leave. We've been safe here."

"I don't trust them."

Max glanced back at Cindy, who shrugged her shoulders. Only now did he spot how disheveled her clothes looked and that there were a few scratches on her face. "Where's Lita?" he mouthed.

Cindy walked towards them and Ell followed her. With the giant creature's movements, the camp's inhabitants let out gasps and faint cries of panic while they flinched as one, and backed away towards the far wall.

"I don't want to go with that!" A woman at the front pointed towards Ell.

Walter jumped slightly when he caught sight of Ell, as if seeing the enormous animal for the first time. "I had forgotten what sort of beasts lived out there." He glanced up at the ceiling as if he could see the worlds beyond.

"His name is Ell and he's highly intelligent and magical. Plus, a very good friend. Come. I want to show you something that might ease your people's fears towards him." Max escorted Walter to Ell. "Put your hand on him like this." Max spread his hand open and put it on Ell's neck.

Walter followed Max's example with a slightly trembling hand.

Max could feel everyone's eyes on him and Walter while they stood with their hands on Ell. The tension in the room was finally broken when Walter started to laugh with glee.

"Amazing." Walter said, still chuckling, with his eyes closed in conversation with Ell.

"What's amazing?" several in the crowd questioned and they seemed to relax slightly, their tight knot loosening a bit.

Walter spun around. "I haven't told you much about my life. But there are things in the universe, good and bad. Ell here, although scary to look at, is an astounding creature. Come! Come!" Walter waved his people closer. "He can speak but you have to touch him to hear it."

Everyone began glancing back and forth between each other and to Ell and Walter, as if silently deciding who would go first. Finally, a small girl about the age of eleven stepped out of the crowd.

"Mandy, come! Come!" Walter waved the girl forward, extending his hand towards her.

The crowd watched anxiously, expecting the worst. When the girl reached Walter's outstretched hand, a woman, obviously the girl's mother, sprang out of the pack.

"Mandy, no..." Her voice a barely audible high-pitched cry.

"It's okay," Walter assured her, and placed the girl's hand on Ell.

The girl, like Walter, started to giggle. "Mommy, he can talk." Mandy spun to her mother. Mandy's actions eased the tension in the room and people moved towards Ell and began communicating with him.

"Where's Lita?" Max finally asked Cindy, while the people spoke with Ell.

"She's out doing a survey of their set up. She wants to know how this place was blocking magic," Cindy reported.

"He'll tell us that." Larry nodded towards Walter, who was still helping the camp's inhabitants who were unsure put their hands on Ell.

Max told Cindy how he and Larry had taken the dam and about Walter knowing Grandpa. Cindy related to Max and Larry how she and Ell were taken captive with large netting, which had electrical currents that negated their magic and trapped them in a pit.

"Once the electricity went down, Lita sent us a message that we should have the use of our powers again. With our magic restored, the people pretty much gave up," Cindy said.

The door to the bunker behind them opened and Lita entered and headed straight for Max and Cindy.

"It's a good thing we found this place. Whoever hit us while leaving town is hunting us pretty heavily," Lita reported. "Plus, this setup is incredible. I can't believe no one has ever tried this before but it's ingenious, blocking magical signals from carrying out their messages."

"I think it is like Larry said, no one ever asked that question. I guess one would really have to understand how spells work. I'm not sure most *magical* people do," Max said.

"Which one is Walter? I really want to talk to him," Lita said. She pulled out a tablet and began typing away.

Max pointed him out. "Let them finish and then I'll introduce you."

"So, what are we going to do about these people?" Cindy questioned.

"Larry had the best idea. We're going to leave them here and either give them directions or send someone to get them in a few days. With the road being watched, it wouldn't be safe for a huge convey to go driving down the road," Max said.

"Hold on a second. I've been thinking about this some more. Don't convoys often travel the road for the safety in numbers factor?" Larry spoke up, glancing from Max to Cindy. "Maybe we do want to go with them. We could disguise the truck and blend in. We still might want to wait out a couple days so the choppers think they missed us."

"I don't know. We might be placing all of these people in danger and there are children here," Cindy said and shook her head.

"That's true. If there isn't any sign of us, they might suspect we are hiding among others," Max agreed.

"Yeah, I didn't think about that," Larry said and hung his head in thought.

"Excuse us for a moment, will you, Larry." Cindy looped an arm through Max's and escorted him away so they could speak alone. When they were far enough away she said, "I still don't believe him. He could be playing us. Our job is extremely important. Are you sure you want him tagging along?"

Lita looked up from her tablet for only a moment but then went back to work analyzing the data she had collected.

"I'm not sure, but he did save me down in the dam. I think he *is* serious about changing. Even Ell thinks he's telling the truth. His experience with the alien was real," Max said. "I think everyone deserves a chance. So far he has been true to his word."

Larry stood watching them for a moment, but when Cindy threw a glance in his direction, he turned his gaze to the crowd around Ell.

"Okay, but let's still keep an eye on him. So, what do you think we should do?"

"If you're through discussing my trustworthiness, I have yet another idea, and maybe it would help prove how serious I am," Larry said loud enough for Max and Cindy to hear but not the crowd around Ell.

Cindy pursed her lips in a doubtful manner, and Max struggled to hide a smile at the look on Cindy's face. Lita looked up from her monitor and glanced from Max and Cindy to Larry.

Max snagged Cindy's hand and walked her back to Larry. "Let's hear it."

"What if we switch trucks?" Larry suggested. "Those choppers out there know what we were driving. Maybe these people have one we can use."

"I'm not sure that's going to work. I'll bet they intercept anyone traveling along the highway," Max said.

"Yes, but what if they do find our truck on the highway, going in another direction?" Larry added.

"Who are we going to get to do that? We can't put…" Cindy said in a loud voice, her dislike for Larry starting to show.

"Me!" Larry offered.

13

A Surprise Reunion

"What do we do?" Kip asked, his head swiveling around, looking at the creatures tied to the horrific wails coming from all directions.

"We hide. They still might not know we *are* here." Sky sprang to her feet and raced down the hill, angling toward the underpass, with Victor and Kip right behind her. They scrambled up the embankment to take cover under the bridge.

Victor slipped and fell on the rain-soaked grass, but quickly popped back up. "They're all around us." He followed Sky and Kip up under the bridge. "I saw them."

"Where? Did they see you?" Sky questioned.

"That blast destroyed part of the building across the way, and I saw shadows moving around in what was left behind," Victor reported.

"How are we going to blend in and search out our target? I mean, how do we mingle with them without being detected?" Kip questioned.

"I brought some of their clothing. It's in the car," Sky answered. "Wait here." She left their place of hiding and sped back to the car. When she returned to Victor and Kip, she passed out the items. "Put these on."

They quickly put on the black clothing of the enemy, complete with head scarves and ISIS writing. The garments of the enemy fit easily over Sky's smaller frame, allowing her to keep all the weapons she normally carried on her person.

"I'm guessing the 'slaves' in this army don't feel super comfortable in the presence of some of these creatures and will be stationed in buildings away from the center of town. I say we search some of the buildings around the airport." Sky went to leave when Victor snagged her arm.

"I say we call in another strike on the city in the general location of the dome. That would give us an excuse for heading away from the dome," Victor suggested.

"Good idea. I'm going to have them send a couple more missiles and space them out. We'll head for the airport after the first blast." Sky took out her communicator and a moment later another blast rocked the city.

The shockwave of heat, wind, and dust particles momentarily stopped the heavy downpour, creating a violent gust of wind that ripped apart any structures that were unstable.

"Go!" Sky sprang from their hiding place and the others followed.

They jogged along Airport Boulevard, heading toward the main building, when the next missile detonated on the other side of the city. The ground shook so violently, they had to concentrate to maintain their balance.

The wails of the creature and several others came at them, muffled through the rain, indicating many had survived the attack. To Sky's relief, more military personnel dressed like them emerged from the buildings. At least for the moment, no one seemed to be paying any attention to her group.

They ran straight toward the main terminal in the airport where a set of automatic sliding glass doors had been propped open, but before they could cross the threshold several large Trogs blocked their path.

"Keep calm," Sky whispered out of the side of her mouth as she slowed to a casual pace, with Victor and Kip following her lead.

"Whar ya think yous goin'?" One of the Trogs growled. "Thisun here place is off limits. Ya knows this?"

"Well, plans have changed in case you haven't noticed, we're under attack." Sky waved at the city behind them while scanning the inside of the terminal at the same time.

"Weuns was told ta admit no ones no matte wha'. So I ain' buyin' it. Yous were told about our arrival and ta rules so turn aroun or else." The Trog folded his arms defiantly.

"Did it occur to you that the arrival might be endangered because of the attack?" Sky stressed.

"Thass none of yer concern. Leave now or die." The Trog drew his sword and pointed the tip at Sky's chest.

Sky put up her hands as a sign of surrender. "Okay. Okay. Come on guys, we're leaving." Sky took a step back and spun on her heel toward the sidewalk.

Sky gave Kip and Victor a quick wink as she caught their glances before they rotated to leave.

Before Sky had taken two full steps, she dropped to a squat and spun with her sword drawn, taking out the closer Trog's legs. It dropped and Sky silenced him before any cries of pain could escape his lips and before he hit the ground. The three remaining Trogs didn't have time to react before Sky cut them down.

Kip and Victor stood in the opening, their mouths hanging open.

'Hurry, help me hide the bodies. I didn't see anymore, but if whoever is coming is that important, I'm sure there are a lot more." Sky could barely budge one of the huge lifeless Trogs.

Kip and Victor helped her stow the bodies behind a ticket counter where the shadows made it difficult to see.

"What's our next move?" Kip peered down the terminal.

"To take captive whoever is about to land," Sky told them, motioning with her head for the others to follow. She started making her way through the terminal, heading for the old security checkpoint.

The group worked their way further into the terminal by jumping from one source of cover to another, pausing to check for any hidden dangers.

"You'd think they'd abort, with our attack on the city," Victor commented.

"I find it hard to believe those three were the only ones keeping guard," Kip added.

"They aren't." Sky lowered her voice and nodded toward shadows moving in the darkened terminal beyond the security checkpoint.

"Judging by the number of shadows, it looks like a dozen or so troops," Victor said.

"Shh, listen." Kip cocked his head, pointing an ear toward the ceiling where a heavy rain continued to create a steady hum.

"The voices?" Victor questioned as the soft sound of conversation from the troops reached out to them.

"*No*! I think there is a plane coming in."

The moment Kip finished this statement, the thunder of plane engines approaching joined the rain, drowning out the momentary conversation.

"We need to move where we can see who it is and maybe what we're up against as far as capturing this arrival," Sky motioned toward another section of gates to her left.

Hunched over, they kept in the shadows of the quickly darkening airport. The storm, plus the setting of the sun, began decreasing visibility quickly. They hustled through another section of gates that had seen heavy fighting in the past. Rain fell through holes in the ceiling and where the glass walls overlooking the runways and docking stations were shattered.

Sky led them into an old snack bar to avoid being spotted by two Trogs standing at the far gate, watching the incoming aircraft. She put a finger to her lips and then held up two fingers before pointing toward the last gate.

"Wait here," Sky whispered.

She poked her head around the corner to determine her next move, while the incoming plane's engine grew louder through the glassless walls.

"HEY!" called a deep trog-like voice from the direction they had just traveled.

Sky's heart leapt as she ducked back into the snack bar like a rabbit taking cover in its hole.

"What ya wan?" questioned a Trog at the end of the last gateway.

"We ain' seen Pak n'ta other three." The Trog shouted as the aircraft came in for a landing. "They ain' at thar post and there was blood."

"Well, we ain' seen nuttin," the other responded. "Are ya sure twas their blood?"

"No, but keep yar eyes opn."

The sound of the plane taxiing toward the building and the pouring rain replaced conversation. Sky slowly let out the breath she had been holding and exchanged a that-was-close glance with the others.

"I've got your back," Victor whispered, holding up his weapon and taking up a position to guard against any Trogs coming up on them by surprise.

Sky nodded and checked the Trogs at the last gate, who had returned to watching the aircraft taxiing closer to the airport. She slipped from the snack bar like a ghost, the rain and plane's engines muffling any sound she made. Swinging in a wide circle, she kept out of the main aisle to avoid possible detection, in case any Trogs returned from behind.

With a knife in one hand and a sword in the other, Sky approached the Trogs from behind. The two unsuspecting soldiers chatted back and forth in their guttural broken language, while a military jet came to a stop fifty yards away, just short of the gate across from their location.

Sky attacked so quickly the guards barely registered her presence before they fell. Sky searched her victims for any useful materials but discovered nothing out of the ordinary.

Victor and Kip joined her in the shadows where they could observe the aircraft as the door opened. Two huge Trogs pushed the motorized stairs up to the open doorway of the plane.

"Don't they know they can drive that thing up there?" Victor questioned.

"Probably not. I didn't realize it either. We aren't from your world, and I've never used your methods of transportation," Sky reported.

A few armed militant Islamic soldiers exited the plane.

"Will our mystery guest please step forward?" Kip muttered.

Just then a gray haired man in an expensive business suit stepped forward and paused barely inside the doorway to keep the rain off. He produced an umbrella and popped it open, shielding himself from the storm before descending the stairs.

"Who is it? Did you see him?" Victor asked.

"I did and I know him," Sky said and sneered. "He was the vice president of what used to be your country."

"You mean our *own* leaders were in on this whole mess!" Victor said. "And I voted for those traitors."

"You obviously weren't the only one they fooled," Kip added.

"What do you think fundamental transformation meant? We need..."

The storm seemed to stop momentarily and a winged shadow landed in front of the stairs, darker than the approaching night, as the expected visitor reached the bottom. The air turned several degrees colder with the arrival of the monster, sending a shiver through Sky and the others.

The vice president flinched at the sudden appearance of the demon.

"I sense you are in great danger." The harsh penetrating voice of the black thing filled the airport.

"Hide!" Sky commanded her companions, who jumped deeper into the gates.

The moment his eyes fell on Sky, he raised a long black crooked finger toward her. The mouth parted and an earsplitting cry issued from the opening. A second later, fire erupted from the outstretched arm and zipped through the air like a flame thrower, toward Sky.

Sky threw out her hands, still holding her weapons, and cast a blocking spell. The beast's fire split on Sky's shield and formed a circle around her, destroying chairs and service desks while spreading fire through the building. Sky inhaled a deep breath as her spell blocked the flames but not the heat, making it difficult to breath.

The winged demon continued to send a steady stream of flames for several minutes. When he finally released the spell, fires continued to burn all around the gate, and steam rose in steady streams while the heavy rain doused the flames.

"Are you still alive, *Witch*?" the vice president called with amusement in his voice.

"If you can hear me, sneak around behind the Trogs when the battle starts, hit them from behind," Sky whispered out of the side of her mouth.

"You got it," Victor responded quietly so only Sky could hear.

"You didn't expect me to die so easily, did you?" Sky taunted in a girlish voice, stepping closer to the window. "In fact, after I take his head, I'm going to take yours." Sky pointed the tip of her sword at the demon first and then the well-dressed former second-in-command of the United States.

"Oh, I'm going to enjoy making you do the things that I want, *Witch*!" The vice president chuckled and the demon joined in with a raspy hissing voice. "In fact, I have a present for you." He snapped his fingers and one of the ISIS soldiers raced up the stairs and back into the plane.

"There is nothing you have that I could possibly want, *except* your head," Sky responded, swinging her sword around.

"Oh, but I know all about your people and their fatal attraction for certain *things*," the vice president teased.

The soldier returned from the plane carrying a small box, which he handed to the waiting vice president. He, in turn, handed the fighter his umbrella, and the soldier held it to keep the rain off the gloating dignitary.

He has a dar! This could work to my advantage. Sky dropped her face while lowering her sword. "*NO!*"

"Yes! You want what's in this box, don't you?" A wicked smile spread across the vice president's face that was barely visible in the flickering fires and the fading light.

"*NO!*" Sky took a tentative step toward the window while stowing her knife back in its hiding place.

"Shall I open the box?" the vice president goaded.

"No!" Sky responded in a shaky voice.

"What does everyone else think?" He raised his voice and a chorus of "Open it" and laughter responded.

"This country used to be run by the majority vote. I think we should carry on that antiquated tradition." The vice president laughed. "All in favor?" A roar of 'open it' issued from several dozen Trogs crowding the windows on the other side, a handful of ISIS troops, and the demon. "Those against?"

"No," Sky responded, to more hilarity.

"I'm afraid I have to open the box." The vice president tormentor slowly opened the lid to reveal a single dar, which twinkled in the firelight.

Sky raised a trembling hand toward the dar and took another tentative step while dragging her sword along the ground in her other hand. "Please. No!" She cried.

"Don't you want a closer look?" The vice president cast a spell which created a small ball of light which illuminated the dar even more. "Come. Touch it and everything will be better."

Sky walked to the edge where a glass wall used to be. She paused for a moment before dropping to the ground, the tip of her sword clanking off the pavement. Her legs shook as she staggered across the tarmac with an outstretched hand, dragging her sword behind her.

"That's it. Come a little closer. Touch the pretty rock."

The rain quickly drenched Sky's clothing on her slow march between the two gates toward the vice president. She kept her eyes focused on the dar sparkling in the light.

"Oh, you're going to feel so much better after you touch your present. And the possibilities of what we can do will be endless. Think...we can end this war."

"Please!" Sky begged, continuing her slow walk toward the dar.

Time and the rain seemed to slow as she approached the vice president and the demon. She licked her lips when she was within a couple of yards, her hand still outstretched.

"You've been fighting for the wrong team. It's time we corrected this problem. Just a little farther and the present is all yours."

Sky's hand started to shake as she hovered it above the dar, staring at its brilliance.

"That's it. Any last smart-alecky comments, *Witch*? Before you are ours."

At this remark from the vice president, Sky's hand stopped shaking. Her eyes snapped up to meet his and a wicked smile crossed her face. "I already own my

dar."

In a flash like lightning, Sky whirled around and beheaded the demon. His glowing blue eyes flashed once and then went out as his head and body dropped to the ground.

The vice president's magical light disappeared as Sky finished off the soldier holding the umbrella before he could respond to the speed of Sky's attack. A second later Sky seized the vice president, spun him around, and held her knife against his throat.

Once, he attempted to cast a spell, but Sky countered, knocking the wind from his lungs.

All the Trogs and the few terrorists pointed their weapons at Sky and her prisoner.

"What's the matter? You don't seem as thrilled about seeing me now as you did a few moments ago," Sky sneered. "Now, tell them to stand down." She pressed the blade of the knife with more force against his throat.

"S—stand…"

Before the vice president could finish his order, Kip and Victor hit the Trogs from behind while their attention was on Sky and her hostage. In a matter of seconds, the entire area erupted into a warzone. Kip and Victor had managed to wipe out the majority of the troops and forced the remaining few to take cover.

"Is the pilot on board?" Sky forced the vice president behind the stairs for cover while scanning the area for anyone coming up behind her. If not for the fires at the other gates, night's arrival would have left everything in total darkness.

"Y—yes." The vice president swung his arm forward and made ready to elbow Sky.

Sky kicked out the vice president's knee, dropping him to the ground and changing his elbow's trajectory so it swung into empty air.

She hammered the butt of her knife into the back of his head, knocking him unconscious. In an instant, she stowed her sword and her knife to replace them with her laser gun.

First she eliminated the remaining Islamic troops on the ground before racing up the stairs to be level with the gates. From this vantage point, she caught the remaining Trogs in a crossfire. The battle was over in minutes.

"Kip? Victor? Are you okay?" Sky called while racing back down to the prisoner.

"Yes," the two men responded.

"Well, get over here and help me." Sky looped her arms under the vice president's shoulders and dragged him to the foot of the stairs.

"How are we going to get out of here?" Kip asked, eyeing the vice president with disdain.

A soft roar from the heart of the city broke the sound of the rain, grabbing their attention.

"Uhh, we need to hurry." Victor stood as if he could see through the airport and beyond.

"Help me get him in the plane," Sky ordered.

"What good will that do? Is the pilot still onboard?" Kip questioned while grabbing the vice president's feet.

Victor assisted Sky with the shoulders and they hauled the vice president into the military plane and dumped him in a chair.

"Secure him." Sky sprang to the cockpit to see that it was empty.

"Do we have a pilot?" Victor asked over Sky's shoulder. "NO!"

"It must have been one of the troops I killed."

"So, who's going to fly this thing?" Victor questioned.

"Me!" Sky hopped into the pilot's seat and began to fire up the engines.

"*YOU*?" Victor questioned. "Have you ever flown a plane before?"

"Do we have a pilot?" Kip joined them in the cockpit.

"No, but I've flown spacecraft before. We need to move the stairs so I don't damage the aircraft. Find a rope so you can get back in," Sky ordered.

Sky took out her communicator while the two men took care of the stairs, and she sent a message to Joseph. Her heart dropped when the response came.

A massive Army is approaching from the south but still a good hour or two away! There were other armies. She flew out of the pilot's seat and began searching the plane. In the back of the aircraft's cargo hold she found a stash of arms ranging from machine guns to missiles.

"What are you doing?" Kip and Victor asked.

"I contacted the camp. A different army is approaching the camp from the south. We need to help them." Sky continued to inspect the items.

"*Whoa.*" Victor flipped a tarp off a device to reveal a high yield bomb. "If this was for us, I don't really think there was going to be much of a fight."

"What?" Sky and Kip questioned in unison.

"This bomb would wipe out the entire camp and anyone within a certain radius of it. It's been modified. I think it can be dropped from this plane." Victor's eyes snapped up to meet Sky's. "Ask them how close the enemy is. And if they are still moving forward or holding back."

"Why would they need an army at all if they're planning on dropping this bomb?" Kip questioned as Victor examined the way the bomb had been secured into the hold.

"To make sure no one leaves alive," Victor added. "And yes, it was meant to be dropped from this plane."

Sky sent the message and waited eagerly for the response. "They've stopped. And they are estimated to be twenty to thirty miles out. I can fly this plane, but you'll have to do the targeting."

"I can do that. What about the vice president? What do we need him for?" Victor questioned.

"Mostly information," Sky responded.

"Let's move him. I have an idea." Victor smiled a mischievous grin.

14

The First Prophecy

Sky tossed a small glass of water onto the vice president's face. He coughed and sputtered, waking up dazed and confused. He shook his head to get the water out of his eyes and squirmed against the ropes securing him.

"Wha...Where?" His eyes met Sky's for a moment before he tilted his head up to see he was secured to the bomb in the hold of the military plane.

"Oh, I just wanted to make sure you were awake for the flight." Sky flashed her most disarming smile. "You know the change in pressure when you've had some kind of head injury can create a serious problem."

"What are you doing with me?" The vice president struggled against his bindings, trying to free himself.

"Well, we figure this bomb," Victor knocked on the metal weapon sending a drumming sound through the hold, "was meant for us. So we thought we would return the favor. We're going to give you and the bomb back to your people."

"You're bluffing." The vice president laughed mechanically. "You killed my pilot and I doubt any of you can fly."

"You keep telling yourself that," Kip said and grinned tauntingly.

"We'll be back once we *are* in the air." Sky nodded for the others to follow.

"I wonder if he will bounce," Victor said and laughed as they began to exit the room, when the vice president's cell phone rang.

The ringer brought them all to a halt. In a mad scramble, they hurried back into the room and retrieved the vice president's cell phone from the inside pocket of his suitcoat. The vice president tried to turn against the ropes so Victor couldn't take his phone. "You answer that and you're dead." The blood drained from the man's face, giving him the appearance of death.

Victor pulled the phone out and held it up for a moment, watching it ring. He exchanged a quick glace with the others and Sky gave him a short nod. He clicked the answer button. "Hello." Victor held the phone at an angle so the others could lean in and listen.

"What's happening? Are we on schedule?" a voice on the other end demanded.

Sky mouthed, "Do you know who that is?"

Both Victor and Kip shook their heads.

"Yes." Victor responded muffling his speech. "We are about to leave now." He pulled a questioning face and shrugged his shoulders.

"Good. I want everyone to know there is no hope for them. This little demonstration should put an end to groups banding together."

"Where are you?" Victor questioned with a smile spreading across his face.

"That isn't…" The voice paused. "Who is this?"

"Someone who's about to put a *kink* in your plans!" Victor shut the phone off.

"We need to get out of here fast!" Sky raced to the cockpit, with the others right behind her. She fired up the engines and started heading down the runway.

"Do you think they will try to stop us?" Kip asked hesitantly. "You do. You think *we're* in trouble."

"Yes! They have people powerful enough to knock us out of the air or alter the course of the bomb. We need to get rid of it as fast as we can. Right now, the only thing in our favor is they don't know where we are or what we are about to do. If they think we are still…"

Little flashes of light caught Sky's attention out of the side window. Victor and Kip sprang to windows on opposite sides of the plane.

"How? Where?"

"Magic!" Sky punched it, sped down the runway, and into the air with spells sparking in the planes wake.

Victor dropped onto a seat and began watching the radar. "I'll bet we can expect something to intercept us. Fly low to the ground. This place is reasonably flat. We want to stay under the radar. I don't think we are going to get more than one pass to drop the bomb. You will have to climb and fast when we drop it. We need to be out of the blast radius."

"Do you want me to cut the vice president loose?" Kip asked.

"Not yet. Go tell him he has twenty minutes to tell us everything we want to know or he's getting off the same time the bomb does," Sky ordered and Kip left.

"What do you want to do if he doesn't talk?" Victor questioned.

"Drop him. We have no use for him. This is war. The sides are divided and there are no fence sitters."

"Do you think we can get the exact coordinates for the enemy from your friends?" Victor inquired.

Sky fished out her communicator, and when the message came back she handed it to Victor to read. Victor typed some information into the plane's computer

"Start climbing at a forty-five degree angle here." Victor pointed out the location on the aerial chart. "That should put us high enough to drop the bomb. Take us straight over the line I entered into the system." Victor hopped out of his seat.

"Where are you going?" Sky questioned.

"To drop the bomb and take a few memories of the occasion." Victor waved the vice president's cell phone in his hand before leaning forward and turning on an intercom system which started piping in Kip and the vice president's conversation. Then Victor bolted from the cockpit.

"Well, I'm guessing you have about fifteen more minutes to live, Mr. Vice President," Victor's voice sounded through the speaker. "Any last words?"

"You people don't have it in you. You're bluffing."

"You keep telling yourself that. The way we figure it, this really isn't the United States of America anymore since you collapsed the system, so you are no longer needed. You aren't worth trading for anything. That leaves the possibility that you know valuable information that could be important to us. If you don't have anything we need and you're not going to join us, what do we need you for?" Victor's voice pointed out.

"What are you doing with my phone?"

"Oh, just taking some keepsakes. My favorite is going to be the look on your face when we release you. I'll forward them to the number that called, of course." The clicking of the phone's camera could barely be heard above the roar of the military craft's engines.

He's doing a good job. A smile spread across Sky's face.

"Anything you want to tell us before your little trip?" Kip prodded.

Sky hit the coordinates Victor had indicated and climbed at a forty five degree angle.

"You feel that? She's climbing to get us out of the blast radius. You have ten minutes. You're going to be a big hit, with a light show and everything, in a few moments," Victor taunted. "I hope it's not too dark so you have a great view and we can get some good footage."

The sound of the bay door opening came through the speakers, along with a rush of heavy wind.

"Any last words?" Kip jeered.

"Wow, that's some wind. I better check those ropes to make sure you stay in your seat all the way down," Victor commented with mirth in his voice.

Sky pressed the intercom switch. "Five minutes until our friend gets off."

"Who are you kidding? You're not going to drop me. You people don't have it in you. That's why you're going to lose this war. You don't have what it takes to win. There will be no peace until you submit to us or are defeated and annihilated," The vice president said in a defiant voice.

"I love how stupid you are. You're just proving our point and our reason to get rid of you. You aren't going to give up until you've killed us or we've submitted. That is the nature of war. So for us to win, we have to either kill you or you submit and we think you are beyond the point of changing. If you're not going to give us *any* information, what good are you? You don't have anything we would want to trade you for and life is tough. We have barely enough food to support ourselves, so we don't need an extra, *useless*, mouth to feed," Victor said. "This way you aren't a total waste. You brought us the weapon that's going to help us win tonight's battle."

A beeping on Sky's control panel caught her attention. "We have ships coming in. We are only going to get one pass before they reach us."

"What do we do with him?" Kip questioned.

"Drop *him*!" Sky ordered.

"You heard the lady," Kip responded.

"Tell me when we reach the mark I indicated. He doesn't have anything to say, so he definitely wants to get off," Victor reported.

"One minute until the drop!" Sky said. "The planes will intercept us in ninety seconds."

They sat in silence, letting the tension around the vice president grow.

"All right, all right. What do you want to know?"

"How about you tell us what you think would be important to us and we'll decide if it's worth keeping you around," Victor said, "and make it quick."

"We're...we're working on a virus that will end the war."

"What's the time frame for this virus?" Sky questioned through the intercom.

"We're testing it now. It could be ready in a couple of weeks."

"Thirty seconds! Where will it be released first?" Sky demanded.

"Over the settlement in the Rocky Mountains," the vice president begged. "Now, *release* me."

"Anything else?" Victor grilled.

"Not until you untie me," the vice president said.

"Sky?" Kip asked.

"*Say goodbye!*"

"NO! NO! You promised! NO!" The vice president started to cry.

"NOW!" Sky ordered.

The screams from the vice president faded rapidly. A moment later a massive explosion created a huge fireball and a shockwave that vibrated the plane. Sky jerked the wheel to the left, taking a sharp turn as Kip and Victor struggled to remain upright while they entered the cockpit.

Machinegun fire zipped through the air around them. Sky worked the wheel and pedals, dropping and rising while zigzagging left and right to avoid enemy fire.

"What are we going to do?" Kip asked in a panic.

"What do we have as far as weapons to fight back?" Sky questioned.

"I'm on it." Victor bolted from the cockpit once more.

"MISSLES COMING IN, HOLD ON!" Sky took the plane into a hard dive while turning the plane back toward where they had just dropped the bomb. She leveled the plane out about a hundred feet off the ground, heading toward the steadily burning flames from the detonated bomb.

"This is going to be hot!" Sky flew through the towering flames, causing the heat seeking missiles to lose their fix on them and collide with the ground.

"We got nothing." A panting Victor returned to the cockpit. "No weapons we could use against other planes. Not even parachutes should we want to bail out."

"We may need some of your magic," Kip commented.

"Can you tell me where those jets took off from? They were on us in a hurry, so it has to be close," Sky asked.

Victor hopped into the chair with the radar. He began searching for what they needed. "I'm guessing they came from Des Moines. That's southwest of our current location."

"Do either of you think you can fly us in a straight line?" Sky nodded to the controls while sliding out of the seat so one of them could occupy it.

"Ahh." Kip's face turned white.

"I can do it." Victor scrambled to replace Sky. "What are you going to do?"

"To keep them off of us until we get to Des Moines. Call out when we have incoming fire."

"And then what are we going to do?" Kip questioned.

"Give you some of my magic!"

Sky hurried to the back of the plane and opened the door where supplies would have been loaded into the hold. Heavy winds whipped her clothing as she tied a rope around her waist and then secured it to the plane. She stepped out into the center of the hold and approached the opening.

Sky's eyes watered from the wind and the cooler air. Night had fully settled over the land, and the stars made it difficult for Sky to spot approaching enemy jets.

"INCOMING!" Victor yelled through the intercom.

"STAY ON COURSE!" Sky threw up a shield spell forty yards behind the plane.

A few moments later several missiles impacted the shield.

Taking a deep breath and using all the energy she had, Sky increased the size of the shield and, thrusting her hands outward, sent the shield farther away from the plane at a rapid pace. Two of the enemy planes collided with the shield, producing a couple of large explosions. The force of the impact created a shockwave that threw Sky backward into the plane. She collided with some shelving, which knocked the wind out of her.

"We're coming up on Des Moines in a hurry!" Victor reported.

Sky gasped, rising to her feet while holding onto the shelf for support. "Can...can you make out the military airport?"

"Yes!"

Sky hurried back to the cockpit, holding her side the entire way. "Where is it?"

Victor pointed to the airbase through the window and then on the radar.

"Get to the back of the plane now!" Sky moved around the back of the pilot's chair, leaned in, and took over the wheel.

Sky set the plane on a crash course with the military base and secured the wheel before following Kip and Victor to the back of the plane.

The two men looked confused while holding on to the walls with the bay door still open. Their jaws dropped when Sky entered the hold.

"Who's *flying* the plane?" Kip gulped.

"It's on auto pilot and we're getting off." Sky stepped out into the middle of the hold, facing the open doorway.

"HOW?" Victor looked bewildered.

Sky extended her hands toward the two men. "Magic." Sky winked. "We need to hurry. Take my hands."

The two men exchanged frantic looks before cautiously stepping forward and taking Sky by the hand.

"What do we need to do?" Victor asked.

"Brace for impact. *Preselimo se* camp!"

The walls of the plane disappeared as the three of them landed in the field before the main gates of the camp they had left yesterday. Sky wasn't able to completely compensate for the speed of the plane, so the group landed hard and rolled along the ground for several yards before coming to a stop.

"That *was* fun," Kip gasped, resting on his hands and knees.

"It got you out of there, didn't it?" Sky sat and wrapped her arms around her knees. The fire raging from the bomb cast a flickering light all around as if they were huddled up against a campfire. "I just hope the plane caused a significant amount of damage."

"I think my arm is broken." Victor tried to stand but then dropped onto his back, clutching his arm to his chest.

"WHO GOES THERE?" A watchman called from the wall.

"It's us. Kip, Sky, and Victor," Kip called.

Sky crawled to the fallen Victor and began examining his arm. "Yep, you have a fracture. Luckily for you, Yelka happens to be here. She'll fix you up in no time."

A moment later, a group of people flooded out of the gate to escort them back into the camp. While Yelka tended to Victor's arm, Sky related all that had transpired since they'd left.

"Your plan worked. The drums started as usual, but since you dropped the bomb, we haven't seen or heard anything," John reported.

"It looks like we bought another day," Joe reported.

"You think they will try to hit us again tomorrow night?" John questioned worriedly.

"Certainly, they can't afford a unified uprising fighting back. They want us disorganized and isolated. They fear what every government fears, its people. Especially, those who still carry the American spirit," Joe said.

"How are we going to withstand those who have a nuclear arsenal?" a woman in the crowd questioned.

"With decisive planning and quick action," Yelka asserted. "We have access to better weapons, but we need to be moving already."

"Yelka and I have to return to the house. It sounds like Linda has translated a good portion of the book we retrieved. Jax and his men will be staying with you, but you'll be in charge and you have top priority with the gateway. I figure this little war will keep eyes away from Max and Cindy," Joe said.

"Speaking of Max and Cindy, there's one more thing," Sky spoke up. "Max and Cindy only have a couple of weeks. The vice president told us they are only weeks away from releasing their virus. You need to tell them there is a time limit."

"That's not good." Joe shook his head. "I suggest you go on the offensive as much as possible and find a bigger camp that can hold more people."

###

Joe and Yelka stepped out of the gateway into the third floor of Joe's house. Rachel's and Cindy's mothers gave them welcoming hugs.

"You both look exhausted," Rachel commented. "How are things going?"

"So far so good, but that could change any minute. We really got Hudich's attention," Yelka informed them.

"One moment." Joe held up a finger on one hand while typing a message to Max with the other. "When's the last time you heard from Max and Cindy?"

"We haven't heard from them for several hours. Is something wrong?" Cindy's mother asked, exchanging a concerned look with Rachel.

"As far as we know they're fine. We just found out the enemy is planning on using the virus sooner than we thought. We need them to hurry," Yelka said.

"Dang," Joe muttered under his breath, staring at the communicator.

"What?" everyone questioned.

"Ah, nothing. Where's Linda? She said she's deciphered some of the prophecies," Joe questioned.

"Tomorrow. I'm not letting you do anything until you've gotten some sleep." Rachel put an arm around Joe and one around Yelka and started leading them toward the stairs. "You're no good if you can't think clearly."

"Give Sky and Jax top priority through the gateway," Joe called over his shoulder before descending the stairs.

The sun shone through a crack in the curtains, pulling Joe out of his sleep. He checked the clock to see he had only slept five hours. As much as he wanted to stay under the covers, the pressing issues of what needed to be done paraded through his mind, chasing away all thought of rest.

He slid out of bed and went to the kitchen where Yelka, Donna, Martin, and Linda sat around the breakfast table, helping themselves to pancakes and eggs. Donna, who had been at the stove, placed another plate on the table for Joe and went back to cooking.

"I was debating on how long to let you sleep," Linda said.

"I take it you've found something important?" Joe lowered himself into the chair and buttered his pancakes.

"Well, we haven't translated everything, but some things are done, and one particular prophecy we've translated has given us great cause to worry. Especially, knowing what Max and Cindy are trying to do," Linda replied.

Joe paused with a forkful of pancake halfway between his plate and mouth and met Linda's eyes. "What is it?"

"Well, they appear to be different types of prophecies. One group are warnings and how to change certain events, while others appear to be markers," Linda said.

"Markers for what? And why do I get the feeling a certain marker has to do with what Max and Cindy are trying to do?" Joe questioned.

"They appear to be things or events that will take place before the coming of The One," Donna said.

"And one of the events is tied to what Max and Cindy are doing?" Joe questioned with confusion written across his face.

"Yes, it states, 'for a desolating sickness shall cover the land,'" Linda said with a drawn expression.

"The virus!" Joe gasped.

15

A Soldier's Confirmation

"You." Cindy laughed mockingly while throwing her hands up in the air.

"Yes...me! It could give you the time you need to get where you're going. I know you still don't trust me and I don't blame you, but it is the only chance you've got unless you want to fight all the way to your destination," Larry said.

"What do you think?" Cindy shot Max a glance.

"I'm thinking it might just work, but I have a few details that really might keep them off our tail," Max responded.

"Like?" Lita questioned.

"Like, I go with him," Max suggested.

"WHAT?" Cindy almost shouted. "HOW IS THAT GOING TO HELP?"

"I have an idea, if you'll just calm down and listen. We're wasting time and we need to get moving. Plus, they know what we look like. If they can see me going the opposite direction, they are more likely to believe it." Max put out his hands in a disarming manner. "We need to buy time. Time to get us where we need to go. Time to get these people to safety. Time for Lita to learn all she can from Walter; his invention could be very powerful in this war."

They spent the better part of two hours planning the events they hoped would keep the military off their backs and get the people to safety. They pored over maps, deciding the best route to take and when each group should reach specific destinations. Several times during their planning session, the military helicopters circled overhead, interrupting their flow of ideas.

"I still don't know about this," Cindy said and shook her head as they watched a group of people from the camp create an imitation of Ell in the back of the truck, using some of his own fur.

"Well, you're not the one who has to dress like a girl." Larry adjusted a blond wig on top of his head.

"I always used to call you a girl, so I'm finding it amusing," Cindy teased.

"I find Ell more amusing with his new haircut," Max said and patted the newly shorn Ell standing next to him.

Very Funny! I'll find a way to get even.

I think you look cool, Cindy thought.

Max checked his watch. It's almost dawn. We need to leave when the light is the poorest," Max said.

"We're just about done," a man called from the bed of the truck.

"It does kind of look like him." Larry referred to the fake Ell.

"It does, and that's a good thing. It might convince them because you make a *poor* Cindy," Max laughed.

"Oh admit it, I'm prettier than she is." Larry fluffed his wig.

"Only you're more feminine," Cindy joked while putting an arm through Max's and leading him away from the others once more.

"I know, be careful," Max said when they were out of hearing range of the others.

"And watch him. I still don't trust him."

"I know, but I have a feeling he's for real." Max glanced back at Larry.

"Don't do anything stupid. These people aren't messing around. Do your job and get out of there. Don't tell Larry the meeting point until the last possible minute." Cindy leaned in and kissed Max on the mouth.

For one brief moment Max felt like everything was right in the world.

"You be careful too. There's no guarantee they're going to buy this little decoy," Max warned after Cindy pulled away.

"I will monitor the area with radar and try to alert you if I see anything around you or heading in your direction. Granted, the farther away you get, the less I will be able to help you," Lita offered.

"Thanks. The more help we can get the better the chance of success. We will play cat and mouse as long as we can," Max said.

After a few final details were worked out, Max and Larry climbed into the truck and started down the forested hill toward the on ramp. Max brought them to a stop before they left the trees and stepped out of the truck, as did Larry.

They checked the early morning sky for any sign of activity, but only the stars and the slightly lightening sky met their gaze. Max strained his ears, but only chirping crickets and other insects made any noise. Closing his eyes, Max decided to send out his sensors to see if there was any magic in the area.

"That's a cool talent," Larry commented.

Max opened his eyes to see Larry watching him.

"So you really can't teach it to me?"

"Sorry, it is the side effect of something really unpleasant. I wouldn't wish that on anyone," Max responded.

"Side effect from what?" Larry asked.

"Slowly dying. I don't see, hear, or detect anything. I think we should get going." Max returned to the truck and waited for Larry to climb in before driving out of the trees. He didn't use the headlights in an effort to avoid detection. Part of their plan involved misdirection. *If they catch us too soon, this plan won't work.*

"You and Cindy almost died?" Larry pushed as Max turned on the ramp and increased speed.

"Kind of. I don't know if I would call it dying or losing one's self. I'm also not sure we—Cindy, Ell, and I—aren't half dead already," Max said. "We were bitten by a spider with dark magic and injected with her venom." Max shivered at the memory of total helplessness. "If it wasn't for our friend Sky, we would have been lost."

"Oh," Larry said and sounded a little disappointed.

"Sorry, but there are other side effects which are not so spectacular," Max continued. "Wounds take forever to heal, look horrific and appear to be necrotic. Plus, I'm sore all the time like I went several rounds with you and your friends on the baseball field." Max laughed.

"Sorry about that," Larry said and chuckled, checking the sky from his door window.

"Oh crap!" Max's communicator started to vibrate inside his pocket.

"What?"

"My communicator. I hope it's not bad news. We're still twenty miles from the junction." Max managed to maintain speed while fishing the device from his pocket. He read the message. "They've spotted helicopters on the radar."

"Where?" Larry made almost a complete circle, checking the ever brightening sky. "I don't see anything."

"Behind us. They are still a ways away on the other side of the camp. We have time. Keep your eyes open for a possible hiding place though. If we can go several hours without detection, that would be ideal." Max increased the speed of the truck. *Give us time. Give us time.*

"There's a city up ahead." Larry pointed as the predawn light revealed a small city not too far in the distance.

"Yes, that's where we make the turn."

"There's probably decent cover somewhere in there."

"There could also be a trap. They know we were heading in this general direction. I figure this is about where they'll see us," Max said. "The bad news is we have to go into town to make the turn. Let's hope they aren't ready for us yet."

Max raced to the ramp that led them into what appeared to be a ghost town. All the buildings had some degree of damage, and trash and debris littered the road. He didn't slow his pace, only swerving a couple of times to avoid trashed cars or large objects in their path.

"There!" Larry pointed to a sign. "We don't have to go too deep into the city."

"Thank goodness!"

Max braked so he could make the turn leading to their chosen route heading north. As he accelerated coming out of the turn, the roar of engines and a flood of lights appeared behind them and to their left.

"Oh crap!" Larry muttered.

"Let's hope Lita's toys will get them off our backs," Max said handing a remote to Larry.

"You can bet those helicopters are about to change course." Larry accepted the device from Max and glanced over the options. "Do these mean what they say?"

"Yes, they do and, knowing Lita, they will pack a large punch!"

"Fantastic."

Max floored the truck's gas pedal in an effort to outrun the half dozen military Hummers racing toward them.

The lead vehicle opened up a line of fire, spraying bullets to the left and right of Max and Larry.

"I think they want you alive," Larry commented. "They have more powerful weapons and I'm sure they are better shots than this."

"Well, unfortunately for them, we aren't playing by their rules. Hold on, we have another turn up ahead." Max let off the gas and cranked the wheel. He didn't brake but started to accelerate once he was into the turn. The tires squealed against the strain of maintaining Max's course but held the road. The truck rocked back and forth for a few moments after they completed the curve before leveling out.

A few explosions joined the gunfire but they continued to happen away from their mark and a little ahead of Max and Larry's position.

About a mile ahead numerous trucks raced onto the highway. Several of them jumped into the air after using the slope of the hill like a ramp and landed onto the freeway. All but two of them sped toward Max and Larry, while the others zipped farther down the highway.

"Ahead of us! Six non-military vehicles," Max shouted.

"Who are they?" Larry whirled around.

"My guess is locals—bought and paid for."

"What do we do?"

"Take them out!"

Larry rolled down the window and put the laser pistol out, taking aim at their pursuers. He had a hard time hitting the mark with Max swerving all over the place. He fired shot after shot until he had destroyed three of the vehicles.

"They're laying down spikes," Larry warned as the remaining automobiles ahead of them turned to block Max and Larry from getting past.

"Use the remote."

Larry glanced down at the control and spotted one that said road cleaner. He pushed the button and a red wave shot out from the truck, covering the road and flowing down both embankments. When the wave reached the section where the two trucks and the spikes waited, it vaporized the spikes and then spread to the vehicles, resulting in two explosions.

"Wow, Lita has powerful stuff."

"I think we need to try a few more buttons." Max nodded to the group behind them as they zoomed past the burning wreckage.

"Right." Larry scanned down the list and found one called reverse laser. He pushed the button.

Dozens of continuous laser beams shot out of the back of the truck, which diminished the truck's power and they began slowing down rapidly.

"What did you do?" Max questioned.

"Swerve back and forth. NOW!"

Max started to jerk the wheel left and right, zig zagging back and forth across all lanes. With each sideways movement of the truck, several explosions followed. Through the rear view mirrors, lasers cut through their pursuers, destroying their vehicles.

Larry turned the switch off and the truck regained momentum. "That was awesome! Right out of a spy movie."

"She must have hooked it into the truck's power," Max remarked. "Now we only have those last few." Max motioned to the three non-military vehicles slightly ahead of them.

"I'm on it." Once more, Larry took aim out of the side window, but before he could fire a shot the remaining pursuers peeled off, leaving dust trails in their wake. "I take it they weren't paid enough to continue the battle once we took out the leaders."

"Nope." With his concentration returning, Max noticed the communicator vibrating on the seat next to him. He snatched it up and read.

Helicopters heading your way!!!

"We need to start searching for a place to hide," Larry said before Max handed him the communicator.

"Yup!" Max scanned the high desert surroundings for any possible hiding place while he sped down the highway.

The sun began to peek above the eastern horizon. Larry pored over the maps where they had previously marked out possible hiding places.

"We're only five miles from the canyon we marked as a possible location." Larry held up the map and pointed out the location.

Max slammed on the brakes and whipped the truck around. "I think I have a better plan."

"What if we hide among the wreckage we left back there?"

"That could work, assuming no one survived. If anyone lived and has access to a radio, we'd be blown in a minute."

Max glanced at Larry. "Yeah!"

"But if we can nestle in close to a couple of the smokers and the helicopters don't get too close and…"

"And? Maybe the two of us working together can use magic to hide the truck while they pass," Larry suggested.

"Smart thinking!"

"There, that looks good." Larry pointed to two burning vehicles on the western side of the road where flames and billows of black smoke rose into the air.

Max floored the gas and zoomed forward. They zipped past the two vehicles that had laid down the spikes, while also watching the sky for any indication of the helicopters' arrival.

"Stay on the road as long as possible and then slowly move next to the destroyed trucks," Larry said, drawing a questioning look from Max. "Remember the dust that got kicked up when anyone drove off the highway."

"There they are." Max nodded out his window as he spotted two small black dots.

Larry leaned across the seat to get a look. "Are they heading right for us?"

They each held their breath for a moment.

"Nope, they're angling north...where they think we're heading." Larry sat back in his seat.

Max slowed to almost a complete stop before turning off the road and slowly positioning the truck between two of the smoldering wrecks. He and Larry climbed out of the truck and, from a position of cover where they weren't inhaling the black smoke, they watched the helicopters head north.

"I'm sure they'll be back sooner rather than later," Max said.

"I wonder if there's anything natural we can do to help hide the truck," Larry commented.

"Good idea." Max went back to the truck and retrieved a couple of water bottles. He passed one to Larry before taking a drink.

"Thanks." Larry accepted it. "You know, I worried whether or not I should join you. I mean, I had seen things but I didn't know if you had what it takes to win."

"What do you mean?"

"I understand the whole thing about mercy now, but we are getting to a point where to win, you are going to have to forget about compassion and be as ruthless as they are. Over the last few days, you've shown you have the ability to do that. If you aren't prepared to totally wipe out the enemy you'll never win because I know them, they will never stop."

"I think it is all in your heart. We would leave them alone if they would leave us alone. I don't like killing or hurting others, but I understand we must in order to survive. I think you still need to really keep your eyes open so you can spot those who are willing to change but are just caught up on the wrong team," Max spoke somberly.

"Like me?"

"Yeah. Aren't you glad we showed you mercy?"

"I am."

"I do realize the deeper we go, the odds of finding those who really want to change are going to be lower and lower. I just hope we still are able to spot those who will."

"What if we pushed dirt up over the wheels and laid pieces of some of the destroyed vehicles across the hood and over the back?" Larry motioned to some large scraps of burned metal.

"That could help. We better check for survivors first. We don't want someone to give us away if they get the chance." Max watched the helicopters disappear to the north.

"Yeah. I don't think we have to worry about the locals. Plus we might be able to get some more weapons. I'll take the ones across the highway, you take this side."

Max hurried to the closest military vehicle, which had been completely cut in half by Lita's lasers. Before looking inside, Max sent a quick message to update the others with what was happening. Then, taking a deep breath, he checked for any signs of life or working weapons. He didn't find anything of use in the first two vehicles but recovered some machine guns and ammo from the third.

When Max returned to the truck, Larry stooped next to a wounded soldier, giving him water. The man appeared to be in his mid-thirties, with a muscular build and thinning hair. Larry had already patched up shrapnel wounds and tried to administer to some severe burns.

"I didn't find anyone." Max set the weapons next to the truck. "I'll get started on the cover if you want to keep an eye on him."

"I think he needs to rest a bit, but I figured we need some answers. He's not with my people, so I'd like to know who sent him," Larry commented.

Using magic, they got a little more creative than they had intended. They magically dug a small crater between the two trucks and tucked theirs into it. Then placed dirt back into the hole and moved things around the truck, hiding it so it couldn't easily be spotted from the air. They even added a few things to the dwindling fires to keep them going with thick black smoke. The sounds of helicopter blades chopping the air reached them just as they had finished putting on the final touches.

They hurried to the truck and pulled the soldier further under the debris to keep themselves hidden. Using holes through the overlaying pieces of burned metal, they watched the helicopters approach.

"We should have mangled the other vehicles a little more. What if they decide to take a closer look?" Larry questioned.

"Well then, we'll have just found a quicker means of transportation," Max said and smiled.

"I like it." Larry shifted his position for a better look. "Wait....do you know how to fly a helicopter?"

"Yes. When they get a little closer, make us look different. I'll hide our heat signatures," Max said, noticing the wounded soldier eyeing them with fear.

"Got it."

After waiting quietly for the choppers' arrival, Larry spoke again. "Do you want to try to lure one to the ground?"

"No, if we take out a helicopter, you can bet jets will be on the scene in a matter of minutes, and I don't think we could fight them. I just had a run in with some last week. They travel too fast for magic. We wouldn't have the advantage."

"Oh!"

A moment later, they each cast their spells. Two helicopters slowly circled the area, hovering only thirty yards above the ground. They stopped over one of the destroyed vehicles for a moment.

The soldier shifted next to Max, and in a flash Max drew his laser pistol and put the barrel against the soldier's head. The choppers circled for another fifteen minutes before heading north once more.

"I think using magic to bury the truck is a good idea. We could move up the road and hide it in a less obvious place. That could get us to the point where we want to be found," Larry suggested.

"Who are you people?" the soldier asked with a harsh voice.

"I agree but what do we do with him?" Max questioned.

Larry waved Max out of the shelter. When they were out of hearing range of the soldier, Larry spoke. "We use him to help us. We could drop him off at some town, maybe let him think he has stolen a radio. That could verify someone saw us farther along this route."

"That just might work. What if we tell him who we are and he wants to change teams?" Max raised an eyebrow. "He's a soldier just following orders. If he's not with Hudich, we might be able to flip him."

"Then maybe we can have someone working for us on the inside?"

"That is a poss..." Max's communicator vibrating in his pocket caught his attention so he quickly took it out and read the message. "Uh-oh."

"What? What's wrong?" Larry moved closer to read the message. "Did something happen to Cindy and the others?"

"No, this message is from Grandpa. We have to hurry. We only have about two weeks to accomplish our objective." Max typed out a response. "I don't think we have enough time to play cat and mouse. Let me make sure Cindy received the same message." Max hammered out another message.

"Maybe our friend in there can help us. He may have information which could tell us what to do or how to proceed."

"Good idea. Either way, I think we need to move in a hurry."

"You do realize, we only really have two options," Larry said.

"What do you mean?"

Larry pointed to the wig he was still wearing and his outfit. "I'm obviously not a girl and Ell is obviously not real." Larry motioned to the back of the truck. "We either have to kill him or take him with us. Are you sure we can trust him if he says he's flipping? Once they learn we are a decoy, they're going to figure out we *are* really going the other way. Just like you haven't told me where to go when we get done here. Not saying I blame you, but see what I mean."

"Point taken. And...we're meeting them in St George, Utah; in case you don't know where that is, you better look it up on a map."

"Don't worry. I'm in this with you 'til the end. And thanks for showing a little trust."

"Oh, I've believed you since you spoke with me and Ell. It's Cindy you need to convince."

They made their way back into the make-shift cover and took up positions on opposite sides of the wounded soldier. The man's eyes were wide with fear as his gaze jumped back and forth between Max and Larry.

"So," Max started. "What are we going to do with you?"

The man clenched his jaw while trying to control his breathing.

"You understand this is war, of course, and in war there are those who live and those who die. Plus, we're not in a position to take prisoners," Larry added.

"The question is: which one are you going to be. You have a couple of options here. One, you don't help us out and we resort to unpleasant measures to get the information we need, and then we leave you out here in the middle of nowhere with only the desert around you. Two, you help us out without much fuss, and we dump you someplace where you would be able to contact your people after we're gone. Three, you listen to what we have to say and see our point of view and start working with us."

The man almost choked on pure air at Max's last suggestion. "Side with you?"

"Yeah, it's better than playing for the losing side, which will be wiped off the face of the earth," Max said flatly.

"What makes you think you're going to win?"

"Hmmm, I don't know. Didn't the two of us just destroy a bunch of you and your highly trained people along with some locals, or did you miss that?" Larry added.

"But...you're just kids. And the world has gone to crap! There's no one organized enough to defeat our full military, should we decide to use it. You're out of your minds if you think you can win."

"I agree as far as conventional weapons from this planet, you hold the upper hand. The problem is, we aren't using those weapons against you in return." Max snapped his fingers and a ball of fire hovered above his hand. "I think you already noticed we have a different kind of power. The look in your eyes tells me you are concerned about us."

"So, we have certain means to interrogate people other than your old fashioned ways. We can induce pain a lot...." Larry paused and cocked his head to the side.

"I hear it too," Max said to the noise of approaching vehicles. "Cars."

"And a helicopter!" Larry took up a position to see what was going on. "This may prove difficult for us to keep going north."

"Shh!" Max shot Larry a shut-up look before turning away to conceal a smile after Larry looked nervous. *I would never have believed I would be with Larry and able to play a game without speaking.*

"I can't see. Are they military vehicles or some of the local boys coming to collect whatever they can?" Larry questioned.

"It looks like…" Max spotted two trucks pulling up and a half dozen men climb out. They paused listening as the helicopter started to draw near. "Locals, but the helicopter won't be. It looks like they're deciding what to do."

"It looks like only one 'copter is returning," Larry commented. "What's our play?"

"I'm not sure yet. The truck's buried. We'll have to take care of them first before we can get away. If that thing lands, it will give us the advantage. I'll let you in on a little trick I learned recently—spells work against machines."

"What do you mean? Of course they do. Fire destroys the living and the dead," Larry added.

"No, I mean you can turn things off or on, etc…"

"Really? Never tried that."

They waited, watching as the helicopter came in for a landing. The leader of the locals stepped forward to meet with a military commander, who exited the helicopter to speak with him.

The two men got together on the highway between the aircraft and the parked vehicles.

"I wonder what they're talking about." Larry changed positions for a better look.

"Probably trying to get details on what went down here or if they've seen us since the battle."

"That should at least confirm we didn't go back to the other highway."

"True. I'm sure the militia hit any small groups traveling the highways around them."

After several minutes of talking, the two men parted and the soldier climbed back into the helicopter. Its blades picked up speed and it slowly lifted off the ground. When it was about forty yards off the ground it opened fire on the locals, ripping through them and their vehicles in seconds.

"Wow!" Larry said with shock.

A fire ignited in Max's gut, propelling him out of their cover. "*Ugasni* helicopter."

Max's spell stopped the engines dead and the craft dropped out of the air. It smashed to the ground, destroying the ship.

Max and Larry sprang forward and opened fire, eliminating the crew. They quickly made sure no one remained who could send out a call to bring more troops.

"Let's get the truck out. We need to leave," Max urged.

Max and Larry used magic to get the truck out of its hiding spot and clean it off. With the soldier sitting between them, they started racing north once more.

"You still don't think we can win?" Larry eyed the soldier.

"My friend pointed out something back there, which I'm sure you've figured out. We can't really let you go. I mean, you obviously know he's not a girl. So, you can either tell us what we want to know and live or you can die."

"Let me clarify for you. You can either keep your mouth shut, suffer a lot of pain, and then die—or you can ride comfortably and tell us what we need to know," Larry interjected.

"I would listen to him. We haven't always been friends. In fact, he used to work for the other side. I'm willing to bet he knows a lot about torture," Max said.

"What are you talking about? You sound like there are more than two sides in this fight," the soldier questioned.

"In reality, there are only two sides, but I'm willing to bet there are factions within your group and a struggle for control. Everyone wants to be in power. The reason I know this is my friend here used to be with the dark side and doesn't know what your people were up to when they tried to capture us as we were leaving town. That means you are working for one of the factions trying to regain their power because he and his friends work for the head guy. The question is: why do they need me to regain this power?" Max said.

"What?" The soldier shook his head with confusion. "I have no idea what you're talking about.

"Let me spell this out for you. What do you want with him and Cindy?" Larry held his palm up and a swarm of fire ants crawled all over it. They appeared to be multiplying as if coming out of a burrow within Larry's palm. Several of the stinging insects fell onto the soldier's knee, which he jerked and swatted to keep from being bitten.

"I was just following orders. How am I supposed to know?" The soldier continued to thrash about as more and more of the ants fell on his leg. "Ouch!" He swatted. "They're real?"

The soldier's thrashing became intense and he pushed up against Max so hard Max had to pull over to keep from crashing.

"Of course they're real, and they love human flesh." Larry wore a wicked smile. Greater quantities of ants continued to fall from his hand onto the terrified soldier.

"It hurts! It hurts! Get them off."

"Why were you after Max and Cindy?" Larry pressed.

"It has something to do with the cure for a *virus*!"

16

The Warning

"A cure for a virus?" Larry acted confused. The soldier's statement shocked him into losing control of his spell and the ants disappeared.

The soldier stopped thrashing and swatted his legs a few more times, just to verify the ants were gone. "Yes. I overheard some higher-ups discussing it." He appeared stunned, continuing to stare at his legs. "They said a virus is coming that will win the war, but may also infect us as well."

"Why would Max and Cindy hold the cure?" Larry regained his composure and the ants began climbing all over his hand again.

"Because we do." Max met Larry's gaze. "You know that special gift you asked about?"

"Yes?"

"This spider's venom runs through our veins. If it would have been able to finish feeding on Cindy, Ell, and I, we would have become its slaves...forever. Death would have been the only release." Max turned his attention to their captive. "Where were you to take us?"

"To a secret base in Colorado."

"Colorado? Not Nevada?" Max questioned.

"Yes, Colorado."

Max took out his communicator and typed a message before putting the truck in gear and starting down the highway once more. He hastily increased their speed. *We are running out of time.*

"Is there anything else you want to tell us?" Larry asked.

"He told me all we need to know. We have to go. We can't play this game any longer. When they come back we will destroy the helicopters, blow the truck, and get out of here," Max said.

"What about him?" Larry nodded to the soldier.

"We can't leave him behind. We've already said too much in front of him. We take him with us. I don't think he is truly evil, just caught up on the wrong team," Max said.

"So, this virus is real?" the soldier questioned with a terrified look.

"Yes, and we only have two weeks to try to stop it," Max reported.

"What about what he said?" Larry spoke up. "That you and Cindy hold the cure. Maybe we're heading down the wrong path?"

Max met Larry's gaze. *Wow! Maybe he's right. Should we go back and work on a cure instead of trying to take down the whole system?* "Well, if they're creating the virus, maybe they've...surely they've created a cure too. I don't know how long it would take us to create a cure. That's still something we need to take into consideration."

"So that's where we're heading?" Larry asked.

Max nodded. *Hudich might not want a cure. He would love the ability to control everyone, even his biggest supporters. There would be no possible uprising among his followers. No other factions trying to overthrow him.* "Hudich probably doesn't want a cure."

"What?"

"Well, whoever sent him," Max nodded to the soldier, "obviously has some power in his organization and they have yet to hear of a cure."

After this last comment, they fell silent. Max was sure Larry had a lot more questions but was holding his tongue in front of the soldier. Max wanted a few answers from Larry as well. He had been around Hudich and his dad is in Hudich's inner circle. *He may know things.*

They had traveled for almost thirty minutes when out of the north two small black dots appeared and gradually increased in size.

"Here they come," Larry pointed out.

"You take the helicopter on the right. I've got the one on the left. Use a spell to turn off their engines."

"Is that how you brought that one out of the air before?" Larry questioned. "So that's what you meant by spells working on machines?"

"Yep!"

"Cool. That is a huge piece of information," Larry said and smiled.

"Yeah, but if the thing is traveling too fast, like a jet, it is almost impossible to hit it with a spell."

"Where did you learn magic?" the soldier questioned, full of curiosity.

"Not now." Max floored the truck, racing toward the approaching helicopters.

A few miles before the helicopters were on top of them they fired several missiles, targeting the highway, creating a massive hole to block Max and Larry's path.

"These boys mean business this time," Larry noted.

One helicopter flew straight for them while the other began to circle. When the circling one reached a good angle, rockets blasted the pavement to keep Max from turning back.

"Now!" Max yelled. "*Ugasni*, helicopter!"

Larry uttered a word Max had never heard but both aircrafts dropped out of the sky. This time they fell from a greater height than the previous one. They hit the ground and exploded into two big balls of fire.

Max stopped the truck at the edge of the smoking pit created by the missiles that had blown up in front of them.

"Wow, that was really simple." Larry followed Max to the edge of the pit. "I totally would have tried to knock it out of the air, which may or may not have been successful."

"Like I said, I just discovered it by accident a little while ago," Max commented. "I'm thinking we drive the truck into the pit and then detonate the charges."

"That works. Although, I think you should rig the gas from a ways back and send it into the pit at full speed. That might make more sense. Like we knocked them out of the air but not before a missile created the obstacle and we couldn't stop."

"I like it."

They returned to the vehicle and removed the soldier and everything they planned on taking with them. Max pulled out a map and he and Larry decided on their landing spot. Then they backed the truck up about fifty yards from the crater and activated the charges. After rigging the throttle, they sent the truck speeding into the pit.

The truck flew into the hole and impacted the northern side of the crater. They watched anxiously for a moment before the charges went off, sending a ball of flames and smoke into the air.

A moment after the explosion, the distant sound of more helicopters caught their attention.

"We need to go now. You take the gear and I'll take the prisoner," Max suggested.

They raced to where they had set all the items on the freeway, and a moment later they landed in the middle of a city park in St. George, Utah. They immediately checked their surroundings for any signs of danger, then hurried over to huddle under a tree to get out of the open. The waist-high grass swayed in the wind. The tall growth plus the tree helped give them cover.

"Do you see anyone?" Larry asked. "Why did we choose St. George?"

"For a couple of reasons. One, the base we're heading to *is* in Nevada about three hours away and two, Utah has many gathering places for the forces of good. There was a massive purge of those against socialism or communism when the government fell, but those who survived and love this country and fight for good are now gathering here."

"Really?"

"Hey, these people were prepared for bad times and were able to help many others seeking shelter and freedom," Max said and smiled. He took out his communicator and typed a message. He only had to wait a few minutes for the response. "Well, Cindy and the others should be here tomorrow. They made it to one of the largest camps preparing to take back our country."

"So our little decoy worked."

"Not only that, because of..." Max looked at the soldier, "what's your name?"

"Rich," the soldier responded.

"Because of Rich and you, we might have other options. I agree we should be working on a cure as well as trying to take down their operation to spread the virus," Max said.

"How are they building a virus that you are immune to?" Larry questioned.

"It's a long story." Max scanned the area for any sign of life.

"We have a day until Cindy gets here," Larry said.

"It all goes back to that book Hudich wanted four or five years ago," Max started. "Let's go to that white building a few blocks away." Max pointed to the spires of an immaculate white building to the east of their position.

"Are you sure this place is safe?" Larry hesitated, eyeing the top of the structure over the roofs of houses obstructing their complete view of the building with the pinnacles. "And yeah, I remember the book."

"Yes, I'm sure, but don't give away details about what we are doing," Max cautioned while they gathered up their equipment.

"How can I? I don't know exactly what we *are* doing," Larry said as they started up the street toward the white building.

They walked down the middle of the neighborhood, trying to demonstrate by their demeanor they didn't pose a threat. They had barely gone forty yards when they found themselves surrounded by a group of armed men.

"Who are you and how did you get inside the city?" one of the men demanded.

Max, Larry, and Rich raised their hands above their heads.

"My name is Max and this is Larry and Rich." Max nodded to Larry then Rich. "We're friends. I'm Joseph Rigdon's grandson. He should have sent you a message we were coming."

"I don't know anything about it. We'll have to clear it." The man took out a wireless radio and called it in. "Are we expecting anyone by the name of…"

"Max Rigdon," Max repeated.

"Max Rigdon."

"Yeah, did he arrive?"

"That's affirmative," the man repeated.

"Bring them to headquarters right away," the voice through the radio ordered.

"Rich, here, isn't really with us. You need to find a place for him, maybe have someone check out his injuries," Max pointed to Rich after lowering his arms.

"Prisoner?" the leader questioned.

"Yep!" Larry added.

The leader nodded and a few of the men took Rich and escorted him away. "Move!" The leader pointed in the opposite direction of the white building. "Headquarters is just four blocks west at the end of the street in an old church building."

"What is the white building there?" Larry indicated the structure that had caught their attention upon arriving in the park.

"That is a temple. It is over a hundred years old and a symbol of love, hope, and peace. But we run day-to-day operations of taking care of the city out of a church down the street."

After Max and Larry had met the leaders of the city, they were fed and given a place to sleep.

"I had no idea there were groups this well organized," Larry commented after they were finally alone.

"Yep. These people have been preparing for catastrophic events for hundreds of years. It's like they knew something big was coming for centuries," Max replied.

"Anyway, about the book?" Larry asked.

Max spent the next half hour catching Larry up on the events surrounding the book and the secret tests and Cindy's blood.

"They still have people who were injected with Cindy's blood?" Larry asked.

"Yes, but I'm willing to bet it isn't Cindy's blood they are using to create the virus. I bet they are using Hudich's blood," Max added.

They sat in silence for a time until the lack of sleep finally overpowered them.

Max received a hard shove that woke him out of his sleep.

"It must be nice to sleep all day!" Cindy jeered.

Max squinted against the light and it took him a moment to figure out where he was. *Oh yeah, St. George.* "When did you get here?" Cindy and Lita came into focus while Larry stirred out of his slumber in a cot by the other wall. "And some of us needed rest after playing the decoy, so you could have a nice comfortable trip."

"Phew!" Cindy blew air through her lips and rolled her eyes.

"Anything new and exciting we should know about?" Max asked.

"I've learned a lot from Walter and his invention to stop magic. It's not hard to replicate, and we have passed the information along to every camp we went through," Lita informed them. "Plus, I think I have an idea how to implement this in battle, but I need to play with it some more. It was difficult without the right equipment."

"They've also agreed to help get us where we need to go or within a decent walking distance. They have known about the base we want to get to for a while, and have scouts watching it all the time. It seems

Grandpa had warned them about it and asked them to keep an eye on it after the fall," Cindy added. "I don't suppose you two geniuses have come up with anything?"

"Actually we, or I should say Larry, had on account of our taking a prisoner," Max said and looked at Larry, who actually appeared to be a little embarrassed. "And it's something we should start looking into right away."

"Well?" Cindy and Lita questioned after a moment of silence.

"The reason the paramilitary wanted you guys, is they think you hold the key to a cure for the virus," Larry finally spoke.

"WHAT?" Cindy exclaimed. "How would they have come to that conclusion?"

"It makes sense, doesn't it?" Max said, and Lita nodded her head in agreement.

"It makes perfect sense, but where would they have…I mean, how could they know?" Cindy questioned.

"I don't know. But Hudich has to know the virus probably won't work on you and me. Maybe he told them to take us. Maybe they were working for him, except why wouldn't Larry have known to watch out for us?" Max scratched his head then stretched.

"I still think they are working for a faction, like you said," Larry commented. "We were always told to kill you if we got the chance. They wanted you alive. Look how they shot around us and blew up the road in front and in back of us."

"True." Max quickly related all that had happened to them since they parted.

"Well, that gives us some more options." Lita smiled.

"I think you should take samples of mine, Cindy's, and Ell's blood," Max looked at Lita. "Again, I'm willing to bet they are making the virus from Hudich's blood so he will have the control, but I will also bet any of our blood would reject the virus."

"There is one thing I've been wondering or maybe scared to ask. If they used my blood to perform tests, why didn't I feel it?" Cindy asked.

"I have a theory about that," Lita said. "I even proposed the same question to Yelka. She thinks when you were, you know, down there before and doing what you were doing, you invoked that magic. You knew what you were doing and you wanted it. Now, if they are using it, you aren't invoking it, you're not trying to control others, so that magic is dormant."

"Hey, if that's the case, wouldn't that make the cure simple?" Max asked. "I mean, if we aren't trying to control anyone, then giving them our blood might just do it."

"Perhaps, but maybe it needs magic to activate it. Without the owner trying to gain control, it might just act like normal blood," Lita mused.

"Then they would definitely need to use Hudich's blood. Who else would be able to activate it?" Max declared.

"Not necessarily. Remember how they had learned magic from the book? Anyone I injected who knows a little magic could be a possible new zombie leader," Cindy pointed out.

"Good point but, again, I don't think Hudich would want to give anyone else that power," Max interjected.

"Max is right, and you're talking to someone who's seen him in person. He wants total control. If there is something out there that would make everyone his subject, he's not going to give it to another," Larry spoke up.

"I agree with Max. I'll take some samples of your blood and at least start looking into a cure. If we can create an antidote, we might be able to abort this mission," Lita said. "I'll go get my stuff." Lita hurried out of the room.

"So, where's Walter?" Max asked.

"Grandpa thought his invention was important enough that they opened the gateway when we were in Salt Lake City and took him back to the house. I guess Sky's got a real war going on back in Iowa," Cindy reported.

"That should be fun for Sky," Max said and laughed. "Did they say when they can take us to the base?"

"I think they said we can leave at nightfall. Are you guys hungry?"

"Yes!" Larry rose to his feet and patted his stomach.

The camp leader had assigned them an escort to take them where they needed to go. He was a tall lanky boy named Randy, with a lot of energy and spiked blond hair.

"What is the world outside like?" Randy asked while they sat around a table eating lunch. "Has it gone all Mad Max?"

"In a way, yes. But the world hasn't been decimated by nuclear war, so the landscape is still how you remember it," Max responded.

"We always believed that good and evil would be separated someday. I guess that day is here," Randy said.

"How many people are in this camp?" Larry questioned with a mouthful of food.

"About seven hundred and fifty thousand," Randy replied.

Larry nearly choked on his food, sending small chunks across the table. He quickly downed a glass of water. "Seven hundred and fifty thousand? How big is the wall around this place?"

"We don't have a wall." Randy flashed a large smile.

"How do you keep the enemy out?"

"Light. Dark doesn't like light," Randy replied.

"Yes, but how do you keep the Islamic terrorist fighters out?"

"Pigs and pig products. We aren't fighting them with weapons only, but a psychological battle as well. We've buried pig carcasses all around the camp and we smear a dab of pig fat on all our bullets. Then we post signs with pictures of pigs and stating these facts all around the perimeter of the camp. Their fear of being unclean when they die keeps them away." Randy grinned.

"That's genius." Max knocked over several items on the table in his effort to retrieve his communicator. His fingers shook as he sent Sky a message.

"What are you doing?" Cindy asked.

"Telling Sky and Grandpa about this. I'm all for using any advantage against these wacko's we can," Max said.

"So when do we leave?" Cindy changed the subject.

"Tonight. I'm to take you to meet your escorts in a couple of hours," Randy replied.

Joe and Yelka stood around a table in a room on the second floor of Joe's house with Walter, looking over his designs to block magic with electromagnetic fields.

"That is amazing," Joe said, completely enthralled by the blueprints. "I have often thought about this type of thing but didn't ever have the time to research and experiment with it."

"Yes, it took me a long time to perfect. At first I used the magic I learned to test it. I often worried I wasn't powerful enough to really experiment with it. After the country fell, I was one of the few who recognized the signs that dark magic had helped topple the country and was spreading throughout the world. Once we broke into camps, I had plenty of opportunities to try my equipment. I had to make minor changes but I haven't found anyone powerful enough to crack it yet."

"Incredible!" Joe admired the design.

"The real trick is complete isolation from the magical signals and absorption. If you don't absorb the signals and then destroy them magnetically, they impact on the shield like any normal solid object. Without absorption, any really powerful being will toss you and the shield around like any other thing. That's why normal electromagnetic fields don't stop spells," Walter reported.

"How much equipment do you need to protect a large camp and also make it expandable?" Joe questioned. "This could help us set up a gathering point."

"Sky?" Yelka glanced at Joe.

"Yes. This could give us a rallying point to move from or help in setting up new places. In order to do what we were asked, in taking back the United States, we will have to move against Washington eventually," Joe said.

"You're planning on taking the United States back?" Walter questioned with raised eyebrows.

"Yes. We've been on the defense for far too long," Yelka said.

"Well, all right then. I've been waiting for an opportunity to strike back at those devils since I had to go into hiding from them all those years ago." Walter rubbed his hands together.

"It's like the messenger told Max. Hope is contagious." Yelka smiled at Joe.

"Yep..." Joe's pocket started to vibrate, drawing everyone's attention. He fished his communicator out and read the message. "This is great news!"

"What?" Yelka and Walter asked.

"Max just sent some info on how to protect camps. It seems the Utah camps have been playing on the superstitions of the Islamic fighters. We need..." His communicator vibrated in his hand. "Sky is already asking for these items."

"What?" Yelka and Walter questioned a little louder.

"Pig byproducts," Joe responded.

"That is shrewd." Walter nodded.

"This day is looking up." Joe smiled as Linda entered the room, breathing heavily, followed by Donna and Martin.

"We found something that may be very important," Linda gasped, carrying the book of prophecy Joe and Yelka had retrieved.

"And it involves Max and Cindy," Donna added.

"A prophecy mentions Max and Cindy?" Yelka questioned.

"No, but it is in relation to the sickness spreading across the land. This prophecy is strange to describe and I'm not sure what it means," Linda said.

"But it could have bad consequences for them," Martin said and frowned.

Linda opened the book and placed it on top of Walter's schematics. "It's on the same page as the sickness prophecy, but harder to decipher as it looks like it is a magical prophecy. It seems to change each day as we move to stop it," Linda reported.

"What do you mean?" Joe asked as the group huddled around the book.

"Well, I took digital photographs of every page of this book so I could work on my computer and preserve the book. Ever since I translated the first part and Max and Cindy left, the jpeg became corrupted. At first I thought it was just a bad file so I took another picture. I looked at it on the computer and it was fine, but then a little while later it wouldn't open. I checked other photos I took and they seem to be fine. Finally, I wrote down the next part by hand and after the last file became corrupted, I checked my written one. It had changed, but the new part wasn't in my handwriting." Linda pulled out her handwritten copy and showed it to the group.

"How can this be?" Walter questioned.

"The book definitely has magical properties," Yelka commented.

"Well, here's my theory," Linda said, "I think we can't stop certain prophesies from happening. They are going to happen no matter what. This next part changes as we attempt to mess with the fulfilling of that particular prophecy."

"That's an interesting theory." Joe scratched his chin thoughtfully. "Well, there must be something Max and Cindy are supposed to do where they are going, or why else would the messenger send them there, even if the sickness is going to spread? So what does this next prophecy say?"

"I don't know if it's a prophecy or a warning."

"How so?" Yelka's eyebrows raised questioningly.

"I've studied all kinds of ancient languages and, in the Bible at least, when there is a woe before something, that's a warning. Three in a row is the worst and, as far as I can tell, this one has three woes in front of it," Linda said and frowned.

"Let's hear it," Joe urged.

"Woe, woe, woe unto those who attempt to interfere with the coming of The One. All things must come to pass to bring about peace. A speedy destruction is pronounced upon the heads of those who attempt to thwart the ways of The One."

"That doesn't sound good," Yelka commented.

"There's more and this is the part that keeps changing," Linda said and eyed Joe.

"Only through great sacrifice of a loved one can they be saved."

17

A Familiar Face

Hudich sat slouched on his throne in a darkened chamber. The hall before him was empty and only torch light flickered around the room. He closed his red rat eyes and enjoyed the euphoria of his new powers.

He looked out of the eyes of his first subject. He could see a room outside of a solid glass wall where people in white lab coats observed him taking notes.

They would ask him to perform certain motor functions, like stand on one leg and Hudich would respond. They also held up charts and had him identify different objects to which Hudich responded in his new subject's voice.

"Was he given an injection like before or was he infected by other means?" Hudich asked.

"This one was administered through drinking water. We are still working on the airborne virus and hope to have it ready for testing in the next week. Our conclusions are correct. You have to activate the virus magically in order for it to work. We tried it on others where you weren't involved, and the virus showed no effect." The scientist looked nervous reporting this information.

"You have one week. Do *not* fail me. I'd hate to have to pay you a personal visit." Hudich detached himself from seeing through the victim's eyes. He could still see the lab in the back of his mind, but he could ignore it and go back whenever he wanted.

The door to his chamber opened and Alan strolled into the room wearing a long black cape over his expensive suit. He walked with confidence across the distance between the doors and Hudich. When he reached Hudich, he bowed to the ground on one knee.

"What news?" Hudich fully blocked the images coming from his latest victim.

"I've set those fools in Washington after Max and Cindy as you ordered," Alan reported.

"Good. They could hold the key to undoing what we are about to set in motion," Hudich said and meshed his fingers together in front of him.

"What would you have me do now, my Lord?" Alan raised his head to meet Hudich's gaze.

"Make a call. Send our little pusher to Nevada. I want to make sure they are properly motivated."

"Now?"

"Yes."

Alan took out a cell phone and made a quick call.

"Now, we are going to take a little trip. Things are not progressing as I had hoped against Israel. We need a little motivational visit to speed things along," Hudich grumbled.

"Why is Israel so important to us? And haven't we already successfully turned the world against them? They are hated among all nations once again," Alan questioned.

"We have, but they are a driven people who have learned from the past. They will remain strong in the face of adversity. They will not be broken as easily as the United States was. And because freedom is contagious, we need to destroy them. Israel is the last living democracy left in the world and we need to crush it. We can't let freedom or hope spread. It could complicate our plans. That is another reason why the virus is so important. We also can't risk a rebirth of the United States, as they were once Israel's biggest ally. We can't risk the two joining forces once more," Hudich responded.

"But I thought the virus will take care of that no matter what." Alan said.

"They still haven't perfected the airborne version and we need to anticipate that old fool interfering with our operations as he always does," Hudich growled, slamming his clenched fists down on the arms of his throne before rising to his feet. He snatched up some robes that had been hanging over the back of his chair.

Alan flinched in response to Hudich's anger. "Where are we landing?"

"A command post in Gaza. Just follow me." Hudich wrapped the robes around himself tightly, even covering his head with a hood that partially concealed his face, and then he disappeared in a flash of light.

Max, Cindy, Larry, Lita, and Ell followed two armed men on a dirt trail. They had left the trucks that had carried them this far in the bottom of a canyon. After loading a lot of the equipment in packs and on Ell, they proceeded on foot into the night. Millions of stars winked down on them from a cloudless sky. The Nevada air had a slight chill to it but otherwise it was a perfect evening.

The trail zigzagged back and forth, climbing up out of the canyon where they had left the vehicles. Max's heart rate increased and sweat formed along his back where the pack rested.

"I don't remember this canyon from last time," Cindy commented while taking a drink of water from a bottle.

"You were here before?" one of the guides questioned.

"Yes," Cindy responded.

"When? Why?" the guide pressed.

"Last year as a prisoner," Cindy added.

"Then how would you remember this?"

"Ah, you're right," Cindy said, shooting Max a sideways glance.

When they reached the crest of the canyon, their guides brought them to a stop before they popped out of the crevasse.

"Wait here. We have a hidden observation station, but we need to let the guards know we are here. Then we will probably have to take the last hundred yards in smaller groups because the cameras and patrols move at regular intervals. We will be out in the open and more bodies are an easier target to spot," the guide said.

Everyone tried to find a comfortable seat on a rock or raised portion of ground while one of their guides slipped away. Ell lay on his stomach in the center of the trail. Cindy went to him and put her hand on his side.

"That's amazing," said the guide who remained behind, watching them. "I wouldn't want to meet him in some dark forest if I didn't know he was a friend."

"Oh, he wanted to eat me at first," Cindy said and laughed.

"Really?" Larry questioned. "How did you meet him?"

"Actually, I have you to thank for that." Cindy quickly related how she had met Ell in the world of the Zeenosees after Larry and his friends had scared her into the gateway on Max's first summer with Grandpa.

"Ell says thanks," Cindy said after she finished the tale. "He didn't know that part about you scaring me though."

"Glad I could help," Larry said.

They waited for twenty minutes before the other guide returned. "Okay, I'll take two of you and the creature," nodding to his companion, "he'll bring the rest in about twenty minutes."

"You and Lita take Ell," Max said and nodded to Cindy. "Larry and I will follow."

"So, how are we going in?" Larry questioned after the others had been gone a little while.

"I'm not sure. But, you'll have to stay with Lita if we do go in. We can't afford to have anyone become a zombie. Cindy, Ell, and I should be fine but anyone else would give away all our plans," Max said.

"What *am* I going to do with Lita?" Larry groaned.

"Dude, she is the smartest person I know. You could learn a ton from her if you wanted. Stuff that would only add to your existing magical talents," Max encouraged.

"Okay," Larry said and exhaled.

"Do you know how far underground this thing goes?" the guide asked. "We've been watching this place for almost a year now and still don't have details about the structures under the surface."

"It is several stories and the structures are connected by a maze of tunnels," Max reported.

"Have you been inside?" the guide questioned.

"Yes, but it is all a jumble. We were trying to find Cindy and fighting our way through. I couldn't find my way around now if my life depended on it. Cindy has details of the whole layout in her mind, but unlocking that could be dangerous," Max said, rubbing his arms from the slight chill his cooling sweat had created.

"Because of what she could become?" Larry asked.

"Yep!"

"What's that?" the guide asked.

"Something none of us want to see," Max added.

"Did she used to work for the enemy?"

"No. She just got caught up in something she couldn't control."

"Well, that's why it is very important to avoid evil at all costs. You never know how playing with something you shouldn't will turn around and bite you in the butt," the guide admonished.

"So true." Max agreed.

The guide checked his watch and then rose to his feet. "It's time to go."

Max and Larry followed the man through a section of hills that kept them out of sight of the base. This lasted for about a quarter mile when they came to a stop behind a large patch of sagebrush, with the base sitting in a valley about a mile away. A fence lining the wide perimeter had lights every twenty yards so that any intruders would easily be spotted. Five warehouse-type buildings occupied the center of the fenced-in area. Men with dogs patrolled the inside of the fence, making regular passes.

"After the next guard goes by we wait about a minute, then we break for that massive rock." The guide pointed to a boulder the size of a house sitting on the side of a hill overlooking the compound.

"Okay," Max and Larry agreed.

The man put up his hand when the next patrol appeared. The sentry walked his dog in the direction of the large boulder. When the guard was far enough ahead of them, their escort lowered his arm and they started forward, hunched over. They moved at a quick pace but not fast enough to overtake the lookout.

When they reached the backside of the rock, Max spotted Ell resting behind the gigantic stone.

"He's too big to get through the door," the man responded, and opened a door cut right into the backside of the boulder.

Max and Larry stepped into a regular outpost behind the guide. There was a small kitchen, a room with cots, a restroom, and a control room.

"Do you have indoor plumbing?" Larry questioned.

"Well, sort of. We have to pump water in and the pipes just carry the wastewater out to an old sewage plant a mile away.

Inside the control room, a glass window about a foot high stretched across the front wall overlooking the camp. Several high-powered telescopes, cameras, radios, and listening devices stood where users could amass information.

"They can't see that window from the base, I take it?" Max motioned toward the glass.

"Nope, it's tinted and the rock has a slight overhang, which helps keep the sun from reflecting off of it," said a man who introduced himself as Wesley. "So, you're here to break into the place?"

"Yes," Max responded flatly.

"I can't wait to hear this plan. I've been here the longest and I haven't got a clue as to how I would break in," Wesley said and whistled.

"We have intimate details of the base that may help us get in," Max said and glanced at Cindy, who appeared to have gone as white as a ghost.

"I'm scared," Cindy whispered, her eyes glued to the base.

"Yes, but I think that's why you can safely visit those memories. You don't want to be like that again." Lita put a comforting arm around Cindy's shoulders.

"Plus, Ell and I will be with you all the way this time," Max said.

"I think that's a good idea," Lita said, giving Cindy's shoulders a squeeze.

Cindy continued to look pale and nervous. "Why don't we get all these people's intel first before we go searching through my mind?"

"That isn't going to take very long," Wesley replied. "We mostly have security detail routines and times. When we first set up shop an occasional truck would show up, but since fall everything is flown in. That is also on a specific schedule, which we have recorded. We pick up ground communications from the surface every once in a while, but it's just regular reports from the guards."

"Nothing strange? No uptick in activity at any time?" Cindy questioned.

"No, not really. It appears all their supplies and personnel are now brought in by planes and are stationed here permanently," Wesley reported.

"From what you know, if we wanted to break into this place, what would be the best time of day?" Max questioned.

Wesley exchanged a confused look with the two guides. "Ah...*Never*. I don't think it can be done. At least, not by any way I've noticed or based on the information we have."

"All right! All right! I'll do it!" Cindy rose to her feet and started pacing around the room. "But, you and Ell definitely have to help me."

"Um, what are you talking about?" Wesley scratched his head, confused.

"Lita can explain it to you as we work. I think we need to get this over with while it's still dark. How safe is Ell going to be out there once the sun is up?" Max questioned.

"He should be all right if he's not moving around too much. The biggest problem for him might be the desert heat in the daytime," one of the guides said.

"It's a good thing we gave him that haircut," Max said and laughed.

Cindy cracked a smile but a moment later her worry returned. She continued to walk the floor, chewing on her nails. She stopped and shook her arms out at her sides while taking a deep breath. "Okay, let's get this over with."

"What do you need us to do?" Wesley questioned.

"I think you should help Lita set up her equipment. Larry, we need you to come watch over us. We will be vulnerable when we take this trip through Cindy's memories," Max said, noticing Cindy's look of 'no-way' out of the corner of his eye.

Everyone followed Max out to the back of the rock where Ell rested comfortably.

"Let me tell him," Cindy said and placed a hand on Ell's forehead.

Lita put the men to work hauling her equipment into the small base, while Max looked for the ideal place for he and Cindy to sit next to Ell.

"You might want to go grab a chair," Max told Larry, who quickly disappeared back into the base and returned a moment later with a folding camping chair.

"Where are you guys going to be?" Larry questioned as Cindy removed her hand.

"I think we could just lay back against Ell's stomach like when we went camping," Max suggested.

"Okay," Cindy agreed with a worried tone. "I just hope we aren't making a big mistake."

Max took Cindy by the hand and gave it a squeeze. "It'll be all right."

They sat and leaned against Ell's massive stomach.

Cindy told you what we are going to do? Max thought.

Keep her from going all zombie-queen-psycho on us again, Ell thought with a teasing tone.

Hey! Cindy responded.

A smile spread across Max's face at Ell's amazing power, which not only gave him the ability to communicate, but to transmit feelings as well.

Okay, how are we going to start? Max asked.

I think the safest way would be for Cindy to relax and let me pull the memories out of her, Ell suggested.

The only problem is, I don't know if I can relax, Cindy said.

Just think about something fun, Max suggested. *You know, like the time you broke Larry's nose.*

You broke Larry's nose? The same Larry who is watching over us now? Was it an accident? Ell asked.

Yes, I did. And, no, it was on purpose, Cindy thought and laughed.

I knew he used to be an enemy but I never heard this story.

Ell and Max listened while Cindy related the events that led up to the nose breaking incident. Ell used his powers of communication to pull these memories out of Cindy's mind, so they could watch the story unfold from Cindy's perspective.

Soon, the images changed to happier memories of the three of them roaming the hills and forest around Yelka's house. They lay on a grass covered hill, looking up at the stars, while a warm summer breeze blew through the tall grasses of the rolling hills.

The scene changed again but this time to the base they had come to infiltrate. Max felt Cindy's body tense up next to him as the images continued to come uninterrupted. They explored above and below ground. There wasn't the tiniest detail that was missed. Max recognized some of the rooms where he and Ell had fought their way to Cindy.

After they had viewed everything about the base that could be seen, they dove into blueprints and diagrams of all the compound's components. Ell took them into large air vents that pulled in fresh air from the top of a mountain on the other side of the base. They followed several paths through these structures that would take them into the base unseen. Then security devices and protocols flashed across their minds, showing them how the base monitored these large air vents.

I think we have what we need, Ell spoke as the images stopped.

That wasn't so bad was it? Max asked.

No. I was afraid I would see the people I had affected and feel their emotions and hear their thoughts again, Cindy uttered.

I thought about that, but when I discovered you had seen more than just what people saw through their eyes at the moment, you also had viewed what guards had seen through security cameras when they were setting up the place. You had also seen the plans to the base through the eyes of those who helped design it. I figured those memories might stir up some bad emotions but not like seeing the people would.

Max sat up to see Larry standing a few feet away, watching the sun rise over the eastern horizon. "How long were we at it?"

Larry looked at his watch. "I'd guess a couple of hours. Did you find what you needed?"

"Yeah, there are some air vents on the mountain on the other side of the complex," Cindy reported.

"Anything happen while we were away?" Max questioned.

"Not out here. I can't answer for Lita. She may have some info but they haven't been out to give me a report," Larry said.

They all went into the base to observe Lita busy at her computer with the other three men looking over her shoulder. Lita had three large monitors set up and each displayed different aspects of the complex below.

"That's amazing!" Wesley said, looking at a 3D image of the top most sections of the underground complex. "And you're building that with sound waves?"

"Yes. Think of it like how a whale or a dolphin uses sonar. My software is learning software. It will decipher different materials by the sounds they emit. It will take a while but it should give us a pretty close representation of the underground complex," Lita informed them.

"What's that?" Larry questioned.

"The start of what Ell, Cindy, and I just saw in Cindy's memories." Max watched the screen.

"Not that. THAT!"

Everyone looked at Larry to see him pointing out the window to where a lot of activity was taking place. Several dozen ground troops had issued out of one of the buildings, along with a handful of military vehicles.

"I don't know. It looks like someone is coming in," Wesley announced. "But, I've never seen this kind of activity for an arrival."

"I have a bad feeling," Cindy murmured.

"Yeah..." Max added.

The troops formed two lines facing each other while standing at attention. A few nonmilitary personnel exited a building nearby and gathered at the end of the formation. One was dressed in a suit while the others wore white lab coats.

"There's a plane coming in," Wesley said with his head cocked at a slight angle.

The others listened as the faint sound of jet engines penetrated the secret outpost and increased in volume. Everyone moved away from Lita's computers and over to the window, several peering through the high-powered telescopes.

"That isn't a military craft." Wesley pointed to the private jet that appeared to be coming in for a landing.

The group watched quietly as the aircraft touched down and taxied to the front of the military lineup.

"It must be someone important. I've never seen this type of treatment for anyone before."

They waited until the stairs had descended and a teenage boy with brown hair shuffled down the stairs.

"It's *Brian*!" Larry said, and then a girl with bubble gum pink hair stepped out of the plane. "And Jo!"

18

A Prize Zombie

"What would Brian and Jo be doing here?" Max questioned, noticing the disgusted look on Larry's face.

"I thought…" Cindy started but stopped at a glare from Max. "*Oh!*"

"Apparently, someone wants to motivate certain people into working harder. They nicknamed Brian The Pusher because of his ability to make people do what he wants," Larry said. "Jo abandoned me when everyone else did, in case you were wondering."

"I'm sorry," Cindy said. "So, how is Brian these days?"

"What do you mean? Besides dating my ex-girlfriend?" Larry responded.

"Is there any hope for him? He didn't want to be with you originally. He was mostly good. And look at you. You changed. Is there any hope he would change?"

"There might have been a few years ago, but I think that light has long gone out. Hudich showed him a lot of attention and gave him a lot of authority because of his abilities. He is now power hungry like the rest of them. I may be wrong, but I don't think he will change. I mean, look how they treat him." Larry motioned to the window and the way the people at the base acted. "You'd think a rock star had just arrived. You know the old saying 'power corrupts.'"

"Yeah, I know it," Cindy said in a sad tone. "I know it all too well."

"Something here is not going the way Hudich wants or he wouldn't have sent Brian," Larry commented. "Or he needs something to stay on schedule."

"What did you guys learn, if anything?" Lita finally pulled their attention away from the new arrivals.

"Ah, yeah," Max said. "We may have found a way in through some air ducts positioned on the top of those hills." Max pointed to the hills on the other side of the compound.

"When we were there a little over a year ago, I set up an account inside their security. I can give you a wireless device that once you are inside, if you attach it to the correct wires, it might give me the ability to control the system. I'm usually pretty good at making my changes permanent and very well hidden. Although, those changes I made were under duress and over a year ago," Lita added.

"The problem might be getting past any security they have before we can get you in. It's not extensive out where the air ducts are but it is still there," Max reported.

"I do have a few tricks to fool cameras, but some stuff I won't be able to change without direct access," Lita said. "Did you notice any difference in the tightness of security during certain hours of the day?"

"Actually, we did. At least for the ventilation structure. They have to turn off some of their equipment during the heat of the day because temperatures here in the desert mess with their instruments," Cindy said, staring at the ceiling as if looking at some image in her mind's eye.

"Good catch, I didn't notice that," Max said.

"Yeah, but you're not that observant or very bright," Cindy jabbed.

"The hottest part of the day is between one and three-thirty pm. That only gives you a few hours to get ready." Wesley checked his watch. "I'd recommend going early, in case you run into a situation that takes time to work through.

"A few hours and my program will have mapped out more of the facility, and I will be able to offer you some more support." Lita nodded to her equipment.

"Let's decide on the absolute minimum we need to carry with us. The less we have to pack, the better," Max said.

They spent the better part of an hour figuring out exactly what they needed to take with them. Most of it was either weapons or electronic equipment from Lita. They loaded the items into packs with some water and a small amount of food, then tried to get a quick nap before they had to leave.

Max only managed a little sleep, which left him feeling more tired than he had been. When he did manage to doze, it was restless and full of dreams with never ending hallways and tireless pursuers.

"Max," Cindy said and put a hand on his shoulder. "It's time to go. Lita has laid out a path for us to follow that should see us safely to the air vents."

"Did you sleep?" Max questioned.

"Not really."

"Me neither."

Lita gave them a landing location and a route that would lead them to the vent. "If they are all on, I'm not sure how you are going to shut them down without anyone knowing, but let's worry about that when you get there." She handed each of them a headset and something that looked like a watch.

"What's this?" Max questioned while securing the band around his wrist.

"It will allow me to monitor your surroundings for all kinds of listening and security devices."

After double checking their equipment and Lita verifying she was getting a good signal, everyone followed them outside where Ell waited. Cindy put a hand on Ell's side to tell him where they were transporting to.

"Good luck," Larry offered.

"Stay on your radios. Let us know if you're in trouble and need help. I brought some toys that can create a nice distraction," Lita informed them.

"And I can use magic if necessary," Larry added.

"Hopefully, we won't need any help," Max said and then transported to a location on the top of the mountains on the other side of the base.

A few seconds later, both Cindy and Ell appeared next to him.

Max touched his headset. "Can you hear me?"

"Loud and clear," Lita responded. "Turn on your security detector."

Max switched on the device that was secured around his wrist. "Is it working?"

"I'll let you know if I read anything."

"That's comforting," Cindy murmured. "Shall we?" She adjusted the pack on her back and started hiking toward the air vents, following the path they had mapped out previously.

Ell followed Cindy while Max brought up the rear. The heat from the desert rose in waves off the surface of the mountain, creating an extremely uninviting environment. Sweat formed where the pack rested against Max's back and all along his forehead.

They worked their way east along the ridge of the mountain top. When they rounded a corner, they spotted three dump truck-sized pipes protruding out of the top of the mountain about fifty yards ahead of them

The vents lay on their side so the openings faced north. They ran for about ten yards before they bent and went right into the top of the mountain. The roar of fan blades chopping the air reached their current location.

"STOP!" Lita ordered through the headset.

Cindy signaled Ell to stop.

"I'm getting a reading on some of their equipment. One moment," Lita reported.

Max tried to see if he could spot anything, but with Ell blocking most of his view he could barely see the fans, let alone hidden security devices. He decided to send out his magical feelers to see if he could detect any magic in the immediate area.

"Good call," Cindy commented in response to Max's actions.

"I don't pick anything up, so we're clear as far as magical traps go." Max breathed a sigh of relief.

"There are heat sensors, but you shouldn't have to worry about those because the outside temperature is hotter than your body heat at the moment, however there is at least one camera," Lita said.

"Where?" Max and Cindy questioned simultaneously.

"About twenty yards ahead of you and on the right. I *think* it's pointing toward the vents so you should be approaching it from the rear."

"I don't see it," Cindy said.

"I will guide you. Start moving slowly forward and to your right."

"Do you detect anything else?" Max asked.

"Not at the moment," Lita replied.

They started forward once more at a much slower pace, while angling to their right. Lita called out direction changes to keep them on course.

"It should be two feet directly in front of Cindy."

"Where? All I see are rocks," Cindy reported.

"It must be disguised as a rock. Does one sit a little higher off the ground than the others? I'm sure they would want to protect it from ground water if it rained," Lita said.

"Yes. I see it."

Lita had Cindy place a small device on top of the rock they decided was the camera.

"Yep! That's it. Give me a second and I will send it a loop of the current image. Then when you go in, I'll turn off my decoy and reactivate it when you come out."

A moment later, "Okay, you can continue. I'm still not picking up anything else, so you should be good."

They approached the ducts, only to find the massive blades blocking their way forward. The noise from the large fans and the flow of air blocked out all other sounds.

"How are we going to get in?" Cindy questioned. "I think they're bound to notice if we just shut down their system."

"We only need to stop one," Max said. "They might not worry about just one. Lita, can you tell if there are any security measures on the pipes?"

"I'm not picking up anything."

"How do we get in?" Max questioned.

Max felt Ell put his head on Max's back. *Why don't we cut a hole in the side of the pipe?*

"Great idea," Max replied.

"What?" Lita and Cindy asked.

"Ell suggested we cut a hole in the side of the pipe," Max reported.

"That should work, if you don't cut through any electrical wires," Lita agreed.

"Is there any way you could tell us where the wires are located?" Cindy questioned.

"I think so, but if they are on the east side and you have to cut the hole on the side facing the camera, it will limit the amount of time you have to get in and get out," Lita reported.

"We'll cross that bridge when we come to it," Max said.

Lita had them use one of her special tools, which they put against both sides of the pipe, farthest from the camera, for several minutes.

"I don't detect wires on either side. They must be on the top or bottom of the pipe."

Max took out his laser gun and adjusted the strength of the weapon.

"Try to get it where you only create a hole on our side and don't go all the way through to the other side of the pipe," Cindy suggested as they stood ten yards back from the pipe.

"What do you think I am, an idiot?"

"Do you really want me to answer that question?" Cindy chuckled.

Max fired a shot at the pipe and they checked to see if the blast went all the way through. It took three shots for Max to get the right setting. Then, after adjusting the length of the blast to continuous, he slowly cut a hole big enough for Ell to enter the large system.

"Uh, guys, I have good news and bad news. The bad news is kind of a big problem," Lita reported. "My mapper has finished creating a diagram for the ventilation system down in the base."

"What's the good news?" Max interrupted before Lita could finish.

"It looks like the pipe runs in a slope so you should be able to slide right down to the bottom."

"And the bad?"

"It appears there are fan blades at the bottom and you, especially Ell, will not be able to stop before you run into it. Your speed will carry you right into the blades," Lita reported.

"We could use magic to clear our path," Max suggested.

"Yes, but my mapping doesn't show workers. You could set off every alarm in the place. You'd have everyone coming down on you before you got a chance to hunt for this virus," Lita pointed out.

"What are we going to do?" Cindy looked at Max while putting a hand on Ell to let him know the situation.

"I don't know. We're running out of time!" Max took out a flashlight and stepped into the pipe. The force of the wind prompted him to grab the lip where two pieces of pipe were joined together and lean backward hard to remain on his feet. "And the wind will increase our speed," he yelled above the wind.

"Ell has another idea," Cindy said in a somber tone, looking very nervous.

Max exited the pipe. "What?"

"It's not something I want to do or even trust myself to do, but it might be our only option. I can try to find someone on the inside," Cindy offered.

"You mean control?" Max raised his eyebrows.

"Are you sure that's safe?" Lita asked through their headsets.

"No. But it might be our only option. Again, I won't do it alone. Max and Ell will be with me. If I can find the right person, I may be able to shut down this vent. When Ell helped me escape what I had become, I was able to control myself and people at the same time in order for us to make our escape. I'm trusting Ell that we can do it again."

"Do you really want to try this?" Max eyed her. He noticed that the blood had drained from her face and she appeared to be trembling.

"Do we have another choice? We aren't going to be able to get inside any other way," Cindy answered. "This is probably our best and only option."

"Okay, let's do it." Max stepped up to Ell and put a hand on his front shoulder.

Cindy took up a position on the opposite side of Ell and stretched out her shaky hand. She paused a moment before touching him but then finally put her hand on him. *Keep me sane!*

How do you proceed? Max questioned.

I'm not sure. But I'm scared by the answer.

Do you want me to try to help you? Ell offered.

Yes.

Once more, images of Cindy's memories flashed through Max's mind. This time the experience was totally different. Back at the rock the memories had just been images, but now a lot of emotions flooded through Max as well. A wave of events from a full range of time, which weren't Cindy's, followed.

A deep, dark sensation crept over Max as he saw and felt horrible things and acts committed by people on one another. He saw and understood how many of these individuals felt at the time of their deaths. Max wondered how long this could go on and how Cindy would ever want to feel these emotions.

Here's one. He worked in security. I can't find any memory of his death. Ell suggested. *Ray Bradley.*

Ray, are you there? Can you hear me? Cindy tried to reach out to him like she was placing a phone call to a friend, with no response.

You're not going to do it that way. You need to command him not talk to him, Ell indicated. *You own him, remember.*

RAY!

A rush of adrenaline flooded through Max and all the hairs on his body stood on end. His mind swam with a warm euphoric feeling and a sense of power and control. Immediately, what Ray was seeing at that moment and time appeared in Max's mind, as if he sat in a chair right behind Ray's eyes.

Ray did not answer and Max could feel Cindy working him like a marionette puppet. Ray's head moved back and forth, taking in his surroundings. Without being told, Max knew Ray was not in the base but out with a military force.

Nope, we need someone else. You need to release him, Ell's voice broke the strange pleasant sensation and a moment later Cindy let go of Ray. *How do you feel?*

I'm good. We can try another, Cindy thought.

Wow! You're stronger than I am. I can't believe what a rush that was, Max commented.

It took you this long to realize I'm stronger than you? You are slow.

I think we need to stick with security personnel so no one will question their movements in the base, Ell suggested.

I agree, Max said.

It took another three tries to locate a security officer inside the base. Again, Max felt like he, Cindy, and Ell sat in a little control room of a large robot, patrolling the halls of the base below. It was like they knew everything he knew, security codes and passwords. It took thirty minutes for Cindy to move the guard through the complex and shut down the fan in the duct they wanted.

What are we going to do with this guard? Max questioned. *Should we let him go? Will he remember what he did or be clueless? We may need him to keep people out of the area until we are out of the shaft.*

That's a good question. What do you think, Ell? Cindy questioned.

Will you be okay holding him by yourself? Max and I will have to let go to slide down the pipe.

More to the point, will you be okay if Ell lets go? I'm seeing how this would be totally addicting. Max added.

I can handle it. Let's get moving, Cindy thought.

They separated to see the large fan had come to a stop. They all stepped inside the vent and cautiously approached the edge. A long dark tunnel greeted them.

Max ran his foot along the bottom of the aluminum pipe. "If we slide, these grooves are going to jar the crap out of us."

"Yeah, my backside is already feeling that." Cindy rubbed her bottom as if it had already taken a beating.

"Lita, we're in the tunnel. How far down is it? We can't slide. I'm thinking we need to transport ourselves to the bottom," Max said.

"One thousand and seventy-five yards at a hundred thirty-five degree downward grade. Be careful. If you're off, you're going to smack into a solid wall or fan," Lita advised.

"Hang here a minute. I'll check it out. I'll tell you if you need to make any course corrections." Max cast his spell and a moment later he landed at the bottom of the pipe. The large grooves in the duct caused him to lose his footing. He fell hard onto the floor of the vent, bruising his arms and hitting his knees. "That was fun." He winced as he climbed to his feet.

"Okay, it's like Lita said, but be careful when you land. I tripped on the grooves and ate it pretty hard," Max reported through the microphone.

A moment later the three of them stood behind the fan at the bottom.

"How do we get out of here?" Cindy stared at the blockade in front of them.

"The same as we got in. My gun is still on the same setting." Max took a few minutes to cut a hole in the side of the pipe, from which they exited. "Now you can tell him to turn the fan back on. It won't be pulling as much air in with the two holes, but it will show as working on any monitors."

Cindy gave the order and the guard reactivated the system.

"According to his shift, he's not allowed in the top secret levels of the base. We're going to need a different set of eyes," Cindy reported when the guard had finished. "Let me send him back to his desk and release him before we find someone else. Pay attention to who he sees as it might give us possible candidates."

"Do I dare suggest you hold on to him? He does have monitors and he knows what's happening up here. We need to be able to move around safely," Max suggested.

"Okay, but I'm going to keep a hand on Ell's side for the rest of this journey," Cindy confirmed.

"Good idea."

Once more, they made their small huddle before Cindy commanded the security guard to return to his desk.

WAIT! Max let go of Ell and fished Lita's security hacking device out of his pack and held it up for Cindy and Ell to see. He then walked to the guard and Cindy had the man take the equipment.

"Lita, we're sending your equipment with the guard. He's going to a main desk. You will need to walk us through hooking it up where it won't be seen by a shift change," Max spoke through his headgear.

"Got it. Tell me when you're ready," Lita responded.

Once Max rejoined the group, Cindy sent the security guard back to his desk and through the security monitors on his desk, they checked the safest route to the lower floors and times of security changes. Then, working with Lita, they acquired her full access to the system. However, the few people the guard passed in the hall didn't yield any solution to working their way to the levels down below.

I think we need to look for a scientist this time, Cindy suggested.

I also think we will need to take the ramp Ell and I used last time, Max recommended.

It didn't take them as long to find a scientist as it had to find the security officer. Cindy soon controlled the actions of a Mr. Knightley on the lowest level of the base. Using the information in his head, Cindy was able to figure out how and where they could get to the other levels, taking the ramp they used for hauling large equipment up and down with vehicles.

"My credentials are still good, I can get you onto the ramp. If you want to release the guard once you're on it, I will be your eyes and ears. I think you still need Mr. Knightley to help you move about the more secure levels, if not for anything other than a diversion, should you encounter anyone. You need to get to Sublevel 6, Room 604. That's where they are working on the virus. They also have a few testing rooms marked with subjects' names," Lita reported.

"Thanks," Cindy responded. "Let's just hope we don't run into any vehicles moving up or down the ramp."

"Does it indicate whose blood they used to create the virus?" Max questioned.

"It just says source unknown," Lita reported.

They snuck through the floor where the vents entered the facility. Going and stopping in response to commands issued by Lita through their earpieces. Twice, they had to use their invisibility spells to avoid being detected. A distracted janitor bumped right into Ell, but before he could put out a hand to search for the object he had collided with, Ell quietly stepped away, leaving the man confused.

After converging onto the ramp, Cindy released the guard and began paying attention to the scientist below. She gave him control of his actions, letting him go about his normal routine while only watching what he was working on. He sat at a computer, entering notes concerning his current workload.

They circled the spiral ramp, following it deeper into the complex. The sound of a garage door opening above froze them in their tracks. A vehicle entered the ramp above them but headed for the upper levels. Max, Cindy, and Ell each breathed a sigh of relief while exchanging looks of disbelief at their luck.

"Brian and Jo just entered the room." Cindy stopped midstride, staring at nothing in particular.

"What?" Max questioned.

"They're in the same room as Mr. Knightley," Cindy reported.

Max and Ell hurried to Cindy and they touched Ell so they could all see what was happening. Events as they were happening before Mr. Knightley's eyes appeared in Max's mind.

"Are you sure we're on schedule?" Brian questioned in a haughty tone, while picking up a syringe filled with a purple liquid from a container on Mr. Knightley's desk.

"Y—yes," Mr. Knightley stuttered.

"He sounds a little nervous." Jo blew a bubble that was the same color as her hair. The bubble popped loudly.

Max could feel the fear that coursed through Mr. Knightley. The emotion was so strong, Max had the urge to run and hide.

"There's no need to be worried," Brian continued in his superior tone. "If you are on schedule that is. Neither Hudich nor I like failure. We have big plans and what you're doing is critical to the success of these plans."

Boy, I wish we could read Brian's mind, Max commented.

What did you say? Cindy questioned.

Cindy, NO! Ell warned.

What? Max asked as the view moved, indicating Mr. Knightley had risen to his feet.

"I can give you a demonstration of our work," Mr. Knightley said and snatched up an empty syringe.

"A demonstration of your progress could be a good thing," Brian said, looking at Jo, who shrugged her shoulder.

"What are you doing?" Jo's eyes grew wide as Mr. Knightley put the needle in his arm and withdrew some blood.

"Come, I can show you under the microscope." Mr. Knightley motioned to one on a table across room.

He worked his way around the desk and when he reach Brian, he sprang on him, injecting the syringe into him.

19

A Dark Secret in the Park

"The word is out," Victor said and joined Sky outside the walls of the city, where she worked with Walter on burying some equipment of Walter's creation. "I was in the military a long time ago and we fought those animals then, but we had to fight by rules created from politically correct ignoramuses. I love that we're free to fight a psychological war. Play upon the fears of these dolts."

"Yeah, we're putting signs out all over the place telling them our bullets are painted with bacon fat and that we're burying pig carcasses everywhere," Sky said and wiped the sweat off her brow with her sleeve.

"I've been thinking, and Kip agrees, we want to go on the offensive some more," Victor proposed.

"Oh, I'm already working on it. I have Sam mapping out possible targets. We were told to wipe out the dark society. We can't do that if we are always playing defense," Sky added.

"It appears I joined this fight just at the right time." Walter looked up from where he was down in the hole. He held out his hands and Sky lowered the bucket-sized piece of electronics down to him.

"This thing you're setting up will block magic?" Victor questioned.

"Yes." Walter knelt down next to the item he had placed in the center of the hole. He made a few adjustments to a control panel on it.

"How long is its battery life?" Sky nodded toward Walter's invention.

"A couple of months. It is more of a reflector and doesn't really generate the field we will create over the camp. The main piece will be inside the camp and that sucker needs a lot of power." Walter began shoveling dirt over the device.

Once Walter had covered the entire piece of equipment he held out his hand, and Victor helped him out of the pit. Then the three of them finished filling in the hole.

"Anyway, hiding and watching evil spread across my country ate at my gut. I'm glad we are taking the fight to them," Walter added.

They paused as the sound of approaching vehicles rose above the construction noises that came from all over the camp. Not only were they fortifying the compound, they were expanding the area of the structure. The news of their victories had spread, and good people from all over the region wanting to be free were gathering to this location.

"You know, I was just thinking. If their eyes are here, they might not expect an attack some place much farther away," Sky said.

"How much farther?" Victor raised an eyebrow.

"Right in the heart of the enemy. Some place like Washington, DC. Let them know they aren't safe even surrounded by their fortified walls." Sky winked.

"I *like* it." Victor grinned.

"Are we done?" Sky asked Walter.

"Yep. At least until we expand and I have to move the anti-magical devices farther out. I don't want to put them out so far we can't protect them from the top of the walls," Walter added.

"Good idea. Let's go check on things and see where we stand. I'm thinking we will need the gateway to pull off the kind of message I want to deliver," Sky said and started walking back toward the camp entrance.

"Hey, a nice message would let them know we are serious after I sent them that text of 'You're Next' with those pictures of the vice president," Victor agreed.

Before they reached the gate, Jax met them with a couple of his men. "I see we have more recruits coming in." He motioned to the approaching vehicles.

"Yup. How's their training coming along?"

"Good. They're excited with the new weapons. You and I have been to a lot of these camps. The mood around here is awesome. It's the first one besides the large ones out west, where there is actual hope. I can feel it in the air and it's contagious," Jax said.

"Yeah, it feels good. Victor and I might go on a little trip that could bring even more hope. Would you like to tag along?" Sky smiled. Ever since Sky had finally accepted that Jax really was on their side, and not a traitor like his brother, their friendship had improved.

"Is it going to be the kind of fun that you and I like?" Jax questioned.

"Naturally. Your men will need to stay here, along with Sam and his troops. We don't want to leave these people on their own yet. They're still new to the equipment. But with Walter's special weapon and our psychological preparations, we might have bought a little time," Sky replied.

"HEY!" Sam called from the top of the wall. "Our missile defense system is up and running. We tied into existing satellites. With Lita's equipment, they won't even get close to us with any rockets or nuclear weapons. Her lasers will shoot them down before they get within a couple thousand miles."

"Excellent," Sky called back.

"It does sound like things might be safe enough here for a little payback mission," Victor said.

Sky, Jax, Victor, and Walter made their way into the command center in the middle of the camp. The number of people working in this area had increased significantly over the last two days until it had become a small city. Not only did they have to make preparations for war, but now they had to handle the influx of new people. This meant entire groups of people were designated to deal with handling food, medical needs, and shelter for everyone. There was another organization which dealt with expanding the compound. In addition to expanding the perimeters of the walls, they were also excavating to create underground levels. John had been selected governor of the encampment and had a constant cluster of messengers around him at all times.

In the middle of the room, they had designated a spot for the gateway to be opened and closed. Every few minutes, a group of people would arrive from areas too far away to travel safely by road. The people would be accompanied by people from John's camp who had been sent to convince them to move.

The new arrivals were quickly ushered off and put to work. The system was becoming like a well-oiled machine. Everyone understood they were in for the fight of their life and they saw this as the best opportunity to succeed against the vast evil spreading across the world.

Sky's group approached John while he conversed with a few others about the ongoing operations. He had noticeable bags under his eyes when he looked up at their approach.

"How are things coming along?" John questioned.

"It looks like we're ready," Sky reported. "Walter's put his magic blocking equipment all around the outer walls, and we've got some serious firepower to protect us from any kind of attack. How are things going in here?"

John exhaled heavily. "Everyone here's wanted to fight back for a long time. I knew it would be a physically exhausting struggle, but I could use a break."

"Well, we," Sky motioned to Victor and Jax, "have the start of an idea that might give you a time out."

"The start...of an idea?" John raised his eyebrows and then glanced to a room off to his left. He started toward it while motioning for the others to follow.

He only let Sky, Victor, Walter, and Jax into the room before closing the door.

"What do you have in mind?" John questioned.

"Well...we had so much success when we hit the enemy before they could launch their large scale assault, we figured we should do it again," Victor proposed.

"You don't think they will be expecting that?"

"They probably are, for any of their hold ups in the surrounding areas. We were thinking of striking someplace a little closer to the nerve center," Sky commented.

"How close?"

"Okay, against." Sky smiled.

"What do you mean against?"

"Into the heart of the enemy, the top dogs, the leadership," Jax added.

"That could be a suicide mission," John indicated.

"Yes, but you've got to admit, they won't be expecting that, which might give us all the advantage we need to pull it off," Victor said.

"We do need things to at least seem stable around here first, as we will need the..." Sky began

A loud warning siren interrupted Sky and startled everyone in the room. They all raced out of the room and then exited the building. They reached the outside just in time to see the laser cannons firing multiple shots in several directions.

They continued to fire for several minutes and then went silent.

Sky sprang up the steps to the weapons Sam had been monitoring and which had been actively firing only a few moments ago. Sky stepped into a small heatwave which had been created by the weapon's fire, when she reached the top where Sam hovered over a computer that was tied into the system.

"What was that all about?" Sky questioned.

"It appears they tried to dispose of us in a much more lethal manner." Sam typed away on a screen showing a dozen detonations from several directions.

"Nuclear?"

"I'm not sure, but Lita's system got them all. Some had just barely gotten off the ground. As soon as they made it above the curvature of the earth, these babies wiped them out." Sam patted the monitors.

"The lack of sleep we've all experienced to get them operational was well worth it." Sky exhaled with a slight whistle.

"WHAT WAS IT?" Victor called from below where a crowd had gathered and was staring up at them.

"We just thwarted a missile attack," Sky shouted down. "We are now a place to be reckoned with."

A roar of cheers spread across the camp as word of their success reached everyone.

"Hope is alive." Sky winked.

"Yes it is." Sam looked up from his monitor with a smile for the woman who had saved his life a little over a year ago when she rescued him from the clutches of the Dark Society.

Sky glanced around to make sure no one was climbing the ladder. "You've done a great job here. I might need you to keep an eye on things for a few days."

"I thought you were staying."

"Well…a few others and I think it might be a good opportunity to strike real fear into the hearts of your old friends. And now, having destroyed their most recent and obvious attempt at getting rid of us, I think we may have some time, as they will have to really plan out their next moves. Now that the easy choice didn't work, they will have to think about a strategy," Sky said.

"That's true."

"Do you think you can keep an eye on things around here? Walter will be staying and all of Jax's men. You won't be alone."

"You can count on me."

Sky patted Sam's shoulder. "Good man. Plus, with the little break we should receive while they contemplate their next move, we should be able to use the gateway."

Sky, Jax, Victor, and Kip stepped out of the gateway and into the third floor of Joe's house.

Joe, Yelka, and Rachel were there to greet them.

"A little war wasn't exciting enough for you?" Joe chuckled.

"Nope. It's okay to deal some small dents in the enemy's armor, but I'd rather penetrate it where we can do some real damage," Sky said.

"We've been gathering all the information we could from the limited flow of news currently available, to help us pinpoint where that might be accomplished," Joe reported. "It appears they are still maintaining their presence in the US Capitol."

"That's what we figured," Victor and Kip spoke at the same time.

"Why would they want to go anywhere else? It has been a symbol of power for over two centuries," Kip continued.

"Yes. Then we started digging through everything we could find about all the buildings related to the area as possible places to strike," Yelka added.

"Good! Let's go look over what you have," Sky urged.

"We've set everything up in a room on the second floor." Joe started to lead the way.

When they reached the designated room, Sky closed the door behind them. "So, how are Max and Cindy?"

"They went into the complex only an hour ago. Lita sent us a message at that time. She has access to everything in the base and will give us updates. But as far as we know, they're safe and fulfilling their mission," Joe said and glanced down at the floor.

"What aren't you telling me?" Sky said. "They're all right, but you *are* obviously worried about something."

"Linda has translated some things from the book we brought back, and they appear to reference what Max and Cindy are trying to do," Yelka spoke up.

"A *prophecy*? One talks about them *specifically*? You know how much stock I put in prophecies," Sky said.

"There is a prophecy about a sickness spreading across the land. Then, kind of a warning about interfering with such prophecies," Joe said with a sad expression.

"But the messenger?" Sky questioned.

"We gave that some thought too. There must be something they are supposed to do where they are currently at," Yelka added. "Or…this isn't the sickness spoken of by the prophecy."

"You believe in such things?" Victor eyed Sky with a bit of skepticism.

"Absolutely. I fulfilled one in my home world long ago, when I was a young girl," Sky said.

"Then this could be the end of times?" Kip asked.

"Yes," Joe affirmed. "Anyway, let's start making plans to take down this Dark Society."

"I'm here. What did I miss?" Linda entered the room.

"Nothing yet. We're just getting started. I thought Linda should be here, as she worked for this Dark Society and might have some valuable insights," Joe offered. He introduced Victor and Kip to Linda and gave them a little background on her story.

"Why don't we start with Linda telling us everything she knows about any individuals tied to the society," Sky said. "Or, maybe about anyone you think might have a connection, especially back east."

"And would still be alive and have connections there," Victor added.

"Well, like most of you know, I was in a secret lab not located in DC. But there may be a few possibilities who could be convinced to help us," Linda said.

"What type of convincing?" Victor questioned.

"A little leaning might be in order, especially the one I have in mind. His name is Stevie and he is a worthless excuse for a human being. He's a weasel and will do anything to be in the know. He'd kill his mother if it would benefit him," Linda said.

"Where do we find him?" Kip questioned.

"I think we will need at least three candidates," Sky proposed.

Linda supplied them with two more candidates who could give them inside information on the Dark Society. They used this information to draw up a plan to capture each individual based upon where they had once lived. Everyone agreed in order to make further plans to attack this Dark Society, they needed some inside help.

"Okay, I say we get a little rest. We've all been going for a couple of days straight and we need to be fresh. We don't know what we will find in the inner cities now. Look how different things are outside with the camps and all," Sky pointed out.

"Agreed." Everyone responded.

Hudich and Alan touched down in the middle of an empty street. The star-filled night sky met them with the sounds of distant gun and rocket fire. The city lay in darkness, with no visible sign of electricity.

They walked down the center of the street, with Hudich leading the way. They weaved down streets and alleyways. Twice, the sounds of hushed conversations floated in the air, but no one moved around them. Most of the buildings they passed had been hit by machinegun fire or worse. Large gaping holes indicated areas where battles had been waged.

Hudich walked at a brisk pace through the city. He led Alan toward an alleyway where two armed men wearing head scarfs stood before the entrance. The men tried to block the way when Hudich put up a hand and flicked his fingers. A shockwave knocked the two men to the ground.

After stepping over the two unconscious men, Hudich and Alan went to a door on the left, midway down the darkened alleyway. Hudich didn't bother to knock but just burst his way into the room, surprising a group of ISIS fighters and two demons making plans around the table.

"Hudich," the demons uttered, and dropped to a knee while bowing their heads.

The terrorists around the table exchanged confused glances before following the example of the demons.

"I *am* not pleased with the progress here. I expected this small country to fall long ago, and yet you don't appear to have made any advantages against them," Hudich growled. "We can't let this become a beacon for freedom. Why haven't you been successful in breaking them?"

Slowly, the demon and the others rose to their feet.

"They are the most prepared people for war on this planet. They are unified and well trained. We have a difficult time cracking their defenses," one of the demons responded in a deep voice.

"They have also managed to weaken our armies along every border. We lose more men than we are able to spare," one of the militant fighters added. "We need more men."

"Hmm!" Hudich responded.

All eyes in the room stared at the tall dark cloaked figure. His face remained hidden below his hood.

"Sir," Alan spoke. "We successfully turned the world against these people through propaganda. We have the numbers, if we just push more lies. I suggest we set things in motion. The world will be a better place without Israel. They are the cause of all this misfortune and suffering. They robbed the riches of the world and left everyone else in ruins. This type of propaganda worked before we overthrew the rest of the free world. Now we just use those we have enslaved and drive them to help annihilate the Jewish state. These armies will come out of the north in huge numbers."

"Set it in motion," Hudich ordered, and Alan gave a slight bow of his head. "It will create a force they cannot deal with. Once this last free society falls, we will rule all. But...just," Hudich paused for a moment. "Do you think you can slip something into Israel's water supply?"

"We have tried poisoning them many times, without success," one of the terrorists said.

"But you know where to put contaminants in the water?" Hudich demanded.

"Y—yes!"

"What are you thinking?" Alan questioned.

"The scientists have the virus in a soluble state where it can be acquired through drinking water. It's something Israel won't be looking for. It's magical not biological. I say we test it here. Go with the other plan but let's try the virus, as well. I don't want this to go on any longer," Hudich growled. "We will pay the lab a little visit after we finish our work here."

"Excellent." Alan bowed again.

"Now, take us to see where you've attempted to poison the water supply." Hudich demanded. "Maybe I can find a weakness."

###

Sky, Jax, Victor, and Kip touched down in the southern section of Anacostia Park, right into the middle of a tent city on what used to be a golf course. Several people dressed in shabby clothing looked up from campfires, confused by the sudden appearance of the strangers. Although everyone peered at them with a mixture of fear and curiosity, the people kept their distance. Many with children ushered them into the closest tent.

"Wow, I never would have thought it would be like this. I used to love golf. I can't imagine why people thought socialism would actually be better. This stinks," Victor said. "But maybe there are still some good people left in the cities."

"We aren't exactly in the city yet," Kip pointed out. "These people might have been forced from there."

At Kip's remarks, the poverty level of these people became apparent. The entire place looked like a large slum. There was trash everywhere, while it appeared that food was scarce.

A small boy in worn out clothing approached the group, holding out his hand. Sky handed him a granola bar. The boy's eyes grew large as he accepted the gift and scampered away.

Jax held a map out in front of him while they walked. "So, according to Linda, this guy might be in an apartment on Gales Street. It's about a thousand yards west of here."

As they weaved their way through the tents the people acted the same, hiding and keeping their distance. When they got within sight of the city, a barbed wire fence appeared to keep people out. They slowed their pace so they remained in the camp but could study the fence. Armed guards patrolled the fence, and towers had been built at regular intervals for spotters to watch for anyone attempting to enter.

"What's this all about?" Sky questioned.

"What do our executioners want with us today?" asked an old stocky man who had been sitting in a camping chair, watching them.

"I beg your pardon?" Sky asked.

"I'm just curious what our rulers want from us now. It isn't that time of the month yet or are you speeding things up?"

"Sorry, we don't know what you're talking about," Jax replied.

"*Sure* you don't."

"We're just trying to reach the city. How do we get through the fence?" Kip questioned.

"Like if I knew the answer to that question, I would tell a government stooge," the man said.

"Do we *really* look like we're from the government?" Victor questioned.

The old man eyed Victor up and down for a moment. "You were in the Marines?"

"Yes," Victor responded, glancing down to see his Marine Corps tattoo showing. "I swore to protect the United States against all enemies, foreign and domestic. Right now, the government is the enemy."

"Amen to that." The old man seemed to soften a bit and then revealed the same tattoo on his forearm.

"What's with the fence," Victor questioned.

"They don't want any undesirables in the city," the old man answered.

"How do they determine who is unfavorable?" Sky questioned.

"It depends on what you have to contribute to the society in there. If you don't have anything they want, they don't need you," the old man said.

"They pushed you out into camps?" Kip asked.

"For a while, but they eventually herd us up and ship us out." The man shook his head.

"To where?" the group questioned.

"I don't know where but only to say the end of the line."

"End of the line?" Victor raised his eyebrows.

"Come on man, what do you think happens every time Socialists and Marxists come into power. Those who are determined useless are eliminated. Oh, they sold it really well, making it out to be this great equalizer. How it would be fair to everyone. And we bought it—hook, line, and sinker. Now all these poor people have to look forward to is a date with death. They will be loaded up and shipped out."

Sky hurried closer to the man and the others followed. She took a knee to be level with him. "We might be able to help them, but we need to get into the city."

"How can you help them? There's no way to get them out of here. That fence goes all the way around the park and there are armed guards and dogs keeping us in," the man said.

"So you don't know a way into the city?" Victor watched a guard about a hundred yards away, walking a dog on the other side of the fence.

"I didn't say that. But most of these people fear going inside so they don't think to try escaping that way. The other side of the park is much more heavily patrolled. Anyone caught trying to escape is shot on sight," the man informed them. "How do you think I know what happens to people in this camp. I've been here a long time because I disappear on shipment days. They aren't registering occupants so there are a few of us who keep slipping through the cracks."

"If you know how to get out of here, why aren't you smuggling people out?" Jax frowned.

"We tried that at first, but we can only get them back into the city. Most are recaptured and placed back here. We don't have the resources to give them true freedom. Now we try to make their last few days bearable. We bring them food and other things to help. It's a sad situation." The man shook his head with disgust.

"What we are trying to do may very well help these people," Sky said. "We don't have time to give you all the details at the moment, but we need to get inside to find someone. This person may have information that will help us topple those who are currently in power."

"You're serious?" He looked at the small group. "Wait a second. How did you get inside if you weren't placed here by them?" He jabbed a thumb over his shoulder to point at those by the fence. "I mean, if they didn't put you in the camp why would you need my help in getting back out when you obviously got in?"

"Let's just say there is a line to use the method that got us here and we just moved to the back of it. I'm Sky, this is Victor, Jax, and Kip." Sky motioned to each in turn. "We could use some help."

"I'm Robert. And what's in it for me?"

"We can get you out of here," Sky said.

"Just me?"

"We might be able to arrange for the whole camp to be moved to a gathering point, where we are waging war against the powers that be, and winning," Sky reported.

"*Winning*, pff!" Robert exhaled through flapping lips. "Last I heard, everything collapsed. And now the government controls all."

"Did you hear about the recent death of the vice president?" A smile spread across Victor's face.

"No. When? Where? It's probably just rumors to give people a false sense of hope and lure them into some sort of trap." Robert waved a dismissive hand through the air.

"That depends." Sky smiled brightly.

"On?"

"Who is telling the story or rumor? Now, say the people who happened to *off* the vice president are telling the story and have proof, it wouldn't be a rumor but fact." Sky stood and motioned for Victor to step forward.

"You're joking, *right*?" Robert looked at them with a little more wonder in his eyes.

Victor stepped forward and showed the footage of the vice president's demise.

Robert sat silently for a moment, shocked. His eyes kept jumping from the phone to the group. "I'll get you in!"

20

Not What it Seems

Robert took a radio out of his jacket. "It looks like clear skies on the horizon."

Sky and the others glanced upward.

Robert held the radio up. "There are unfriendly ears and they're always listening. Follow me." He rose out of the chair and escorted them deeper into the camp.

Robert walked with a slight limp but still had a good gait. He took them toward a section of the camp nestled under a group of trees. There, tucked under the largest tree, a makeshift tent had been constructed by tying several tarps to the tree and then staking them to the ground in a large circle around the trunk. There were no sidewalls, only the roof.

Two men, identical twins with dark curly hair, sat in chairs next to a small campfire where the hole in the tarp above them let the smoke out. One of the men bounded out of his seat and collected additional chairs for Sky and the others. He quickly positioned them all around the fire.

"Everyone, this is Mike and Jason. Jason is the one with the goatee," Robert said and motioned to the tall lanky men.

After Sky and the others had introduced themselves, they each took a seat around the fire.

"Robert, you think these people have brought more favorable weather with them?" Mike asked.

"Show them your phone." Robert held out his hand toward Victor.

"Technically speaking it isn't my phone, but the owner died you see." Victor passed the phone to Robert who showed the two men the video.

"It *can't* be!" Jason gasped. "Where? When? How?"

Sky, Victor, and Kip related details of their capture and release of the former vice president of the United States of America.

"Rumors of an uprising in the Midwest have been broadcast over the old radio waves, but we didn't put much stock in it. Now..." Mike mused.

"But it does look promising," Jason added.

"What do you need from us?" Mike questioned.

Sky spent the next half hour giving them the details of their mission. "We need to get into the city to extract one of these men, or at least interrogate them," Sky finished.

"We can get you in. We even know where to find one of these persons, but what can you do for us?" Mike inquired of them.

"We can get you out of here," Sky offered.

"Maybe if we can get the information we need from this man we can accomplish our greater goals, and the fence can just come down," Jax suggested.

"What if we'd rather help deliver some payback?" Jason asked. "This city was once our home and they forced us out, murdered our friends and families."

"Depends on how fast you can get us to our target," Sky responded.

"We can get you in there tonight. How soon can you help these people?" Mike pointed at the camp around them.

"We can probably have some supplies here within the hour, but I don't think we should move anyone until after we are gone. Wouldn't that draw the attention from the troops watching the camp, if all the people suddenly disappeared?" Sky asked.

"It would. But how are you going to get supplies here?" Mike questioned.

"The same way we arrived." Sky smiled and took out her communicator and sent a message. She waited a moment. "You should have a shipment of food and clothing here in a short amount of time. Now, how do we get into the city?"

They spent the next hour developing plans that would take them out of the park and into the city. The man Linda suggested as the best source for information, and who was their target, no longer lived at the address

Linda had given them. They agreed Robert would stay behind while the twins would accompany the group in and help them accomplish their objective.

The gateway opened under the trees an hour later, and Sky and the others helped unload the supplies. They did it in secrecy so as not to be noticed. Robert informed them that they constantly worried about spies within their ranks. Sky even had some military equipment sent through for both Jason and Mike since they would be going with them.

Although they kept the supply delivery method quiet, the news of food and new clothing created a great deal of excitement in the camp. Robert, Jason, and Mike used a few trusted individuals to pass out the items so no one congregated under the tent.

"Well, you certainly have my attention now. I mean, the fact you disposed of the vice president was impressive, but not as much as that machine or whatever it is that brought you and those things here. You've given this old man hope for a better world," Robert surmised as they sat around the fire waiting for the sun to set.

"Yeah. Now instead of watching people being sent off to some extermination camp, we can see them go to where they can live and be free again," Mike added.

Sky and the others tried to get some rest, but constant interruptions from the people after they had received the supplies, kept them awake.

Finally, after the sun had gone down behind the western horizon, they gathered up their equipment and followed Mike and Jason to Kingman Lake, after the pair had indicated the best way to sneak into the city was at night via the river.

"Wow, these night vision goggles are incredible. This should make our trip across the river and under the fence a lot faster," Jason responded as they paused beneath a tree.

"Yeah, usually we have to wait until the guards move, and even then we wait until we are sure there aren't any we haven't seen. With these, we will be able to spot them, so it will be more like a pause," Mike added.

"Do you have a boat to get us downstream?" Kip asked.

"Nope, we swim." Jason started the group moving toward the river again.

When they finally stopped again, Kip started to speak but Mike held up a hand to silence him. He then pointed to a few guards patrolling the bridge on Benning Rd. Two men dressed in military garb slowly walked toward each other in the center of the viaduct. When they met they spun on their heels and headed back toward the opposite ends of the bridge.

"Yes, we swim," Jason whispered after he was sure they couldn't be overheard.

"But I don't want to walk around wet all night," Kip complained. "Plus, squeaky wet shoes won't work well when we are trying to be quiet."

"We strip down to our skivvies and put our clothes in a waterproof bag," Mike added, slapping a bag in Kip's hand and then passing more out to the others.

Everyone removed their weapons and outer layers of clothing. Sky had an impressive pile of weapons hidden all over her body. Most of the items were some form of a blade in various lengths and sizes.

"Are you sure these bags are strong enough to hold her stuff?" Victor chuckled quietly while motioning to Sky's pile of weapons.

"You had all that on you?" Mike questioned with wonder.

"Hey, I need this stuff," Sky said and smiled in the dark.

"Okay. We won't be able to talk until after we are through the border. You will have to dive at least three feet down to get under the fence. The water will be cold and we will be in it for about thirty minutes. Once through, we let the current take us downstream to the East Capitol Bridge. It is the best spot to get out without being seen. If I spot trouble, I will put up my hand," Jason informed them as they gathered up their equipment and stuffed it into the waterproof bags.

Jason checked the position of the guards once more before motioning the others to follow him out into the open. He headed straight for the river. Once there, they all put their headgear into the waterproof bags and quietly slipped into the cold water.

Sky fought the urge to gasp loudly when she had finally lowered herself fully into the water. She followed the others as they floated along toward the bridge. She struggled to keep her teeth from chattering in the cold water. Her fingers and toes started to go numb and she did a little dog paddling to try to generate some heat inside her frame's core.

Time seemed to crawl while floating in the cold water, but eventually they reached the bridge and everyone held on to the fence. The current was too slow to trap them against the chain-link fence which had been placed in the water. One by one they all dove down and underneath the bottom of the barrier.

After everyone was through and they had floated a good distance from the Benning Rd Bridge, they all swam a little harder. Sky welcomed the physical activity as she had begun shivering once they were some distance away from the structure.

When they finally climbed out of the water under the next bridge, they were all cold. Jason passed out towels he had stowed with the other gear. "This should help."

Sky was so glad to be back in her clothes. It took her longer than usual to stow all her weapons in their hiding places because her arms and fingers were so cold, they didn't respond normally. She cupped her hands and blew into them to try to help the circulation.

When everyone had warmed up again, Jason lead them east into the city, keeping them off the main roads. The once busy city was quiet. Only the occasional car drove by them, lighting up the area with their headlights because most of the streetlights were out.

Their night vision allowed them to move through the city relatively quickly and to avoid any people who might be trying to keep an eye on the streets. They changed their course several times to avoid areas where there were more people on the streets.

The march through the city quickly restored Sky to her normal body temperature and allowed her to concentrate on the task at hand.

Jason and Mike stopped them on a darkened street.

"The building we want is in the center of the block. It will be heavily guarded as Stevie, the weasel, has moved up in the world. He's making a living off of other people's misfortune. I would love to see him taken down," Mike said.

"This street is rather well lit," Sky commented, while taking a peek down the road.

"I make at least five armed guards on the street," Victor added.

"And do you want to bet there are more in the building and on the roof. Believe me, he's in with the big players now," Mike said.

They all ducked for cover as a car made its way up the street and past their location.

"That car passed without any trouble. Maybe we need to *borrow* one and take a couple of trips around the block," Jax suggested.

"Good idea, but it just can't be any vehicle. There are rules in play here. Only certain cars are permitted in some areas. Some might only have rights to drive in daylight," Mike informed them.

They spent twenty minutes searching for the correct vehicle. They then debated on whether to do a drive-by to gather information or to get into their goal.

"Listen, I think two passes would look rather suspicious. Here's what I propose we should do. Jax and I will go in alone under the invisibility spell. A couple of you wait in the car and be ready to pick us up. Everyone else take up positions at opposite ends of the street to watch for any unwanted attention. As dead as this place seems, I'm willing to bet a large force could show up in a hurry," Sky said.

"Oh yes. There is a rather large Islamic terrorist army stationed here. That's who rounds up people and expels them to the park," Jason said.

"And I would bet many people don't even make it to the park with those brutal people," Kip said.

"Jason and I will drive the car, since we know the city better than any of you," Mike suggested.

"That leaves me and Kip for lookouts. Just be sure you don't exclude us from the fun," Victor said. "I'll take the other end. You better give me twenty minutes to get in position. I'll let you know when I'm ready."

"Do you think you can find your way back to the bridge where we got out of the river?" Jason asked.

"Yeah."

"If all hell breaks loose, that will be the rendezvous point," Jason determined.

"Be careful and stay on com," Sky warned.

Victor smiled at her and then hurried off into the night.

Everyone waited quietly for Victor to get into position. Exactly twenty minutes after he had left, he called in.

"I'm ready. Everything is quiet on this end."

"Are you ready?" Sky asked Jax.

"Let's do this," Jax said and then disappeared, to audible gasps from Mike and Jason.

Sky disappeared and the two of them made their way down the street toward the building Mike and Jason had indicated. They scurried from one hiding place to the next, not knowing if any thing or any one who could detect magic was about. They continually whispered through their headsets to make sure they were on the same page and not bumping into one another.

They finally came to a stop in the shadows of an entryway across the street from their target.

"I still only make out five guards," Jax observed.

"Six. There is one standing on our side of the street about three buildings down," Sky said.

"Well, he definitely needs to be taken care of first," Jax said.

"You take him and I'll take the others," Sky ordered. "Do it quietly and let me know when you're done."

"Okay."

Sky only had to wait ten minutes before she received confirmation from Jax that he had disposed of the one security guard.

"Do you see any more other than the five still standing on the other side of the street?" Sky questioned.

"Nope!"

Sky released her invisibility spell, removed her headgear, and began to stroll across the street. It took several moments for the guards to realize she was there, and she had made it almost all the way across the street before the group of five men had her surrounded. They were quickly joined by a sixth, who had been watching behind the glass doors of the building's entrance.

"Who are you? How did you get here?" one of the guards barked.

One of the men flipped on a flashlight and shone the light directly into Sky's face. Her stunningly beautiful looks, with her bright red lips, changed the mood of the men instantly.

"Well, well, well. What do we have here, boys? We've been wanting some fun and look what walks right into our laps."

"What's your name, sweetheart?"

"We've been very lonely," another added and the group laughed, closing tightly around Sky.

"You boys what to have some fun?" Sky batted her eyes at the men.

"Oh yeah," several flashed wicked smiles.

One of the men reached out to grab her when Sky struck. From out of her clothing she retrieved two long knives. She caught the surprised men completely off guard. The speed of her attack didn't give anyone in the tight circle a chance to respond. They only managed to produce shocked looks on their faces before Sky cut them down.

The fight only lasted a few minutes before Sky stood alone in the center of the street, surrounded by the lifeless bodies of the guards.

"There. Wasn't that fun," she sniggered.

Jax hurried to her and together they dragged the bodies out of the street and piled them on the sidewalk. They slipped into the entrance of the building to find a waiting area, which was completely empty.

"Luckily, you drew the guard in here out," Jax said.

"Yeah. Never underestimate the stupidity of men," Sky said and winked at him.

"I won't argue with that. So, how do we find him?"

"If he is as big as they say he is, I'm willing to bet he's pretty much the only person living here," Sky said.

"Where do powerful people live in buildings?" Jax questioned.

They looked at each other and spoke at the same time, "The top floor."

"Should we take the stairs?" Jax nodded toward the open stairwell.

"The elevator. Let's not play this like anyone else would. That should give us the upper hand." Sky headed for the shiny gold doors in the middle of the room.

The moment Jax stepped in, Sky hit the button for the top floor. She got out her long knives, while Jax held his laser blaster at the ready. They watched the light for each floor flash and then go out as they climbed to the top.

Springing out of the elevator at top speed, Sky disposed of one guard, while Jax blasted a second at the other end of the hall.

Stevie came flying out of the room in a full on rage. "I TOLD YOU IDIOTS TO KEEP THINGS QUI..." He froze with a raised fist in the air when his eyes locked on the fallen guard and Sky.

His jaw dropped but before he could retreat into the room, Sky was on top of him, holding a knife to his throat. Jax made a quick sweep of the hall before helping Sky drag Stevie back into the room.

"We got him. Hang on," Jax reported to the others.

"Any signs of activity or alarm?" Sky questioned.

"All clear," the others reported.

"Who are you? What do you want?" Stevie demanded, but a quick blow to the gut from Sky silenced him.

"Shut up! We're the ones who *will* ask the questions." Jax practically shoved the barrel of his weapon up Stevie's nose. "So..."

"Shh," Sky interrupted while glancing around the room. "Do you hear voices?"

They stood silently for a moment. Stevie's eyes jumped back and forth from Sky to Jax.

"Yes," Jax whispered after a few moments. "It's coming from that hallway." Jax pointed to a long wide corridor to his right where light filtered out into the passageway from under the double doors.

"Check it out," Sky ordered.

"You don't want to be disturbing what's in there." Stevie regained his composure and a wicked smile spread across his face.

Jax paused and glanced at Sky.

"Let's all go." Sky yanked Stevie to his feet, spun him around, pulling his arm behind his back while still holding the blade of her knife to his throat. She pushed him down the hall, keeping him between them and the door.

"You're making a huge mistake," Stevie taunted.

"Why would he warn us?" Jax questioned Sky about halfway down the hall.

"I think he's trying to protect someone," Sky responded.

"He could be walking us into a trap." Jax raised his eyebrows.

"Don't say I didn't warn you," Stevie taunted as they stood in front of the closed doors.

"I'm not worried." Sky cast a spell that blew the two doors completely off their hinges as she and Jax pushed Stevie into some sort of conference room.

A group of nine shocked people and something dark and sinister sat around a conference room.

A demon so vile his mere presence darkened the area of the room around him presided over the gathering. A strange red glow, like the embers of a fire, filled all the cracks in his skin, eyes, nostrils, mouth, and clothing—while a shadowy smoke rose off of him.

The fiend rose slowly to his feet and the strange shadowy smoke increased with his movements. "You know magic!" it said in a high-pitched voice and its eyes seemed to blaze with a greater fire.

21

Breaking into the Dark Society

The demon threw his arms out to the side and it was as if the entire room grew to three times its previous size. Then with a flick of his fingers, all the chairs holding the people at the table rolled back against the wall. Another twitch of his hand and the table melted into the floor. The creature laughed—a screeching, unnerving sound.

"I told you," Stevie said, full of glee.

Sky jabbed him in the ribs once more, knocking all the air from his lungs before passing him to Jax. "We told you to shut up. If you think he's going to rescue you, you're wrong!"

"I'm going to enjoy killing you. Your screams will be a song that will please me for the rest of my life," the demon said.

In a blur of movement, Sky's daggers disappeared and her long sword appeared in her hand. "Bring it!"

The demon opened his mouth and a high-pitched wail of rage threw fire across the room. Sky tilted her blade and with a small blocking spell, angled the flames into a section of people who had been sitting at the table. Their screams filled the air and then went silent as they turned to ash.

Sky's trickery in disposing of the devil's own people enraged the beast, and it launched itself forward with outstretched clawed black hands, the same reddish glow emanating from his nails. Its speed of attack was a black-reddish blur.

Sky spun away and countered, slashing her sword through the demon. To her horror, her blade passed through the evil creature, as if his entire body were made of black smoke. Her strokes only managed to disturb the strange dark wisp for a moment before it re-formed into the demon's body.

The monster cackled insanely before throwing out another spell. Sky attempted to block it but it hit her with great force, slammed her into the wall behind her, pinning her against it. "Your pitiful weapons are no match for me." It zipped across the room and held Sky's throat in its hand as it lifted her off the floor.

Sky swung her sword up and through the creature's arms. Once more, it passed through them like they were nothing but air. This resulted in the beast's solid hands turning to smoke, and at the same time releasing her. Sky hit the floor and rolled away. "That's a nice trick, but it won't save you."

"Don't you know you're looking at death, witch? You *are* outmatched."

Before the demon could attempt a new strategy, Sky attacked. Her sword strokes were barely visible to the naked eye. She drove right into the center of the creature, her sword flying.

The creature tried to zip away, but Sky threw out spells to repel him back into the path of the weapon she brandished. A counter spell from the fiend sent Sky backward across the room. Again, the he flew to catch her mid-air by the throat and tried to squeeze the life out of her.

Sky responded by swinging the sword she gripped back through the creature's arms, forcing him to release her, but this time before she could drop too far, the demon smashed his head against hers.

Tiny lights popped in front of Sky's eyes and her head swam dizzily. Before she had a chance to recover, the demon blasted her across the room to snag her by the throat while she was still airborne.

The same event happened again. After Sky cut through his arms, the demon would head butt her to the ground. The force of the impact buckled Sky's knees. She began to fall, but the beast caught her by the throat and flung her up against the wall.

Sky swiped the sword instinctively through the creature's smoky arms, but as she fell she drew a dagger from inside her clothing. As the demon's thick head swung forward, Sky buried her dagger into its skull. Sky landed on her feet as a horrible cry filled the room. The devil staggered backward, grasping the handle of the dagger sticking out of its head.

With all the strength she had left, Sky swung her sword through the creature's arms at the base of the beast's skull, lopping its head off. The demon's head dropped to the floor, while its smoky body evaporated into thin air and the reddish glow went out.

Everyone stared in stunned silence for a few moments.

"I don't believe it," Stevie gasped.

Sky kicked the skull, which created a dull clunking sound before it rolled across the floor. "It's metal...and empty." Sky walked over to it, stepped on it with one foot, and pulled her dagger free.

"What?" Jax questioned. "If it was all smoke, how did you kill it?"

Sky glanced at Jax with a weird look. "I'm not sure. I wonder if it had to do with the fact it was unable to re-form with the blade in its brain. Maybe he could only not stay solid for so long. When he passed that point, the dagger killed him. I'm only guessing of course."

"Who are you?" questioned one of the remaining six people who hadn't been destroyed by the demon's fire.

"Someone who's here to put an end to your power." Sky smirked. "We're here to tear down your reign and restore freedom. Now, face the wall with your hands over your heads."

Jax forced Stevie over to the others and helped him put his hands on the wall. Jax touched his microphone. "It looks like we have a few more hostages. Stand by."

One of the men in the group attempted to retrieve a revolver out of the back of his pants. Before he could withdraw the gun, Sky hammered him in the back with the butt of her knife. The man dropped to his knees, and as he fell she snagged his weapon.

"Really? You just saw me take down that demon and you think you're going to pull a gun on me."

"What do you want to do with them?" Jax asked. "We only came for Stevie."

"Yes, but now I'm wondering who is the top dog in this room. Is it Stevie? I know the demon was, but why was Stevie checking on the noise level? That's more of a job for an errand boy," Sky said.

"Good point," Jax agreed.

Sky activated her microphone. "Hey, everyone come inside."

"Are you sure? There seems to be a little activity out here," Victor reported.

"What sort of *activity*?"

"A truck just pulled up in the street and a dozen troops jumped out," Victor reported.

"It looks like they're headed into your building," Kip added.

Sky glanced at Jax. "Watch them." She nodded to their captives before bolting for the door. "Any chance you can hit them from the rear?" she spoke into the microphone.

"You got it," Victor responded.

"Jason and Mike, hold your position in case we need to make a getaway," Sky ordered. She hid the sword beneath her clothing and retrieved a laser blaster.

"Some are taking the stairs, with a handful coming up the elevator. What floor?" Kip questioned.

"All the way to the top. I can hold them in the hall, if you take them from the rear. Wait. Wait. Wait. Victor and Kip, don't come unless I tell you. Jax, I'm coming back to you."

Sky bolted back into the room where Jax watched the other prisoners.

"What do you have in mind?" Jax questioned.

"When that demon expanded the room, he knocked holes into the joining apartments." Sky used her weapon to point to a hole in the back wall. "You, bring up the rear. Everyone, follow me through the hole. If you make a sound, you will be the first casualty in the battle before it even begins." She led the group to a small hole in a corner of the wall and stepped through into a darkened room on the other side. She used her magic to create a small amount of light for the others to see by.

Jax had just stepped through the hole when the troops knocked on the door. "At least they're not sure if anything's wrong. Although, the bodies in the street should have told them otherwise. That should give us a very small amount of time to come up with a plan," he whispered.

Sky led them into another room of the adjoining apartment and closed the door behind them. She hurried to the window to see a fire escape attached to the back of the building. "Everyone down the ladder. Victor, Kip, meet us out back."

"Aren't they going to notice everyone's missing?" Victor questioned.

"You didn't see the room. It looks like a bomb went off in there. They might assume everyone was killed." Sky hurried down the steps ahead of the others. When she stopped on the landing of the second floor, she paused. She went to the window and, with a device of Olik's making, opened the locked window. "Change of plans, everyone inside again."

"What do you want us to do?" Victor questioned through the microphone.

"Hold outside and keep an eye on things but be careful. They know someone killed those guards in the street. Mike, Jason, continue to maintain your position. We're going to determine the best hostage," Sky ordered.

After everyone was back inside the apartment on the second floor, Sky pulled the blinds shut and used magic to create a little light to see by. Sky and Jax forced their prisoners back into a positon with their hands over their heads against the wall. One by one, they secured the prisoners hands behind their backs and then spun them around to sit on the floor, facing them.

"On second thought, one of you come up. We need an extra set of eyes in the building." Sky stared down the group while Jax went to the front door to listen for signs of trouble.

"Hold on, someone is peeking out of the top story," Kip replied. "When the coast is clear, I'll head up."

"Would you please tell us who you are?" whispered a round bald-headed man with a reddish face.

"Who I am isn't important. It's *you* I want to know about. You see, we have this problem we need to get rid of and we need your help to do it," Sky answered in a hushed voice.

"Why would we *help* you?" Stevie spoke with a hiss, his eyes reflecting a hatred toward his captors.

"Because," Sky smiled broadly, "if you don't," Sky kicked him hard in the side, "I'm going to beat you black and blue."

"We have troops in the hall," Jax whispered from the front door while peering through the peephole.

Just then Kip entered through the window, startling Sky for a moment.

"Watch them." Sky pointed at the prisoners and then hurried to Jax. "What are they doing?"

"Not much. It looks like they are just making a quick sweep. They haven't entered any of the apartments. They checked a couple to verify they were locked but that's it."

"Hopefully, they think we hit them upstairs and made our getaway," Sky added.

"We have more ground activity out here," Victor reported. "I think Jason and Mike should abandon the car. It appears they are going to widen the search. Some of the troops have exited the building."

"Everyone, make your way to us. Jason, Mike, we're on the second floor. Use the fire escape on the back of the building toward the west side," Sky ordered.

Sky went back to Kip and the hostages.

"I'm willing to bet you are all expendable to those you work for or with." Sky squatted to be eyelevel with the group of seven individuals, which consisted of six men and one woman. "Do you agree?"

The people exchanged worried glances but no one spoke.

"Do you think if I offered some kind of trade, your people would follow through?" Sky shook her head while laughing quietly. "You people are all dumber than you look."

"Maybe we should prove it to them. When Victor arrives, we can activate the vice president's phone and make a demand," Kip added.

All the color drained out of the prisoners' faces and they continued to glance back and forth at each other.

"That's a great idea. What you don't know is we have a way to contact people in your inner circle. This should be fun. But what shall we ask for in trade?" Sky rose to her feet while tapping her finger on her chin in thought.

"How about they pull out of a large section of the US for us to live in peace and for them to leave us alone?" Kip suggested.

"I like it," Sky said as Victor, Jason, and Mike arrived. "Victor, get out the phone."

"You're bluffing," said the man with the fat red face.

"Why does no one believe it?" Victor wore an incredulous look. "Although, I do enjoy sharing that video with others."

"Me too," Sky agreed.

The vibe in the room grew thick with fear. The woman in the group visibly trembled after Victor showed them the video.

"Now that we've established how serious we are and the great lengths we will go to get what we want, let's talk business," Sky commented as Jason handed her a chair.

Sky plopped down on the chair across from the group.

"I think they've pulled out of the building," Jax reported. "Do you want me to take a quick look?"

"I can go with him," Kip spoke up. "I'm not too good with this sort of thing." He motioned to the people.

"Okay, but stick tight with Jax. He has some tools to detect any surveillance equipment that may have been activated or left behind," Sky ordered.

"You know in my experience, things always go a little quicker if we off someone up front," Victor said with a stony face.

"Yes, but do it here. It always works better if they get to see it as well," Sky encouraged.

"Okay, who's first?" Victor pulled out a long, hunting knife.

"I vote Stevie. We've determined our weasel is just a messenger boy," Sky said. "What do you guys think?" Sky turned to Jason and Mike, who had just been watching.

"If you've determined Stevie holds no value, I have no problem with getting rid of him. He's been a huge pain in our rears," Mike said.

"Yeah," Jason agreed.

"Sorry, Stevie. Nothing personal." Sky nodded for Victor to continue.

Victor spun his knife through his fingers, finally catching it by the handle, and then advanced on Stevie. He grabbed Stevie by the hair and yanked his head back. "Adios."

"ALL RIGHT! ALL RIGHT! I'll TELL YOU WHAT YOU WANT TO KNOW!" Stevie belted out.

Victor jabbed him in the ribs. "Keep it quiet."

"Stevie, shut your pie hole," the red faced, fat man said.

Suddenly, Stevie started to choke and his face turned purple as he struggled against unseen hands.

Sky rose to her feet, a dark expression on her face. "*Nejhaj!*" A shockwave blasted the entire group, slamming them up against the wall. The maneuver worked. The strangle hold on Stevie was broken.

"Somebody in this group has some type of magical skills." Victor wore a surprised look.

"Someone in this group isn't who they appear to be. I sure could use Max or Cindy right now. They'd find you in a snap." Sky snapped her fingers. "Hmm, let's see, whoever you are, you can speak up and not do anything stupid again, or I will find you and you *will* be the example."

The people exchanged frightened looks once more but no one spoke.

"Have it your way." Sky held out her hand palm facing upwards and a ball of fire appeared in the air above it. Sky blew into the fire and it divided and jumped from her hand onto the legs of all the prisoners but Stevie.

The people all squirmed against their bindings and cries of pain filled the room. Suddenly, the fire on the fat-faced man's legs went out. Sky leveled her gun at the man but then turned it toward the woman and pulled the trigger. The woman sagged within her bindings and Sky extinguished the flames.

"Are you sure it was her?" Victor questioned.

"Look at her pantsuit. The fabric isn't burned. Everyone else's clothing caught fire," Sky pointed to the differences.

Victor leaned in to Sky and whispered, "I think they will all tell us what we want to know now."

Sky gave him a slight nod as he moved away. "Anyone else want to test me?"

The entire group shook their heads back and forth slowly, while staring at her.

Jax and Kip returned to the room after being gone for a few moments, drawing questioning looks from Sky and the others.

"We're trapped on this floor. Or at least from going anywhere on the inside of the building," Jax reported. "They have trip alarms set up all over the place. Even in the hall outside. I almost gave us away before I had activated Olik's little toy to reveal security traps. There is a trip sensor about every ten feet, all the way down the hall."

"Would you be able to lead us out should we need to go that way?" Sky questioned.

"It's possible, if there aren't alarms that go off when we open the stairwell doors."

"Check the back. Make sure we didn't miss anything that way," Sky ordered.

"Got it. I'm assuming if they did anything it would have to be on the ground or we would have heard them on the stairs, plus we all came in that way." Jax flipped down his night vision goggles and went to the window and cracked the blinds. "Okay, they are watching the back. I can see two of them. One at each end of the building."

"Well, if they don't know we are here, we can probably wait them out," Victor said.

"Okay, back to business." Sky returned her attention to the people on the floor. "What can you tell us about those who arranged the downfall of this country and where can we find them?"

"You want us to give you the names and locations of people in the inner circle?" the red faced man said and gasped. "That would mean our deaths for sure."

"No, it will lead to your freedom. If we cut off the head of the snake, their evil chokehold will be broken and freedom can return. We will protect you," Sky offered. "But if you aren't with us you're against us, and we will have no use for you. An enemy with no use is not worth keeping around, if you know what I mean." Sky nodded to the dead woman on the floor. "We don't wish to shed anyone's blood, but this is now a life or death struggle. There is no time for political correctness and fighting by rules. It's kill or be killed. I don't like it but I choose to kill rather than be killed. Now, we are giving you the choice. Help us or be killed."

"Wow, you are so attractive to me right now." Victor laughed while winking at Sky.

Sky flashed Victor a big smile and then turned back to the prisoners. "What's your choice? Let's be clear. If you're not with us we can't trust you, and we have no use for liabilities."

"But you don't know who's in charge. A demon more powerful than the one you fought upstairs," Stevie said.

"Hudich, we know about him. I'm not talking about him. We want the people who were in charge of this country before Hudich arrived on the scene," Sky said.

"You mean the president of the United States?" asked another prisoner who was so skinny he resembled a skeleton in a suit.

"Yes, and those who were pulling his strings. He wasn't smart enough to pull off all the things that brought down this country. Do you know where we can find these people?"

"You want to kill the president of the United States?" Stevie questioned.

"Or take him prisoner, for what it's worth." Sky smiled a wicked grin. "Can you help us find him?"

"YES!"

22

Unexpected Arrivals

Cindy, what did you do? Max felt a surge of panic.

It's okay. I didn't do it out of the need for control or power, but the information we can gain, Cindy responded.

The image changed from Mr. Knightley's perspective to the view from Brian's eyes.

Jo turned her rage on Mr. Knightley and blasted him against the wall and held him fast.

"Wait. It's okay." Cindy controlled Brian. "I'm all right."

Jo released the man and turned her attention back to Brian. "For the moment. What if he gave you something that hasn't kicked in yet?"

Cindy changed the view back to Mr. Knightley for a moment. "I actually gave him something to protect him. I know something you don't."

"What's that?" Jo shot him a venomous gaze.

"Hudich wanted to test the virus on him. I just gave him the cure. Hudich wants to control everyone and that includes you." Mr. Knightley spoke Cindy's thoughts.

Hey, that was really good, Ell thought.

Thanks. Cindy changed back to Brian.

"Hudich wouldn't do such a thing," Brian said, and a second later Brian's thoughts and memories began to flood through Max's mind.

Max was amazed at how Cindy could control two men at the same time as she created a story and a conversation, all for Jo's benefit.

Why don't you just take Jo as well? Max questioned.

I don't want to be in that freak's head. Cindy said.

Plus, I don't think we should risk Cindy's control. I'm helping her maintain it but the more people we add, the more difficult it will be, Ell commented.

A moment later, Cindy had the three of them walking the hallways of the lower level, all while they were reading Brian and Mr. Knightley's minds.

Crap! If we survive this thing, it will be a miracle. Hudich's forces are massive, Max said after seeing details about Hudich's organization that they never knew before.

Yes, but we came here to do something other than learn about all of Hudich's other ventures, Ell pointed out, and he drew their attention to details that were inside Mr. Knightley's brain.

They are secretly working on a cure, Cindy said as they watched a few victims of the experiments, who were locked inside glass cells. *But they haven't figured it out yet.*

And I was right. It looks like they started with your blood, Cindy, but now they are using Hudich's, Max proposed.

That means if they spread the virus, I wouldn't be able to break the link, Cindy said.

I'm not sure I will be able to either. I think we need to look in the direction of the cure, Max said.

"I thought you didn't have a cure?" Jo eyed the doctor suspiciously. "Hiding things from Hudich isn't a good thing."

"Would you rather I let your friend be infected?" Cindy had the doctor say.

"Well, no, but I don't like crossing Hudich. Things don't turn out well for those who do," Jo added. "Plus, won't he know if Brian isn't infected? You might have just saved Brian but I don't know who will save you."

"I'll take my chances," the doctor replied.

"Yes, but you may have sealed yours and Brian's fate. If that was Hudich's plan, who knows what he'll do," Jo growled.

Boy, do Hudich's followers fear him, Max spoke almost in awe.

That's not freedom, Ell added. *And it just goes to show evil doesn't want to share power.*

HOLD it, I think I've found something important that I didn't know, Cindy interrupted.

They all watched as Cindy played the scene where Dr. Knightley explained the virus had to be activated magically. Cindy showed them this piece of information, all while keeping her subjects moving. She used the doctor's knowledge to lead Jo and Brian through the underground complex, giving them a tour and updates on the tests.

I've found where they've been working on the cure, Ell said. *Cindy, continue what you're doing, I'll make it so Max and I can process what they have as far as a remedy.*

Max felt grateful for his two companions. He didn't know how Cindy controlled the two subjects with such precision and kept them moving about as if everything were normal. Ell's ability to mine the data from Cindy's and the other's thoughts astounded Max. If it were up to him, he would have been lost.

The information Ell had mentioned flashed in Max's mind.

It appears they have been more concerned about a cure or prevention, than getting Hudich's virus created, Ell commented.

Yes, and it looks like we may have to have one of Cindy's subjects go to the computer. Dr. Knightley has only been getting updates on the antidote's progress. His main task has been getting the airborne virus working, Max noted.

Cindy had Dr. Knightley show Brian and Jo those currently infected with the virus and explain to them how they were administered the altered organism.

Wow, this is the way to learn. I've learned more about genetics and how they work in these few short minutes than in my entire life, Max said.

Yeah, it is rather ingenious mixing some of Hudich's blood with current forms of the flu and making sure the magical part is intact, Cindy added. *Hey, since the blood is from Hudich and thus from you, maybe we need to have you try to see if you can control some of their subjects.*

I think that is a good idea, but let's use Brian and the doctor to get all the information we can first. For one, we don't know if it will work and two, you will have to teach Max how to do it, Ell thought.

Yeah, lets tackle one thing at a time, Max agreed.

A garage door opening above them brought them back to the fact they were still out in the open and vulnerable.

"Cindy, get on Ell so you can concentrate on what you are doing. Ell and I will find a place from which we can work," Max ordered.

"I think it is coming down." Cindy climbed on Ell's back after he lowered himself to the ground.

"Lita, we need an exit," Max spoke into the microphone, with the sound of the vehicle growing louder by the second.

Max and Ell ran to keep ahead of the approaching group.

"I'm going to open the next door you come to but there is a problem," Lita said.

"What's the problem?" Max questioned.

"Jo went to report what's going on to higher-ups," Cindy interrupted, increasing the sense of panic Max was feeling.

"There are five people in the room. The good news, they aren't armed and I've deactivated all electronic devices in the room. The bad news, you're going to have to take them hostage," Lita reported.

"*Terrific!*" Max forced his response through gulps of air.

They rounded the next full circle to see the five occupants behind the open door, staring at the ramp with puzzled looks on their faces. The moment they caught sight of Ell, panic took over and they turned to flee.

"FREEZE!" Max yelled as he, Ell, and Cindy raced into the room and Lita closed the door behind them.

"You're one level above the bottom floor," Lita informed them.

Max fired a few shots over the heads of the people fleeing toward a door on the opposite side of the room. The laser blasts impacted on the wall above the door, sending small particles of debris and sparks raining down in front of the scrambling workers. They all put on the brakes and turned to face Max and Ell. All eyes came to rest on Ell.

"Get on the floor and put your hands behind your back," Max ordered, while keeping the gun pointed at the group.

"I don't know where Jo went. Brian doesn't have any memory of them having to check in," Cindy commented.

"She's in a room, making a phone call," Lita indicated.

"You can bet that's not going to be good," Max murmured. "We better hurry. If Jo isn't with them, there is no longer a reason for pretense. Get them to the cure!"

Hudich and Alan stood with a few of the Hamas leaders on the side of a hill, eyeing the Israelis main water treatment facility. Gun and rocket fire flew all around them as they stood in a somewhat protected area. The ongoing battle made the area look like a continuous fireworks display filling the night sky. Even in the dark and with the light of the constant flashes from explosions, Hudich could see the place was heavily guarded. "We really need the airborne virus to be a success," he grumbled out loud.

"It should only be a week away, correct?" Alan questioned. "Surely, we can wait a few days?"

"The longer we take, the more time that old fool Joe has to meddle in our plans. We have remained a few steps ahead of him this past year, and I want to keep it that way. I'm sure he has a hand in what's happening in Iowa," Hudich growled. "They have thwarted everything we have thrown at them when they were just a small camp."

"Do we need to activate our secret weapon?" Alan questioned more than said.

"We may not need to. Should the virus work, we will have a swift victory and total control," Hudich sneered.

"It can wait then. Until you activate it," Alan said.

"I don't think we will have much success hitting their water supply," Hudich declared, then turned to the terrorist next to him. Keep up the siege. Don't give them a break."

"What the?" Alan began patting his pockets and then finally fished his cell phone from an inside pocket of his jacket. "Something must be up for someone to call me on the satellite phone." He pushed receive and put the phone to his head. "Yes?"

"What is it?" Hudich questioned.

"It's Jo. It seems the group at the underground base has plans of their own, which are contrary to yours." Alan repeated the conversation.

"Tell Jo she will be rewarded for her loyalty. We need to pay them a visit, *now*!"

"Yes." Alan gave a slight bow.

Hudich disappeared in a flash and Alan followed.

A second later, they landed between two buildings on the secret base in Nevada.

Joe worked the gateway, after convincing both Rachel and Cindy's mother to finally take a break. Yelka went to work aiding Linda, Donna, and Martin in translating the book of prophecy to see what other helpful information they could glean from its pages.

The parade of supplies and people moving to the camp in Iowa continued around the clock. Joe found some amusement in the shocked look on the people's faces as they were transported for the first time.

The vibrating of his communicator in his pocket drew his attention. He took it out of his pants and read the message. "The prophecy," he muttered, as a sinking feeling spread through his body. "YELKA!" He called, knowing they were working just a floor below.

After stomping on the floor while continuing to work the gateway, he realized he wouldn't be able to get their attention with the noise from the gateway creating a constant hum in the house. He typed out a message to Yelka on his communicator.

It only took a few minutes for Yelka and the others to join him on the third floor.

"What's the emergency?" Yelka questioned.

"THIS!" Joe passed his communicator to Yelka.

"Oh no!" Yelka gasped.

"What is it?" the others asked.

Yelka showed the others the message and received the same reaction she had given.

"Keep that under your hat!" Joe flashed a stern warning look. "Go wake Rachel. You and I need to leave. Max and Cindy might be in big trouble, but don't tell Rachel," Joe ordered.

"She's a smart woman. She knows where Max and Cindy are, she'll see where she's sending us," Yelka commented.

"I'll think of an explanation. Go!" Joe said.

"I'm sending them to the area where they have been doing all the research on a cure," Cindy said.

"Lita, can you get the information for us?" Max hopped forward and began securing their captives' hands behind their backs with plastic zip ties. He then helped get them into a seated position.

"No, it must not be on the network. I've tried everything to find it and I have access to pretty much everything. Perhaps they wanted their work isolated so no one outside the base would discover it," Lita surmised.

"They're in the room. At the computer," Cindy reported.

"See if you can download everything to a flash drive," Max said, after gagging their prisoners.

"I'm working on it. I'm trying to convince the man with the password to give us all the information," Cindy reported. "Crap! Jo found us and is questioning everything!"

Max hurried to a door that contained a small window. "Has Jo…Whoa, did you feel that?" A shadow passed over Max, and a twinge of fear spread through his body as if something terrible had happened. He glanced at Ell and Cindy to see them staring at him. He thought he could detect Cindy shiver slightly.

"HUDICH IS HERE," Lita yelled through the headset, snapping them out of their momentarily frozen state.

"WHAT?" Max and Cindy responded.

"I just made Brian and the doctor scream 'What.'" Cindy's face was full of trepidation.

"Yes, he and that Alan just arrived; they are entering a building right now," Lita responded.

"You need to get out of there," Larry piped in. "You're history if they catch you."

"Cindy, can you access Brian's powers?" Max asked, returning his attention to the hall where the workers appeared to be going about their business as normal.

"Yes."

"Use them to get the info we need now and deal with Jo if you have to. Lita, can you tell me how to get through the complex to where Brian is at?" Max questioned.

"Yes, I can get you there but what about security?"

"I'll deal with it when I run into it." Max bolted out of the door and into the hall. "Tell me where to go!"

"You realize this is going to let Hudich know you are in the building?" Lita tried to warn him, but Max was already in the hall.

Max raced forward, surprising people in lab coats, but no one tried to stop his progress or question him. Lita spoke directions in his earpiece. Max turned a corner and plowed into a worker carrying a box of supplies, sending the man to the floor and the items in his box scattering everywhere.

"Hey. Who are you?" the man questioned.

Max jumped back to his feet and sprinted away. He had just made it to a stairwell down another hallway when alarms sounded throughout the building, accompanied by flashing red lights.

"The guards are organizing and heading your way," Lita reported.

"How does the stairway exit look at the moment?" Max's feet thudded against the metal stairs as he took them two at a time. He started breathing heavily.

"You're good for the moment. I've made it so they can't see anything on their security monitors," Lita warned. "Just be ready. They are searching for you, but it is mainly concentrated on the floor you just left."

Max leapt down the last five steps and burst through the door into the hallway below, almost colliding with the opposite wall. He quickly regained his balance and turned in the direction Lita indicated.

"The data is downloading, but there is a ton. Might take a few minutes," Cindy reported through the headset.

"How's Jo taking things?" Max asked between gulps of air.

"Okay, is it wrong if I'm getting a kick out of the way she is cowering in the corner? She's afraid of Brian. I had him confront her about reporting to Hudich and how he was trying to protect himself and she had betrayed him. He has a lot of power in his voice. Scared the crap out of her," Cindy relayed.

Cindy's humor helped ease the pressure Max was feeling while scrambling through the complex. He continued to pass shocked people, but everyone gave way after spotting the weapon in his hand.

"Get ready. You're going to run into a group of guards," Lita warned.

Max sent his spell before the group rounded the corner to block his path. His spell caught three guards the moment they entered Max's path and threw them out of the road like dry leaves on the wind. The force blasted them into the wall at the far end.

"Turn down the hall on your right—now," Lita ordered.

As Max dove down the new hallway a few shots whizzed past him from behind.

"They gained on you faster than I thought. Get ready to take a left and the room will be four doors down."

When Max turned into the hall with the room he wanted, doctors and lab technicians were loitering in the hall, trying to figure out what was happening. Max fired several shots into the air.

"OUT OF THE WAY," he screamed, scaring the workers back into their respective work areas.

"You need to hurry. Hudich has entered the building and more troops have reached your floor," Lita urged.

"Cindy, after I have the drive, do you think you can use Brian to give me cover?"

"Yes, just hurry. We're no match for Hudich," Cindy stressed.

Max burst into the room to see a nervous doctor standing in front of a computer, with Dr. Knightley standing next to him. The man almost jumped at the sight of Max. Jo stood in the corner like a wounded animal, while Brian faced her.

"Just keep working," Dr. Knightley said in a kind of monotone.

What little color that was left in Jo's face drained away at the sight of Max. The sudden whiteness of her skin, combined with her makeup and pink hair, gave her a psychotic clown look.

Jo's finger shot out like a striking snake. "It's Max! Brian, behind you," she warned in a high-pitched voice.

Max joined the man at the computer. "How long?"

"W—who..."

"*How* long?" Max demanded.

"A minute." The man pointed to the progress bar on the screen which read a little over a minute.

"This is going to be close." Lita exhaled.

"Brian, what's wrong with you?" Jo cried. "Hudich will kill you for sure."

"She's right," Cindy commented.

"Well, we are going to use him to get out of here, so it looks like he might be coming all the way with us," Max responded to Cindy, drawing a strange look from the man at the computer.

"Don't follow us." Brian warned Jo in the same strange flat voice that Mr. Knightley spoke in, with Cindy pulling the strings.

"Y—your g—going with, with them!" Jo seemed to grow taller and her face, which had been deathly white a moment before, turned a beet red.

Max adjusted his gun to stun, whirled around and blasted Jo, knocking her flat.

"Oh, that had to feel good." Cindy beamed.

The man behind the computer pulled the flash drive out of the USB port and held it in the air. "It's finished."

Max snatched it out of his hand. "Thank you. Bring Brian."

"There are troops in the hall," Lita warned.

Max readjusted his weapon before poking his head out the door. The way back was blocked by a dozen guards.

"PUT DOWN YOUR WEAPONS AND COME OUT WITH YOUR HANDS UP," a guard shouted.

"HURRY! Hudich is almost there," Lita warned.

"It looks like…" Max started when the marionette puppet Brian strolled past him into the hall with his hands above his head.

He stopped in the center of the hall facing the blockade. "Put down your weapons and step aside," he commanded.

Max felt the surge of magic fill the hall. It took all the strength he had to not obey the command, which was extremely powerful. To his surprise, the troops did as Brian commanded.

"Piece of cake against the weak minded," Cindy said with satisfaction.

"What do you mean weak minded? I had to fight to maintain possession of my gun," Max said. He took off down the hall while Cindy had Brian follow him.

Max followed the same pattern he had used to reach the room where he retrieved the necessary data.

"WATCH OUT!" Lita screamed

Max flinched at her words and ducked just in time to avoid a spell, which caught Brian square in the chest and crushed him like a tin can. Max turned his head away from the gruesome sight and ducked into the nearest hallway. He peered around the corner, holding his weapon at the ready.

"Max," Hudich said while stepping into view, with Alan right behind him.

23

A Horrible Choice

A powerful, wicked spell flew down the hallway, destroying the walls and widening the hallway, sending boards and sheetrock flying through the air. A cloud of sheetrock dust filled the air. Max dove back the way he had come.

"Lita, I need another exit," Max shouted while fleeing in the opposite direction.

"Max, we're coming," Cindy yelled.

"NO! Head for the exit. I'll meet you there," Max ordered.

"Stairs coming up on your left. There are troops heading down so be careful," Lita warned.

Max bolted into a stairwell seconds before a wall of fire filled the hallway behind him. The air current created by the sudden wave of extreme heat acted like a vacuum, almost pulling the exit door off its hinges as it slammed shut. Max bounded up the steps three at a time. The pounding of boots on the stairs above him drowned out his own footfalls.

"What floor is the ventilation shaft on?" Max questioned while puffing for air as he raced up.

"Sub level 2."

The steel banging from the soldiers heading down toward him grew louder and louder. Max took up a position with a clear line of sight, when they rounded the landing above him. His heart pounded in his chest while he took aim at the location. From the lack of any rhythm to the footsteps, Max knew there were several combatants coming at him.

The guards stormed recklessly down the steps. Max waited until at least four of them were in his line of sight and then opened fire. The laser blasts cut down the leading soldiers, and then he sent a massive surge of fire up the steps to force the others to retreat. Max sprinted up the steps after them, firing shots at all who came into view. He had to send more fire to keep the troops from stopping and engaging him.

Max had just rounded one set of stairs when the door in front of him began to swing open. Lowering his shoulder, Max slammed into the door at full speed, catching the soldiers trying to enter by surprise, knocking them back into the hall.

"*Zakluci!*" Max yelled, sealing the door shut.

"Get off on Sub level 3. Hudich and Alan just got off on Sub level 2," Lita warned. "There is a stairwell closer to the maintenance room or the ramp."

"Thanks. Did Cindy and Ell make it out?" Max questioned.

"They're waiting for you but they made it to the room," Lita reported.

"We aren't leaving without you," Cindy pipped in. "I've activated a number of workers, along with a few troops, and I am moving them to Sub level 3 to help occupy the soldiers' attention. You should be able to get through with only a minimal amount of resistance."

"If you can turn some on Hudich, that would be awesome." Max gulped air, lines of sweat running down his forehead.

Joe and Yelka stepped out of the gateway next to the rock which held the hideout overlooking the secret base. Warning sirens from the base rang loudly from the valley below, and troops rushed back and forth between buildings.

"It looks like they aren't messing around," Yelka commented.

"Let's find out how we can help." Joe hurried to the door behind the rock, with Yelka right behind him.

They entered to see Lita, Larry, and the others huddled around Lita's computer screens, watching the events inside the complex from its security cameras. Larry and the others would point out troop movements while Lita relayed information to Max.

"What's happening?" Joe asked, momentarily drawing their attention so they realized they had new arrivals.

"Hudich and my dad are in there. Cindy and Ell are waiting at the exit, and Cindy is trying to help by controlling people. Max has the information on their cure research and is trying to reach Cindy and Ell," Larry reported.

"Bring up a layout of the building where Max is on one of the monitors," Grandpa ordered.

Lita continued to relay information to Max all while she typed in a few commands to show the schematics Joe requested. Joe had to force himself to ignore the events on Lita's other monitors and the information she was relaying to Max, to find what he was looking for inside the complex.

"How much activity is around Cindy and Ell?" Yelka questioned. "Could we help Max from that location?"

"I don't think so. That floor is the center of the activity, but they don't appear to know that Cindy and Ell are there. If you enter there, you might give Cindy and Ell away," Lita reported.

"But we could send Cindy and Ell back if we open the gateway there," Yelka said and turned to Joe, whose concentration was on the screen in front of him.

"I don't think they will go for that. Max tried to order them out a while ago," Larry reported.

"There." Joe pointed to the monitor, drawing everyone's attention once more. "I think that would be a good place to go in. It's isolated and we might be able to hit the enemy from the rear. Plus, it is a floor below all the action."

"Yes, but once we're in, we won't be able to get everyone out that way. We will have to eventually open the gateway at Cindy and Ell's location or take their planned exit," Yelka reported.

"There is some more headgear in my bag on the floor. I will be your eyes once you are inside too," Lita offered with her microphone still activated, and then quickly switched off the send option. "Max heard that and doesn't want anyone else to go in." She then turned it back on.

"Don't tell him any more info until we *are* inside," Joe ordered, fishing out a headset for Yelka and himself. "What other weapons do you have? We left in a hurry. Do you have a schematic mapper?"

"There's one in the bag as well."

"Can you preprogram it?" Joe asked.

"Yes," Lita reported.

Joe dug out the schematic mapper and handed it to Lita. "And the weapons?"

"Over there," Larry said and motioned to another bag in the corner. He hurried over and dug out two laser blasters and passed them to Joe and Yelka. "Do you want another hand?"

"Thanks, Larry. It isn't that I don't trust you, I just don't want to have anyone else to worry about." Joe put a hand on Larry's shoulder. "Plus, we may need your help on the surface once we are out."

"I'll be ready," Larry vowed.

"Here," Lita called and tossed Joe a small square silver-colored device.

"Are you ready?" Joe glanced at Yelka, who gave a slight nod.

Joe took out his communicator, and a few moments later he and Yelka were back to the third floor of Joe's house. They had to wait a few moments while Rachel changed the new exit point into the middle of the complex.

They dropped out of the gateway into an empty darkened room in the middle of the compound. Spinning red lights from the hallway beyond flashed through a small window on the door, and the ringing of alarms and the distant sound of battle filtered in as well.

Hustling to the window, they paused to take a quick look. From inside the room, there wasn't much to see except a small portion of the hall.

"Are you ready?" Joe questioned.

"Let's go get them." Yelka adjusted her weapon's fire power.

They burst into the hall, scaring a few technicians in lab coats trying to find safety. Joe activated the device to get their bearings. A small hologram of the complex appeared above the small screen on the gadget.

"Which way is Max heading?" Joe questioned.

"Northwest, across the floor above you," Lita reported.

"GRANDPA!" Max's voice sounded through the headset. "WHAT ARE YOU DOING?"

"We're coming to help you. Don't head back to the ventilation room. Turn full west and come down the stairwell there. We can meet you and use the gateway to get out. Cindy, you and Ell take the exit now," Joe ordered.

"We need to stay to make sure Max can make your exit. We're keeping the troops away from him," Cindy reported.

"Lita, let Cindy know when Max makes the stairwell and then Cindy, you, and Ell leave," Joe ordered.

"This way," Joe said and nodded down the hallway to the right. He and Yelka took off as fast as their old legs could carry them.

Panic pumped through Max's veins while he flew down the hallway. Normally, help in the form of his grandfather and Yelka brought relief, but it only spoke to the desperation of the situation. His heart raced with fear and exertion pounding in his ears while his breath came in labored gulps.

He rounded a corner and ran into the back of a battle between the security forces and Cindy's zombies. He put on the brakes and took cover behind the bend in the hallway.

"That's the best route," Lita reported in his ear. "And you better hurry as troops are circling and coming around behind you."

"Got it!"

Max sprang out with his weapon ready and engaged the already occupied troops. With his help in eliminating a half dozen troops, Cindy's minions took down the rest.

Now Max had a full escort roaming the halls with him. Cindy dispatched others to occupy those trying to attack Max from the rear.

With the aid of his weapon and the use of his magic, Max cut a path through the complex to the stairwell on the other side. The door had just come into sight when the ceiling above came crashing down. Max dove backward to avoid the collapsing structure.

Out of the dust and debris, Hudich rose like a dark menace. His red-rat eyes burned with a dark fire. He threw out a spell which snatched Max by the throat, lifted him into the air, and pulled him toward Hudich's outstretched hand.

Before Max reached Hudich's grasp, a dozen of Cindy's victims attacked. Several leaped onto Hudich, while others bounded in between Max and Hudich. The force of Hudich's spell pulling Max to him caught three of Cindy's subjects in its wave. The three people and Max slammed into the unsuspecting Hudich, knocking him backward and breaking the spell.

Max sprang to his feet and fired several shots at Hudich, one of them making its mark before Hudich could block it. Hudich roared with pain and fury. A shockwave of rage blasted Max backward down the hall.

Max slammed into the wall before dropping to the ground. He struggled to regain both his feet and his wind. He barely managed to duck around the corner of another hallway before Hudich blew a hole in the wall the size of a dump truck where Max had been a second before.

"Grandpa...Hudich is on my floor, be careful." Max ran as fast as his tired legs would carry him.

"I have an idea," Lita pipped in. "Max, there is a garbage chute in the main hallway. Take a right at the next intersection and then it should be about twenty yards beyond that. It will take you to the lower level. Joe, Yelka, start heading down. You should be able to use the gateway to get out from there. Cindy and Ell, I'll let you know when they are clear so you can get out as well."

"I'm on my way," Max agreed, while picking up speed.

"Heading down now," Grandpa reported.

"I'll try to keep them occupied and give you enough time to get out," Cindy offered.

"Lita, find me a good location to open the gateway," Joe ordered.

"Searching," Lita responded.

"Make it quick. I'm telling Rachel we need the gateway open in five," Grandpa reported.

Max followed Lita's instructions to the garbage shaft. He opened the metal door to see that it was going to be a tight squeeze to get in but, once inside, he would have plenty of space. He poked his head in to try to locate the bottom. "What's at the bottom?"

"There is an open dumpster, but you might want to use the transportation spell to ease your landing," Lita reported.

Max debated for a moment when gunfire and shouts for him to freeze echoed through the hall. He sent a shockwave into his attackers to give him enough time to squeeze into the garbage chute. He barely managed to cast the spell to soften his landing before he reached the bottom. He hit the bottom of the dumpster, which only had a few items in it.

"That was fun." He rose to his feet, rubbing his knee before swinging himself out of the dumpster. A sharp pain spread through his right knee and up his leg.

"Are you okay?" Lita questioned.

Max spotted the camera on the wall and flashed her a thumbs up. "Where's the gateway?"

"I've got a large room on the southeast corner with a few technicians, but there is more than enough space," Lita informed the group.

"Send the coordinates to Rachel. We're on our way," Joe gasped.

"I've lost track of Alan. Hudich is heading down fast. I'm trying to slow him down, but he isn't sparing anyone in his path," Cindy reported. "He will kill everyone in the place to get his hands on you."

"Which way?" Max asked as he stepped into the hall and checked both ways for trouble.

"Left."

Max tried to run but the stabbing sensations in his knee hindered his speed. He had an obvious hitch in his gait. The pain pushed into his concentration, making it hard to think of anything but finding relief. He had to pause for a moment to regain his strength.

"MAX, get moving. They're coming!" Lita shouted.

"What's wrong?" Grandpa asked.

"Nothing. I'm on my way." Max swallowed hard and pushed through his pain.

"At the next intersection, turn left again," Lita directed.

"Max, we're coming up behind you," Grandpa reported.

Max whirled around to see Grandpa and Yelka rushing toward him. When they reached him, Grandpa looped Max's arm over his shoulder to help him run. They paused for a moment as a group of scientists and security personnel approached them.

"I'm sending them to slow Hudich. Keep moving," Cindy ordered.

They only had to stop once to fight a small handful of guards. They kept Max, Grandpa, and Yelka pinned down for a few moments before Cindy brought a few of her troops up behind them. They forced the resistance out into the open where they laid down their weapons and put their hands in the air.

After collecting the guards' weapons, they started forward once more. Lita continued to help them navigate the complex, calling out directions.

"When you make the next right, the gateway will be in the second room on the left," Lita reported.

They made the turn and bolted for the door thirty yards down the hall. When they rounded the entrance to the room, they smacked into a group of what looked like patients. The group lunged forward and clamped on to their arms and legs.

"Cindy, what are you doing?" Max yelled as the group started dragging them to the ground and pulling them back out into the main hallway.

"It's *not* me! Those *aren't* my zombies," Cindy responded with a hint of panic in her voice.

"WATCH OUT!" Max panicked as he caught sight of needles in the zombies hands.

One tried to inject Yelka, but she blasted the three zombies trying to hold her down outward in three different directions. A zombie tried to inject Max, but his blood immediately responded and shot back up the needle stuck in his leg, forcing the serum back inside the syringe.

"*Premakni!*" Max launched the one on top of him back across the hall and then kicked and punched his way free. He'd turned to check on the others, when another zombie sunk a needle into Grandpa's leg.

"NO!" Max screamed along with Lita in his ear. Max then took up his laser blaster and destroyed all the zombies around Grandpa.

Max and Yelka rushed to Grandpa and tried to help him to his feet.

Grandpa trembled violently and pushed their hands away. "You have to go!"

"WHAT?" Max cried.

"Hurry, I can't withstand him much longer." Grandpa's voice was weak. "I will hurt you." Grandpa's eyes were wet.

"No, I won't leave you." Tears streamed down Max's face, still trying to get Grandpa to his feet.

"Yelka, get him out of here," Grandpa ordered. "You know I'm right. Max go. Go now!"

"We have to leave him. We can't help him. He will turn on us. You know it." A teary- eyed Yelka pulled a struggling Max back toward the gateway.

"Max," Grandpa called. "I love you." He then dropped to the floor.

"I...I—love...y—you," Max struggled to speak against the lump pushing its way up into his throat and the dizzy sensation stealing over him. He didn't seem to have control over his legs and dropped to his knees.

Grandpa suddenly rose up on his hands and knees. His head snapped up. "Run!" Grandpa yelled and then a twisted expression crossed his face and an evil cackle issued from his mouth. "You can't escape me." Grandpa said in a monotone voice.

"No! No! No!" Max continued to cry.

"Max." The shaky voice of Lita spoke into his earpiece. "You have to kill him!"

The world froze and Max felt like he was encased in ice.

"Listen to me! Hudich will know all our plans and secrets, if he doesn't already. Grandpa would want you to release him. Death is the only freedom," Lita said.

A blurry Yelka came into view through Max's tears as he glanced at her. Yelka looked stunned and appeared as if she had lost the ability to speak. "Make it painless," she said, after what seemed like hours.

Max felt like a zombie himself as he adjusted his weapon to full.

Grandpa had risen to his feet and Max did the same. Max raised his weapon but he was shaking so bad, he couldn't take aim.

The twisted expression on Grandpa's face turned to a calm peaceful expression. "You're doing the right thing. You're so strong. You can do it. I love you. You must do it. I can't hold him out much longer."

"I love you," Max cried and pulled the trigger.

A huge flash filled the hallway and when it cleared, Grandpa was gone.

Spell Pronunciations and Definitions

The following words are from the Slovene language

Stress marks: [bold type] indicates the primary stressed syllable, as in news·pa·per [nooz-pey-per] and in·for·ma·tion [in-fer-mey-shuhn]

pridi (pri·di) [prē-dē] – Moves objects towards you.
zaspi (za·spi) [zä-spē] – Causes sleep.
prizgaj (pri·zgaj) [prē- 3g ī] – Use to create fire.
ugasni (u·ga·sni) [oo-gä-snē] – Use to extinguish fire.
premakni (pre·ma·kni) [prā-mä-knē] – Moves objects away from you.
vstani (vs·ta·ni) [oos-tä-nē] – Stops moving objects.
pochasi (po·cha·si) [pō-chä-sē] – Slows moving objects down.
izginem se (iz·gi·nem·se) [ēz-gē-n ām- sä] – Makes one invisible.
prikazi se (pri·ka·zi·se) [prē-kä-zē-sä] – Makes one visible.
izbrisi znamenje (iz·bir·si·zna·men·je) [ēz-brē-shē znä-menyē] – Removes
curses.
preselim se(pre·se·lim·se)[pre-se-lēm-sä] – Transports one to another world.
vrnim se(vr·nim·se)[vr-nēm-sä] – To return from transport.
odkri (od·kri)[ōd-krē] – Reveals something hidden.
razkrij zlo (raz·krij·zlo)[räz-krē-zlō] – Reveals a person who has been using evil magic.
razkrij dobro (raz·krij·do·bro)[räz-krē-dō-brō] – Reveals a person who has been using good magic.
unichi (u·ni·chi)[oo-nē-chē] – To destroy something.
vrtinchim se(vr·tin·chim·se)[vr-tēn-chēm-sä] – To twirl like a tornado.
zadravi (za·dra·vi)[zä-drä-vē] – To heal something.
oviraj (o·vir·aj)[oo-vēr- ī] – To block something.
beri misel (beri·mi·sel)[berē-mē-sel] – To read another's thoughts.
gori (gor·i)[gōr-ē] – To lift something up.
zakluci (za·klu·ci)[zä-kloo-chē] – To lock something.
zapri (za·pri)[zä-prē] – To shut something.
snezi (sne·zi)[sne-zē] – To create snow.

raztrgaj (raz·tr·gaj)[räz-tr-gī] – To break or tear.
odpri (od pri)[ōd prē] – To open
rasti (ra sti)[rä stē]] – To increase or expand
zachni (zach ni)[zäch nē] – To start or ignite
nejhaj (nej haj)[nā hī] – To interrupt or stop

Symbols and their examples:

ē bee
ä father
3 vision
ī pie, by
oo boot
ā pay
ō toe
e bet

James Todd Cochrane was born in California in 1969. He received his BA from Utah State University, where he majored in Business Information Systems with a minor in German.

A writer since elementary school, he published his first novel, Max and the Gatekeeper, in 2007.

The author writes part-time while working as a computer programmer.

BOOKS

Max and the Gatekeeper (Max and the Gatekeeper Book I)

The Hourglass of Souls (Max and the Gatekeeper Book II)

The Descendant and the Demon's Fork (Max and the Gatekeeper Book III)

The Dark Society (Max and the Gatekeeper Book IV)

The Reign of Hudich Part I (Max and the Gatekeeper Book V)

The Reign of Hudich Part II (Max and the Gatekeeper Book VI) in progress

The Prophecy of Sky

SELF HELP

How I Corrected My Nearsightedness Naturally in progress

NOVELLA SERIES

Centalpha 6 Part I

Centalpha 6 Part II

Centalpha 6 Part III

Centalpha 6 Part IV

Centalpha 6 Part V

Centalpha 6 Part VI

Centalpha 6 Part VII

Centalpha 6 Part VIII

Centalpha 6 Part IX

Centalpha 6 Omnibus

Centalpha 6 Part X in progress